Jim Harrison told me to write this book.
Cinderella told me first.
You were both right.
This is for her.

My niece Emilia Urrea was a shining example
through times that inspired events in this novel.

And for Chayo, who danced at the funeral.

Juan Francisco and the Urrea family showed
me how this story was possible.

Must I go alone
like flowers that die?
Will nothing remain
of my name?
Nothing of my fame
here on earth?
At least my flowers,
at least my songs . . .

—Ayocuan Cuetzpaltzin

This is my confession of love.

—Rick Elias

The House of Broken Angels

Luis Alberto Urrea

JOHN MURRAY

First published in the United States of America in
2018 by Little, Brown and Company

This edition first published in
Great Britain in 2019 by John Murray (Publishers)
An Hachette UK company

1

A CIP catalogue record for this title is available from the British Library

Hardback ISBN 9781529359299
Export Paperback ISBN 9781529375015
eBook ISBN 9781529359312

Printed and bound in Great Britain by Clays Ltd, Elcograf S.p.A.

John Murray policy is to use papers that are natural, renewable and
recyclable products and made from wood grown in sustainable forests.
The logging and manufacturing processes are expected to conform to
the environmental regulations of the country of origin.

John Murray (Publishers)
Carmelite House
50 Victoria Embankment
London EC4Y 0DZ

www.johnmurray.co.uk

Contents

Delirious Funerals

Big Angel's Last Saturday

Big Angel was late to his own mother's funeral.

He tossed in his bed, the sheets catching his feet in a tangle. Sweat tickled his sides as he realized what was happening. The sun was up—it was bright through his eyelids. The burning pink world. Everybody else would be there before him. No. Not this. Not today. He struggled to rise.

Mexicans don't make these kinds of mistakes, he told himself.

Every morning since his diagnosis, he had the same thoughts. They were his alarm clock. How could a man out of time repair all that was broken? And on this morning, as he was awakening to these worries, cursed by the light, cursed in every way by time, betrayed by his exhausted body while his mind raged, he was startled to find his father's ghost sitting beside him on the bed.

The old man was smoking one of his Pall Malls. "That's a lot of weight to carry around," his father said. "Time to wake up and let it go."

He was speaking English. His accent had gotten smoother, though he still pronounced "weight" as *gweitt*.

"Es mierda."

The old man became smoke and rose in curls to vanish against the ceiling. "Watch your language," Big Angel said.

He blinked his eyes. He was the family's human clock. If he was still asleep, they were all still asleep. They could sleep till noon. His son could sleep till three. Big Angel was too weak to leap up and start shouting. He poked his wife in the back until she started, looked over her shoulder at him, and sat up.

"We're late, Flaca," he said.

"No!" she cried. "Ay Dios."

"Sí," he said, deeply satisfied somehow to be the one to lay down a rebuke.

She sprang from the bed and raised the alarm. Their daughter, Minnie, was asleep on the living room couch, visiting for the night so she'd be on time. His wife shouted, and his daughter crashed into the coffee table. "Ma," she complained. "Ma!"

He put his fists to his eyes.

The women came into the room without a word and levitated him out of bed, then helped him to the bathroom to brush his teeth. His wife took a comb to his bristly, stand-up hair. He had to sit to pee. They looked away. They wrestled him into slacks and a white shirt and planted him on the edge of the bed.

I am going to miss Mamá's funeral, he told the universe. "I never cry," he announced, his eyes bright with hard light.

They ignored him.

"Daddy's always watching everything," his daughter said.

"Es tremendo," her mother replied.

No measure of psychic strain could budge the world or his body into faster motion. His family? Why should today be any different? Chaos. In his house, they were suddenly all awake and moving around like crashing doves in a cage. Raucous flutter and no progress. Time, time, time. Like bars across the door.

He was never late. Until now. He, who endlessly combated

his family's reliance on "Mexican time." They drove him crazy. If a dinner gathering was announced for six o'clock, he could be sure it wouldn't start until nine. They'd walk in as if they were early. Or worse, they'd say "What?" as if he were the one with a problem. You know you're Mexican when lunch doesn't show up till ten at night.

Qué cabrón. The morning had crept downhill like brown sludge. Muffled. Yet sounds were violently silver in his ears, all reverberations. Noise shocked him. His bones wailed deep in the midnight of his flesh, as white and hot as lightning.

"Please," he prayed.

"Daddy," his daughter said, "tuck your shirt in."

It was loose in the back—it kept coming out of his trousers. But his arms couldn't reach it. He sat on the bed glaring.

"My arms don't work," he said. "They used to work. Now they don't work. You do it."

She was trying to get into the bathroom to spray her hair. Her mother had laid waste in there, scattering brushes and girdles and makeup everywhere. Combs lay across the counter like fallen leaves from a plastic tree. Minnie was already sick of this whole funeral thing. She was almost forty, and her parents made her feel sixteen.

"Yes, Father," she said.

Was that a tone? Did she have a tone just then? Big Angel glanced at the clock. His enemy.

Mother, you were not supposed to die. Not now. It's hard enough already, you know. But she wasn't answering. *Just like her,* he thought. The silent treatment. She had never forgiven him for her suspicions about his past, about his part in the fire. And the death. He wasn't telling anyone, ever.

Yes, I did it, he thought. *I heard his skull crack.* He turned his face, lest anyone discover his guilt. *I knew exactly what I was doing. I was happy to do it.*

His mind kept playing a cartoon of a traffic jam made entirely of coffins. *Really? Not funny, God.* He'd show them all—he'd be early for his own pinche funeral.

"Vámonos," he shouted.

There was a time he could make the walls crack with his voice.

Across the bedroom, above his mirror, hung a crooked gallery of pictures of his ancestors. Grandfather Don Segundo, in a vast Mexican revolutionary sombrero: *I feared you.* Behind him in the picture, Grandmother, faded brown. To Segundo's right, Big Angel's mom and dad. Father Antonio: *I mourn you.* Mamá América: *I bury you.*

His daughter stopped trying to get past her mom and bent to Big Angel's shirttail to take care of him.

"Don't touch my nalgas," he said.

"I know, right?" she said. "Grabbing my daddy's stringy butt. Too exciting."

They faked a laugh, and she shoved back into the bathroom.

His wife burst out with her hands clamped to her hair, the strap of her full slip falling off her shoulder. He loved her collarbone and the wide straps of her bra. He was fascinated by the dark brown skin on either side of her straps, her shoulders scored by the weight of all the milk that had made her breasts so heavy and long. Dark grooves in her shoulders that always looked painful but that he could not stop kissing and licking in the days when they had still made love. He was soft inside his trousers, but his eyes were focused. The slip shimmered as she hurried, and he watched her bottom wiggle with each step.

She insisted on calling the slip "mi petticoat." He had always meant to look that up, because he was sure a petticoat was something else entirely, but then he realized he didn't want to correct her. When he was resting in the dirt, he was going to miss her little phrases. And her sounds: her stockings made frantic *shish-shish-shish* noises as she rushed to the closet to destroy it the same way she had wrecked the bathroom. Even her little grunts of panic pleased him. She sucked in a sip of air and made a sound: *Sst-uh. Sst-uh.* She stepped out of the closet and waved her hands.

"Look at the time, Flaco," she said. "Look at the time."

"What," he wanted to know, "have I been telling everybody?"

"You're right, Flaco. You're always right. Ay Dios."

"They're all waiting for me!"

She made a tiny grunt and *shish*ed back into the closet.

He sat on his side of the bed, his feet barely brushing the floor. Somebody was going to have to put his shoes on him. Infuriating.

Children outside raised hell with a legion of dogs; they were all absolved of the sin of noise—even of the sin of time.

Big Angel de La Cruz was so famous for punctuality that the Americans at work used to call him "the German." *Very funny,* he thought. As if a Mexican couldn't be punctual. As if Vicente Fox was late to things, cabrones. It was his calling to educate them.

Before he got sick, he had arrived early at the office every morning. At every meeting, he was seated at the table before the others came in. Old Spice in a cloud all around him. He had often set out Styrofoam cups of coffee for each of them. Not to show them respect. To tell them all to go to hell.

Like Nature Boy Ric Flair said on the TV wrestling shows, "To be the Man, you gotta beat the Man!" "Be a Mexi-Can," he told his kids. "We're not Mexi-Can'ts." They snickered. They had seen that in, like, an El Mariachi movie—Cheech Marin, right?

He didn't care about the job—he cared that he had the job. He brought his own colorful Talavera coffee mug to work. It had two words painted on it: EL JEFE. Yeah, the employees all got the message. The beaner was calling himself their boss. But what they didn't know, of course, was that "jefe" was slang for "father," and if he was anything, Big Angel was the father and patriarch of the entire clan. The All-Father, Mexican Odin.

And, by the way (bi de guey), the de La Cruz family has been around here since before your grandparents were even born.

His bosses could never have known that he was one of many fathers who had walked these territories. His grandfather Don Segundo had come to California after the Mexican Revolution, crossing the border in Sonora on a famous bay stallion called El Tuerto because he had lost one eye to a sniper. He carried his wounded wife into Yuma for help from gringo surgeons. Stayed in a burning-hot adobe close enough to the territorial prison so a person could smell it and hear the shouts from its cells. Segundo then stole a wagon and brought his wife all the way to California to try to enlist in World War I as a U.S. soldier. He had learned to kill while fighting General Huerta, and he was good at his job. And he had come to hate Germans because of the military advisors from Bavaria he'd seen with their ugly spiked helmets, teaching Porfirio Díaz's troops to use air-cooled machine guns on Yaqui villagers.

Dad had told him the story a hundred times.

When the United States denied Granddad's request to serve, he stayed in Los Angeles. Big Angel's father, Antonio, was five.

He wasn't allowed to swim in the public pool in East L.A. because his skin was too brown. But he learned English and learned to love baseball. The de La Cruz family became Mexican again when they went back south in the great wave of deportations of 1932, joining two million mestizos rounded up and sent across the line in boxcars. The United States had apparently grown weary of hunting down and deporting Chinese people for the moment.

What. Time. Is it? When are we leaving? Is Perla dressed yet?

He held his hands to his head. The entire history of his family, the world itself, the solar system and galaxy, swirled around him now in weird silence, and he felt blood dribble down inside his body and the clock, the clock, chipped away at his existence.

"Can we leave now?" he asked. But he could not hear his own voice. "Are we ready yet? Anybody?"

But nobody was listening.

Here We Go, Pops

Do I look good?" he asked Perla.

"Very good," she said.

"I used to look better."

"You were always handsome."

"Tie my tie."

"Stop wiggling."

He knew his siblings gossiped behind his back, of course. *Big Angel wants to be a gringo*, they said in their richly rewarding family sessions of tijereando, the ancient Mexican art of scissoring people. He knew this without anyone telling him. *He thinks he's better than all of us.*

"I am better than you."

"Excuse me?" Perla said.

He waved his hand.

Big Angel simply aimed to show the Americans something. His family was welcome to observe and learn if they wanted to.

A 43mm Invicta Dragon Lupah watch perched massively on his wrist with its magnifying glass crystal, as if he were some bomber pilot. It reminded the bosses that he was perpetually on time—American time. Minnie had bought it for him off a cable TV watch-shopping show. It was one of her 2:00 a.m. insomnia gifts. They were all prone to sleepless nights.

Now his watch circled his wrist freely like a collar too big for its dog. He watched Minnie spray her explosion of dark hair. She smiled at him in the mirror.

My beautiful daughter. We have good, strong blood. But I don't like the men she sees.

He winked at her. Only Big Angel could wink and denote wisdom. He tapped his Lupah.

He wasn't legendary only for his punctuality; he also had been the head of the computing division for the gas and electric company. He was proud that the company was so famous there had been a rock band in the '60s with the same name: Pacific Gas and Electric. He was pretty sure he could sing better than they could. Just not rock music, which everybody knew wasn't music at all. Hairy fairies in tight velvet pants and girls' shirts. Except Tom Jones. Ese sí era todo un hombre.

At his office desktop, he could access the records of every San Diegan, as well as organize and maintain the activities of all employees and executives in the network. Big Angel could see how often, for example, people in every neighborhood turned on their stoves to cook. The rich bastards in La Jolla and Del Mar used less gas than the rabble in the southside or Barrio Logan. Or his neighborhood, close to the border— Lomas Doradas. Judging from his gas and electric records, his Perla cooked about twelve hours out of every day. She had just discovered Kentucky Fried Chicken, though, and was starting to slack off a bit.

Computers weren't the point for Big Angel. He didn't even like computers. A Mexican doing what these rich Americanos couldn't do was the point. Like his father before him, with a piano, playing Ray Conniff into the night and stealing their wives right out from under their noses.

"I saw everybody's secrets," he called.

"Muy bien!" his wife shouted.

Real people cooked. He could see the use-rate digits every day. Street by street if he had the time. That was the theory he concocted: rich people must be ordering deliveries or eating cold food or going to fancy restaurants that cost as much as a sofa. Mexicans liked food hot, home cooked, and lots of it. Though for some reason his family had recently developed an addiction to pancakes. It must have come from their father, who called them "hotcakes" in Spanish: los jo-kekis, los pan-kekis. Legend had it that pancakes were the first American food he ever ate. Those and chop suey.

Many of Big Angel's executive colleagues thought Mexicans pushed brooms or scrubbed the restrooms, maybe wore hard hats in the field. He had done all these things. But a Mexican computer center director and cyber-systems manager was some sort of anathema that defied explanation and demanded whispered quorums deducing the impact of such upheavals.

Big Angel was aware of it all. He wasn't interested in affirmative action. He hadn't asked for help. His family had never accepted government checks or cheese or those big silver cans of federal peanut butter. He had never seen a food stamp. He wasn't some peasant holding his straw hat in worried hands, bowing to some master. He was Emiliano Zapata. He wasn't living on his knees. In his mind, he was showing his long-dead father his own worth as a son. His name tag said HOLA! instead of HELLO!

He shook his head, hard. Rubbed his face. Had he been napping? Chingado!

"Move," he said. "All of you!"

"Yes, Daddy."

"Now!"

Out in his room in the garage, Lance Corporal Hungry Man got his beret neatly positioned on his head. He had moved back in with them when Pops got so sick.

Favorite son, he told himself. He glanced at the plastic trophy Pops had given him. It said: LALO #1 SON! He looked at it all the time. He cocked the beret a little, down over his eye. Bruce Lee glowered from a poster behind him. And a bumper sticker from one of his attempts at a recovery program was above his bed: ONE DAY AT A TIME.

His former sponsor had made him a little placard with this motto wood-burned into it: SHORT FORM OF THE SERENITY PRAYER—FUCK IT.

He had done stuff. Bad stuff. He was working on it. Pops was always saying this was not *West Side Story*. Whatever that was. He got it—wasn't about no gangbangers. It wasn't about fights and creepy shit. Lalo knew this much: he was doing his best.

His high-and-tight haircut made him look like he was still in the service. It had been a good while. He tugged down the hem of his tunic. Squared away. Head of De La Cruz Security.

Days like today called for a uniform. Moms made sure it was always pressed and sharp. He maintained his dress tunic and trousers, his dress blouse and hats—all clean, crisp. Black shoes shined like dark mirrors. His little rows of fruit salad ribbons and medals neat, a gap where he had removed his Purple Heart and pinned it on his father. He still limped a little, but the leg wasn't too bad. He had some magic pills. He didn't think about it, if he could help it. Got a Chinese dragon tattooed all along the scar. Tail wrapped around his ankle, which still crunched like cereal when he walked. Didn't talk about it.

Ain't no thing. Every homie had his secrets. Too bad those old-timers didn't have no secrets. Or maybe they did. He had kids himself—Gio and Mayra. He wasn't planning to tell them shit.

Lalo knew he had tragic eyes. Dark, like his father's. He looked like someone who had lost a lover. Or one who had tried to stop what sick sadness he was doing and could not, and was exhausted by acting like life was a sunny Fourth of July picnic.

His great-grandpa had been a soldier. And Gramps Antonio had been some kind of a badass cop. Grandma América—she had been a trip. She had managed to be sweet as she kicked everybody's ass. She had been badder than Abuelo Antonio. Sorry to be burying her today, for reals. He wasn't about to even begin considering burying Pops.

Pops. Hungry Man didn't know what his dad had done in the real world aside from raising the fam with Moms. Life, man—did Pops have a life? That was its own little war, being a dad. Lalo knew that. He laughed once, making a *skitch* sound with the side of his mouth. It was war for sure with him and his brothers and sister. And Moms.

Freakin' Moms, laying down the law and order with her slipper. La chancla. Every vato feared the chancla. A million bug-eyed, pissed-off Mexican mamas whacking the bejesus out of their kids, holding one arm and flailing ass with the free hand, the whole time dancing in a circle as the homie tried to run away but couldn't get out of her grip. And Moms getting all formal as she lectured, every word coming down with the whacks on the ass: Usted-va-a-aprender-quién-es-la-jefa-aquí! It was all "thee" and "thou" when the Old Ladies started smacking you. And once the poor criminal escaped, Moms launched that chancla like a guided missile and beaned him in the back of the head.

"Worse than a drill instructor," he told his reflection.

Outside, all the shorties and peewees were laying siege to the yard and the house. Squabbling and screaming and passing a half-flat soccer ball from foot to foot as they ran. The girlies were as loud as the fat boys. It was a freakin' chicken coop out there, but Pops liked all his grandkids and grandnieces and neighbor kids and waifs eating all the food and breaking stuff. Above their incessant caterwaul, he heard his dad shouting: "Lalo!"

"Coming, Pops!" he called.

"Hurry, mijo!"

"On my way!"

It seemed to Lalo that some days everyone shouted at everybody else, like they were all deaf or didn't understand English. Well, Moms—that was arguable. But she probably understood more than she let on.

"Lalo!"

"Coming!" Hungry Man snapped a salute in Big Angel's general direction. He looked in the mirror again, tugged the hem of his jacket down one last time, trying to hide that civilian gut. He had a little silver .22 automatic strapped to his ankle like some narco. You do what you got to do, no lie. "Good to go," he said to himself and stepped out to find his sister smoking in the backyard. "Minnie," he said. "Check it." He posed. "I got my hair did."

"You look sharp," she said. "Bubble butt."

"You're too funny, Orange Is the New Black. Look who's talking."

"Hey," she said, tossing her smoke into the geraniums, "I never got arrested or nothing."

"Yeah? You're the only one."

She lit up a fresh one, smoked, studied the end of her cigarette, elegantly tipped off some ash with her ring finger, looked sideways at him. "You know what? Most people don't get arrested."

"What planet you from?"

She blew smoke at him.

"You smoke too much," he said.

"Said the junkie."

"Say what?" he said. "Keep flapping your big ol' duck lips, girl. See what happens."

She sneered.

"I hate it when you look at me like that, Mouse," he said.

"Really."

"I'm okay, okay?"

"Right." She blew smoke rings.

"Look," he said. "I'm clean. No lie."

"You sure about that?"

"I don't got a problem. Just takin' the edge off. I got reasons." He tapped his thigh, but sympathy moves no longer worked on his sister.

She held the cigarette away from herself and nodded. "Yeah, who doesn't?" Then, "And you stole my car last week."

"At least I ain't Braulio," he said.

"We don't talk about Braulio."

"I know, I know." But Lalo also knew, if he wanted a conversation to change, all he had to do was mention his dead brother.

They stood there, out of insults and accusations. Out of anything else to say. They looked at their feet.

"We have to get going," Lalo said.

"Pops," she replied.

"Yeah. Good ol' Pops. Got needs."

"It's what we do."

"Fuck it."

They went inside the house.

⁂

"I was never sick. I was never late. I banked my vacation time."

"How nice, Flaco," his wife said, patting his shoulder.

"And for what."

"I don't know."

"I wasn't asking, Flaca. I was saying."

"Right."

"Maybe asking myself."

"Eres muy filosófico," she said.

Minnie was back in their bathroom, ratting and spraying. Why did she drink so much last night? Her head was pounding. Big Angel knew. He could see it in her eyes.

"I don't care about my job," he said. "It was foolish, Flaca. I wish we'd gone to the Grand Canyon."

"How nice."

Perla was trying to hook her girdle snaps to the tops of her stockings. He watched her. Did anyone wear girdles anymore? Snap them to nylons? It had been his erotic fantasy to see the skirt rise and the fingers pull the sheer stockings up those dimpled thighs.

In his youth, he'd knelt at the feet of older women sitting in chairs as they pulled the nylon high. Opening their legs. "Don't touch! Look." Their gift to him. Their warm scents of baby powder and secrets. Him glancing at the shadowed white latex mounds between their thighs. And their dexterous fingers hooking the girdles to the nylon. "Just watch," those women ordered, knowing from his blush the power they were unleashing.

Nobody did that anymore except for his Flaca.

"I like your legs," he said.

She stared at him. "We do not have time for that," she scolded.

"Says who?"

"You do," she said.

As if he could anyway. "All right. Time to go," he replied. "But I still like to look. I like your thighs."

"Sí, mi amor."

"Delicious."

"Travieso," she said, that delightful old Mexican word for "bad boy." She pulled up her skirt and showed him herself.

"Your beehive is full of honey," he said.

"Cochino!" she said. But she didn't drop her skirt.

"Mom!" Minnie cried from the bathroom. "Stop that!"

Mother and father smiled at each other.

"How do you think we made you?" he called to Minnie.

"TMI!" she said and hurried from the bathroom and through the bedroom with her fingers in her ears. "La-la-la-la-la!"

The parents laughed in her wake. He gestured for his wife to collect herself. He was temporarily out of words. He, who had taught himself English by memorizing the dictionary. Competing with his estranged father to see who learned newer, stranger, more American words. His father, once a monument of a man, later small and gray and watery-eyed, charming and brutal as ever, but whittled down. Sleeping in Big Angel's back bedroom for a season — Big Angel ascending to patriarch. Nobody could imagine such things. No Mexicano or gringo.

No way of knowing how language re-created a family. His own children didn't want to learn Spanish, when he had given everything to learn English. The two men at the kitchen table with cigarettes and coffee and used dictionaries. They captured new words and pinned them like butterflies of every hue. "Aardvark," "bramble," "challenge," "defiance." One called out a word: "Incompatible." The other had to define it in less than three minutes. Five points per word. Scores tallied on three-by-five-inch index cards. At the end of each month, a carton of Pall Malls was at stake. If the caller's accent was too hard to understand, he lost three points. And so, with verbs and nouns, they built their bridge to California.

English exams, followed by paperbacks bought at the liquor store. His favorite gringo phrase at work, which he seldom used at home, was "By golly." He learned that a mighty lover, in James Bond books, was known as a "swordsman." He learned from a John Whitlatch action novel that a man with a prostitute for a wife was an "easy rider." Americans in the '60s said "easy ice" to bartenders when ordering a cocktail, thus sounding very current and ensuring a bit more liquor in the glass. Big Angel maintained a mental data bank of American secret spells and incantations. Hard-on. Johnny Law. What can I do you for?

Why was he thinking about work? About the past? It was over. It was all over. He was never going to work again. "This second," his father liked to tell him, "just became the past. As soon as you noticed it, it was already gone. Too bad for you, Son. It's lost forever."

(*Muy filosófico.*)

Minnie stood in the shadowed living room, listening to Lalo chase the kids around the patio. Mom and Daddy were so dirty. It made her laugh a little, then grimace at how gross it was. Beehive. Honey. It was filthy. He was going all Prince in his old age. But he made it sound pretty. She rubbed her eyes and tried not to smear her makeup. Nobody said anything that sexy to her. Nobody said pretty things about her parts anymore.

Maybe when you've had three boys, those days are over.

She yelled at the kids: "Be quiet!"

She had the worst hangover. All this death. All this responsibility. On her. She was carrying this whole weekend. Lalo? Useless. Moms? Too broken up. Her friends had come over to her house last night to cheer her on. They were all like "Mija, this weekend's a bitch!" And they were making fireballs and micheladas. She had never laughed so much. She half remembered texting her uncle, Little Angel.

Why did she do that? They had some connection she couldn't figure out. She rubbed her forehead. How badly had she embarrassed herself? She grabbed her phone to check her texts from the night before.

At 2:00 a.m., she had written: "OMG, Tío, I am so buzzed right now!"

She thought he'd be asleep or something. But he had texted her back. "Me too," he said. "Funerals."

She had gotten here, somehow, late last night. She hoped she hadn't driven drunk. She thought one of the guys from work had brought her. She felt like everything was slipping out of her hands.

She wore her laciest purple underwear, in case her man came around for a look. It was a kind of prayer.

❦

Big Angel and Perla were just staring at each other, so many things still to be said, when Minnie suddenly appeared back in their room and fell to her knees and wrestled his shoes onto his feet. He patted her head. The shoes were tight. They hurt him, goddamn it. *Sorry, Lord.*

"Watch it, Minnie!" he said. "If Braulio was alive, he'd know how to do it right!" He kicked at her.

Braulio. Her big brother. Dead and in his grave for almost ten years now. The son inflated by his absence into the position of family saint. Poor Pops. His two big boys—his greatest failure. Nobody was invited to mention either of them. And here he had Lalo to fool himself with. The good boy, supposedly. Damn, her head was banging.

Minnie just looked up at Big Angel. "Love you anyway, Daddy," she said.

Lance Corporal Hungry Man stepped into the room. "Y'all ain't ready yet? Yo, Pops. What's the holdup?"

❦

Lalo had arranged the peewees all over the house. Surveillance teams. He announced: "Maggots! Listen up!" They knew to fall in and stand at attention. "Big Papa Actual on the move! Say again: Big Papa Actual, rolling! Over."

"Roger!" a chubster in the kitchen cried.

"Man your positions."

They scattered and created faux checkpoints all through the house. Uncle Lalo, #1 Babysitter.

A girl in the living room shouted, "All clear!"

"Be advised: snipers have been spotted—watch your six and niner!"

"Roger!"

Big Angel slumped in his wheelchair and hung his head. "Yeesus, Lalo," he muttered, fingering his son's Purple Heart pinned to his own tiny chest.

"Just playin', Pops."

"There's nothing funny, mijo."

"Always something funny, Pops," said Hungry Man. "Coming through, maggots!" he yelled.

Minnie and Perla followed, carrying handbags and the folded walker. Out the door and down the yellow scrap of lawn. They shoveled Big Angel into the minivan. They didn't let the All-Father drive anymore—his feet couldn't reach the pedals anyway. He sat in the middle-back seat, rocking in place, swinging pendulum strokes of his desecrated body, as if his anxiety could force the vehicle through traffic. The inertia of will, striving to overwhelm all tides and hit that far shore.

Big Angel's best friend, Dave, had told him, "There is a far shore. We are all like these little lakes. And when there's a splash in the middle, ripples flow out from the center in perfect circles." "Dave," he'd replied, "what the hell are you talking about?" "A life, pendejo—you. The ripple starts out strong and gets slighter till it hits the shore. Then it comes back. Almost invisible. But it's there, changing things, and you're in the middle wondering if you accomplished anything." Big Angel shook his head. That damned Dave.

"Dale gas, pues!" he said.

"On it, Pops."

Once, Big Angel would have roared it, but now he thought

he sounded like some mewling cat urging somebody to fill its saucer with cream.

A little American flag fluttered on the antenna. Lalo driving, his Perla in the navigator's seat, fretting in Old Mexican Woman fashion: "Ay Dios. Dios mío. Por Dios." God, being worn down by faithful repetition. There was some evidence that he might be deaf.

Maybe, Perla thought, God didn't speak Spanish. Then she crossed herself in penance. "Diosito lindo." It was always smart to compliment God. He liked to hear how handsome he was.

La Minnie was in the third row, rubbing Big Angel's shoulders from behind. And the wheelchair sat folded up in the way back, clattering against the walker to announce every infuriating application of the brakes in this unmovable traffic.

He punched the seat. "Today, of all days," he said.

His two great messages to his kids, without fail, were: be on time; don't make excuses. And here he was, late and thinking up alibis by the dozen. Burying his mother on the day before his own birthday party. His last birthday, but nobody else knew it. He was collecting his scattered family by decree. It was going to be a puro party that nobody would forget.

"You're a good girl," he said as an afterthought. He patted Minnie's hand.

He looked at his giant watch. He had to squint. His eyes going now. Wonderful. He had always been proud of his eyesight. He resolved to abandon time and let it go. But he was not about to get glasses. Enough was enough.

"Turn the radio down!" he snapped.

"Radio ain't on, Pops," his son said.

"Then turn it on!"

Lalo did so.

"Turn it down!"

Everyone in the van bent to his whim, but the sky and the clock and the pinche traffic seemed to ignore his dictates. A guy on the overpass held up a BUILD THE WALL sign, facing south.

"My mother," Big Angel said, "would expect more from me than this."

He had so much to prove to her. He had failed her a hundred times. He couldn't bear confirming her suspicions about him: incapable. Not even close to what his father had been. And of course she had never granted him a pardon for marrying Perla. "That señora," she called her. Implying that Perla was used goods. Experienced.

"You're doing your best, Daddy," Minnie said.

"If this is my best, kill me right here, right now."

"Ay Dios," his wife prayed.

A Prayer Before the Rain

Where did all this traffic come from?

Mother had died the week before, but his birthday party had been announced a long while before that. Long at least in terms of Big Angel's diminished prospects. A week was a long time when you were racing the Lupah.

People were coming from everywhere: Bakersfield, L.A., Vegas. Little Angel, his youngest brother, was coming all the way from Seattle. People had made reservations. Taken time off from work. High rollers and college students, prison veteranos and welfare mothers, happy kids and sad old-timers and pinches gringos and all available relatives.

It would be tight.

So he courted outrage by having Mama cremated. There was no time left for a big Catholic funeral in a big Catholic church. What church would they have picked? Half the family had briefly become Mormons, and some of them were in a UFO-worshipping group awaiting the return of the Anunnaki when Planet X came back into Earth's orbit. Some of them were evangelicals. Or nothing. Lalo was probably an atheist. Or a sun worshipper. The eldest son of Big Angel's brother César seemed to think he was a Viking. Big Angel truly had no time for these details.

He had made the even more daring move of arranging for

her funeral to take place a week later than expected so his birthday party would be the day after. Ashes could last forever. No worries.

Nobody seemed to care—they were happy he was handling everything. That's what he did. They didn't want to be responsible, because the Great Mother would have found fault with any funeral they conspired to offer. And Big Angel was reliable. It was simple to get orders from him and follow them. So they had adjusted to the funereal addendum to the birthday party agenda without a fuss. Most of them were relieved because they didn't have enough vacation days available to make two trips. They certainly didn't have the funds. One weekend worked for everybody.

More traffic? Where is everybody going?
Big Angel put his hands over his eyes, if only to avoid looking at the blackness seeping up the backs of his wrists. His hands had black splotches on them too. He never looked at his legs, afraid of what he'd see.

Outside, the afternoon sun burned apertures in the clouds, charring the floating crevasses red along their edges and shooting hauntings of yellow light across the city. Like curtains of golden mesh, blowing in a cool breeze. Big Angel calculated in his mind how far toward Hawaii the sun must be; he saw angles and degrees etched into the blue above the flaming clouds. Heaven was a blueprint.

Mother had never been close to him after La Paz. She had coddled his siblings, including his half brother, Little Angel, who wasn't even her son. She had seen some charm in him that Big Angel had never managed to fully accept.

He watched the sky. He was amassing evidence of any kind of signal sent from Beyond. Anything at all. Braulio? Mother?

Anybody? Rain was good. He could work with rain. Many messages in rain. Rainbows were even better.

When he was a boy, Mother had taught him that a rainbow was a bridge where angels walked down from heaven. In Spanish, it was an *arco* iris. This was so much more lovely than English, like the name of a butterfly or hummingbird or daisy. He felt smug about this: go, Spanish! *Sunflower: girasol*, he thought.

> *girasol*
> *mariposa*
> *colibrí*
> *margarita*

But no rainbows were visible.

"It was good of Mother," he said, "to die first."

"Ay, Flaco," his wife said in Spanish. "You know. She could not stand to see her son die before she did."

"Who's going to die, Perla?" he said. "I'm too busy to die."

He said that a lot. But he also said "I am ready to die," and as often.

He had confessed it to his priest. Almost as soon as Doctor Nagel told him the gushes of fresh blood returning to his urine signaled the collapse coming. That moment, oddly, made him feel calm: he had stared at the doctor and thought, *Her name is Mercedes Joy Nagel, and I wish I had bought a Mercedes because I would have felt joy.* The x-rays had shown grape clusters of death all inside his abdomen and two dark knots in his lungs. He sat small and alone in that office, putting his most stoic warrior face forward, staring the doctor down. "How long?" A shrug, a pat. "Not long. Weeks." "Can I have a lollipop?" he said. She opened her glass jar. He liked cherry.

He called his priest and confessed over the phone, then told Perla he had been talking about baseball with a friend.

"Pops," said his son. "I ain't gonna lie. Grams done it on purpose. Took care of business. For reals."

"She was like that," Big Angel said.

"Rainbow, Daddy!" his daughter cried.

Big Angel looked where Minnie was pointing and finally smiled. *Good work, God.*

◈

Little Angel had landed.

Baby Brother, he announced to himself, *in the house!*

Big Angel's half brother had thought he'd be late. As old as he was, they all thought of him as the baby, including himself. The oldest twenty-eight-year-old on Earth, an age he had managed to remain for an extra twenty years.

You couldn't miss the matriarch's funeral. There was no way he was going to be late. She wasn't his mom—he was often reminded of this in small, pointed ways. He was the footnote to the family, that detail everybody had to deal with when he deigned to appear. Son of an American woman who had been branded in the family legends as the gringa hussy who had taken away their Great Father, Don Antonio. Somehow they even resented his mother's death. She had managed to join Father in the afterlife before Mamá América could go over to wrestle him back from the American's clutches.

Little Angel didn't want to be in California, land of sorrows. And he didn't like breaching the thousand-mile buffer zone between himself and his origins. But the fear of Big Angel's displeasure drove him forward harder than his reluctance held him back. He'd forced the plane from Seattle to fly faster by the sheer strength of his will. The overwhelming mural of sunlight ricocheting off coastal peaks and spilling over them to the ocean—going from burning red to blue, then green, then purple—hypnotized him. Then the harrowing plunge toward San Diego, the feeling that his plane was passing between the buildings on its way to the runway...and he was home.

He realized he was at the car rental office before eight in the morning, and he felt silly. Yet relieved. No missing the funeral. No smoldering, wounded stares of reproach from Big Brother. He was on Big Angel's schedule—always early.

When they were in their cups, Big Angel called their brotherhood "the Alpha and the Omega." Little Angel thought the tequila really suited him. Let him out of his self-imposed sanctity. The first and the last, eh? Little Angel had parsed the meta-messages in that text enough to earn a PhD in cross-border gnostic sibling ontologies. He smiled, more or less.

Big Angel seemed to think, when he was loaded, that they were some sort of wrestling tag team. He'd announce: "Coming into the ring, weighing two hundred pounds, from parts unknown—the Omega!" Baffled women and kids would clap as Little Angel raised his hands.

Little Angel, somewhere inside himself, felt good when he heard this. He felt witnessed. None of the rest of them had ever paid attention to his boyhood. Hell, they hadn't even seen it. Their father had made sure they were kept far apart.

But Big Angel saw. He was the eldest, and by then had his own car and job. He came to visit their drab Clairemont house, to the consternation of Little Angel's American mom. But she made him chicken potpies and tried hard to be a good sport anyway. By then she had learned that Don Antonio would come to their San Diego home with lingerie tucked in his jacket pockets. She was done with him but had nowhere to go. She smiled at the boys even though she was exhausted and always nervous. Even though Big Angel frightened her with his black-eyed glare. She knew he hated her.

Big Angel knew what his baby brother's Saturdays were like: morning cartoons, Three Stooges reruns, followed by some fat boy lunch of cold spaghetti or frijoles sandwiches on white bread, and chocolate milk and comic books. Or *Famous Monsters of Filmland* magazine. Monsters were his mania. And nobody in his version of the family approved. Don Antonio would begrudgingly buy him a copy at the liquor store, even though he berated the kid afterward. Little Angel didn't care; his mind was crowded with King Kong and Reptilicus, the Wolf Man and King Ghidorah. The monster magazines made his mother despair even worse than Superman comics or *MAD* magazine.

And after lunch, it was Mutual of Omaha's *Wild Kingdom*. Followed by wrestling. Big Angel had taken part in this ritual perhaps three times, but he never forgot it. His little brother's fervid insistence on these things, in order, without interruption. The ridiculous wrestlers falling around the ring in grayscale black and white: Classy Freddie Blassie, Pedro Morales, The Destroyer, Bobo Brazil. Little Angel seemed to think he was friends with them all.

At 3:00, Moona Lisa appeared on channel 10—*Science Fiction Theater*. She lounged around a cheap set that looked like the moon, dressed in Morticia Addams skintight dresses. Big Angel thought she was hot. But Little Angel didn't seem to notice. He was holding his breath for *Them* and *The Brain from Planet Arous*.

Big Angel made Little Angel his research project. He had

never seen his own isolation mirrored in the world. Little Angel finally understood this, years later, when his brother shouted his faux ring announcements.

They even shared an English slang exclamation they picked up from Dick Lane on KTLA, brought in fuzzy and snowy on the rabbit ears. "Whoa, Nelly!" Lane called whenever The Destroyer made Blassie kneel in the corner of the ring, begging for mercy.

So when Big Angel ring-announced him, sometimes Little Angel would shout back, "Whoa, Nelly!"

The fam had just stared.

≈

The Dollar car-rental office had only a Crown Victoria available. Black. In his fantasies, Little Angel had imagined snagging something more dramatic. A Mustang GT500 convertible, perhaps. Or a Challenger Hellcat. Something with a horsepower of 700. Kid brother makes good. Bad to the bone.

He initially balked at this fossilized cop car, a car for granddads taking their golf friends to a tasty brunch in La Jolla. But in the end it amused him, and he took it. He could have put ten bags in the trunk. He tossed his overnighter in there—it looked huddled and unloved. His shoulder messenger bag went on the couch-like back seat, and he settled in the front. Professor Little Angel, with a satchel full of notebooks and William Stafford poetry. He would ignore the ten papers that needed grading.

Time to boogie on down there to the south side. Time to think, make up his strategies. Doctor Think Too Much, back in town.

Sometimes, when Big Angel was in one of his moods, he

called Little Angel things other than his name. "The American." What the hell. How was that an insult? But it had some inexplicable sting. Especially coming from a Republican. Or at least he thought Big Angel was a Republican. Why didn't he just say "The Liberal"? They'd had their only fistfight over it. Just once. Blood on their lips.

Did it have bearing on this day?

The car was vast and pillowy. Little Angel felt like he was driving a square acre of 1979. It smelled like cigarette smoke—reminded him of his dad. He took the turns wide and hit I-5 like a cloud being pushed by a sea storm. Being in no hurry, he decided to go on a slight expedition to the north. He hadn't been back in years, but you never forget the hometown. Even though it seemed he came home only for funerals.

He could have gone left and rolled up Clairemont Drive to his old neighborhood. Stared at his sunburned house on the Indian-themed streets above Mission Bay. Mohican Ave. He knew his mom's jungle of succulents and bamboo, geraniums and jade trees, was gone now. It had been dust long before the drought. He knew the front and back yards were bare San Diego dirt, and a dirty Japanese pickup slouched in her driveway, a Ski-Doo beside it. A crooked basketball hoop screwed in above the garage door. People he had never met.

His old Goth sweetheart, Lycia, still lived on Apache. A grandmother now. He could almost smell the scent of sandalwood that came from her thighs.

*

Before the family had even gotten Big Angel dressed, Little Angel was speeding off the freeway at Midway to hit Tower

Records. He wanted to hear some Bowie. Ziggy Stardust always made it better. The Crown Vic had a CD slot. *Keep your electric eye on me, babe.* He and Lycia had cried every time that song played, and then they'd made love. And now Bowie was gone.

Even if Tower wasn't open yet, he was willing to hang out in the parking lot and wait. But he couldn't find the record store anywhere.

He drove past the Sports Arena. When they were kids, they'd called it "The Sports Aroma." He pulled a U and rolled back. He never saw Tower. He drove down the long block slowly. People honked, but he didn't care. Tower was gone. That was some happy horseshit right there.

Back on the freeway, but he wasn't going to be bested by this disappointing turn of events. He couldn't seem to find 91X on the radio. He headed south to Washington Street and sped up the slope toward Hillcrest. Off the Record would ease his itch. Damn right—best CD bins in town.

But that was gone too.

Someone had come into his memories and erased whole blocks with an invisible bulldozer. He rolled on to the empty parking lot where The Rip Van Winkle Room used to stand. Alberto's Tacos was there now.

He pulled in and just stared. His dad had once played piano in there for tips. Rip's Room, the hipsters had called it. The piano lounge was up a half set of carpeted stairs, in red light. The whole place smelling of cigarettes and liquor and perfume and Aqua Velva. Little Angel's memory was echoing and ripe: candied cherries, vanilla Cokes, Patsy Cline on the juke when his dad was not tinkling "Red Roses for a Blue Lady." Cocktail waitresses with lips the same color as the cherries, wafting clouds of White Shoulders and musk oil, tracing Dad's back with their fingernails as they passed. He was there most Friday and Saturday nights.

Walkin' After Midnight
I Fall to Pieces
Crazy

Little Angel never understood what those songs were about. But he sure understood what those red nails on Dad's back meant. Don Antonio, with his carefully pomaded hair and his dapper little Pedro Infante mustache, used Little Angel's charm to help him reel in waitresses and bowling wives and bored retirees looking for a night of passion. He trained Little Angel in the art of making women feel visible. "If you teach a woman to feel like a work of art, you will make love to her every night." *Uh-huh, Dad. Right. Got it.*

Dad gifted him with porno cocktail napkins featuring cartoons of busty and idiotic farm girls romping in barns with salesmen. Why were these guys in barns wearing suits and little hats, he wondered. And tricky books of matches with naughty zingers built in. Like the Rip Room's legendary Baby Bobby matchbook. Wherein Baby Bobby could be observed on the cover fiddling between his legs with chubby fingers. And when Little Angel opened the cover, a single red-headed match in a little pink plastic tube popped out at him, a delighted Baby Bobby with arms outstretched in rapturous erect joy.

Little Angel was in fifth grade.

Love Is Blue
Perfidia
The Girl from Ipanema

The painted ladies loved him. He was like a little darling dog to them. They hugged him as he sat upon his stool, looking at Batman comics, their stout, encased breasts rolling across his cheeks, and he could smell the hot spaces beneath their arms. He tried to hide his personal Baby Bobby situation from them.

A brandy snifter full of ones and fivers glistened on the piano. Swingers sent a steady stream of cocktails to the piano man, but by agreement with the barkeep, they were all ginger ale on the rocks. Who could play a lick after fifteen manhattans? Let alone drive home. Dad split the overage the drinkers paid with the bartender.

Nobody there knew it was his night job. That he spent all day cleaning up after bowlers. Putting sanitary cakes in urinals. Clearing the white tin bins in the ladies' room. At night, in a dapper cream smoking jacket, he did his Ricky Ricardo routine for drunk Americans. Slicked back hair, no wedding ring, and cigarettes.

This was how Little Angel remembered his father.

He sat there staring at the taco shop and wished he had learned how to smoke. Memories. Game for losers. He had places to be. Too much time travel before 10 a.m.

"To hell with this," he said, and pulled out of the lot. He drove south again and blissed out on the glittering blue of the sea on one side, the epic sweep of the Coronado Bridge ahead, the dry hills across the freeway with huge jets dropping toward the airport like some invasion of gargantuan moths. And in the southern distance, always there, the mother of them all, the hills of Tijuana.

Nobody went back there now. Not even to visit their father's grave.

The American, Big Angel called Little Angel. The Assimila-
tor. Little Angel has an American mother—not as classy as the
women in the bar. Laughter. All eyes on him. Little Angel's job
was to take it and smile.

When Little Angel got as far south as National City, he still
had hours to kill. His hotel was right off Mile of Cars, where the
funeral home awaited. He shook his head. It was tawdry, in a
way that only the gnomes of his English department in Seattle
would appreciate. How California, they'd say. How San Diego,
though a couple of ironic-eyeglasses and small-brim-hat types
would call it "Dago." How Latino, though nobody in his family
had ever spoken Latin.

Early check-in. Bags on the bed. Someone had left a crum-
pled tissue in the bathroom. It had lipstick on it. It reminded
him of the cocktail waitresses. He was disturbed to find this
vaguely erotic. They'd all be eighty now, or dead, those alarming women. In Father's neon cocktail lounge in the sky.

A maid came for the trash.

"Gracias," he said.

She seemed startled that he spoke Spanish.

When he stepped back outside and walked to the enormous
car, it had begun to drizzle. *Damn it,* he thought, *Big Angel broke
my nose in that fistfight.* He didn't realize until then that he'd
been thinking about that fight the whole time.

A week earlier, Big Angel's arrival at his mother's deathbed
was the most heroic thing his wife had ever seen. This, after a

lifetime of watching her Flaco be a hero. And the old woman refused to accept it. Perla didn't like that old witch. But dying, well, that earned her several points.

She knew how much the day had cost him. She could envision him walking back through all their history to be his mother's child one last time.

He didn't talk to Perla about La Paz much. He was broody by nature except when he was overtaken by good moods. Or feeling naughty. She still blushed at the memories after half a century. Oh, the things he did with her. Until he got sick.

Even when he brooded, she knew when he was thinking about La Paz and his father and all the things that had happened back there. He just hung his head and stared at the floor. Now that he didn't smoke anymore, he drank many cups of black instant coffee and thought. And ate too many sweets.

Her thoughts were not of La Paz but of coming north. It was the biggest decision she had ever made, and she relived that terrifying moment almost every day. It wasn't the trip that had been terrifying, or the destination. Rather, she had known that with this one step she would join her fortunes to his. Forever. Risking everything. A romantic choice, yes, but also one that could have left her with nothing.

She was already the mother of two fatherless boys. She didn't understand why her Angel had taken to calling her his "Perla of Great Price" when everyone in La Paz saw her as damaged goods, another silly girl used and forgotten by a man whose name she chose not to remember. She wanted to believe what Angel said, and yet she feared it was no more than his nature. She saw how he charmed—and was charmed by—other women, and she was frantic to keep him from their beds. She wasn't always sure what was real. Only that she needed to be with him. There would be no going back home after this decision.

She and the boys headed north before there was a modern highway. Her bigger boy, Yndio, was a toddler, and Braulio was only a baby. It was one long bus ride that cost all the money she had. Rough roads, sometimes over dirt and boulders. The stops were at terrible taco shacks with outhouses, or gas stations with drooling, stinking toilets much worse than outhouses. The people aboard the bus had brought their own food. She had carried a kilo of tortillas, a clay jug of water, and goat cheese. Four days riding.

South of Ensenada, police had set rocks across the road to stop the bus. They boarded and pointed their pistolas at the passengers and went through their bags. Perla had no money to offer. They ignored her boys. But they put their hands on her breasts. She looked out the window and held her breath and pushed them away with her mind. Angel's father would have stopped them, she told herself. She didn't have a father.

She looked at them with her hateful stare. *One day, you'll beg.*

The three policemen snagged a man by the arms and dragged him from the bus. They kicked at the doors to let the driver know he should leave. Nobody dared look back or listen to what the man was yelling.

Everybody smelled by the end of the trip, and they were mortified—no Mexican wanted to smell like a barn animal.

Tijuana was another world. Perla and her boys huddled outside the bus terminal on the north end of town, near the riverbed, in clouds of exhaust smoke. La Paz was all deserts and sea, perched at the tip of Baja. It caught ocean breezes and crushing subtropical heat and hurricanes.

She had cooked in her mother's restaurant. Her sisters beside her—all slaves to the old woman. Her boys had grown up near the ferry terminals, watching huge white boats groan in from Mazatlán. They watched boys not much older sell chewing gum and trinkets to visitors. When the fishermen docked, children haggled for cheap crabs or begged for a tuna. Sometimes they swamped out the boats for sodas.

Yndio considered this training for his future. This was how he was going to care for the family. Sometimes he was able to bring his mother a bottle of Coca-Cola. And though they'd been hungry, it was home.

But now they found themselves afraid and excited, as if Tijuana were El Dorado and all good things awaited them. It was loud and pushy. Scary and tumbledown. Too bright. Too colorful. Perla's overwhelming impression of Tijuana was twofold: symphonies of noise and endless swirls of dust. And stringy street dogs all of the same stumpy build, the same yellow-red tinged fur, the same black patches of bare skin. All of them moving through traffic with insouciance, like dancers or bullfighters, seeming to bounce off the bumpers of old Buicks and under the two-tone city buses called burras, but bobbing out of the dust clouds again and hopping onto curbs unharmed, where they stretched out in the sun and slept with flies in their eyes. Perhaps the most amazing thing about Tijuana was what they never imagined: the unexpected gringos. Downtown Tijuana was an endless parade of towering, noisy, apparently rich Americans. Perla was astonished to realize the kids were already learning English. That was something she did not expect.

She remembered how Big Angel chose to go hungry so everyone could have a tiny bit of food, even if it was only a mouthful. He'd divide his portion among her sons. That's when they had taken to calling each other Flaco and Flaca. They would never be that thin again.

Sometimes he brought candy for her two boys, though she scolded him. "Perla," he said, "life is sour enough. Let them enjoy this." That first Christmas, he bought the boys a bike to share and bought her a new dress. She had knitted him a sweater, and even though it was hot that year, he wore it every day.

Big Angel was her hero. She did not know his heroism was fueled by fuming rage. He fought anyone who insulted her or her children. He even fought off his own family's rebukes and married her, then snuck them into the United States when it became obvious that only hunger and dirt and rats and evil police waited for them in the poorest of the colonias where they could afford to live.

Perhaps his biggest mistake was his believing that rage could help him be the perfect father. It was really all he knew about being a father. On some days it almost worked. But Perla was so afraid of losing what she had won that she became more strident in her defense of her man, insisting to the boys that Angel was always right, even when she knew he wasn't. And the boys' occasional bruises told them otherwise as well. It fell hardest on Yndio, the oldest. The one who had been his mother's protector and defended her honor in the streets of La Paz, scrounged for food, done odd jobs, and still remembered his birth father. Yndio, the older brother, who found himself usurped and then disciplined, began a lifelong resistance Big Angel could never overcome.

Families came apart and regrouped, she thought. Like water. In this desert, families were the water.

Poor Mother América.

Big Angel's sister, MaryLú, had watched over the old woman at the hospital. Perla's sister, La Gloriosa, had helped. Retired women themselves, they were called "the girls" by all the older women. The younger women called them "Auntie" whether they were their aunts or not. That was the rule in Mexican families: all older women were your tía or your nina.

They had presided over Mother's hallucinations in those hours of her dissolution. She saw dead friends and dead relatives and angels and Jesus Christ, and she greeted them and extended her hand to them and laughed with them. The sisters-in-law believed this was really happening, or one of them did. The other didn't believe anything but was willing to debate it. Besides, Mother was completely blind and half deaf, so how could she be seeing or hearing anything?

She kept misunderstanding the script of their daily lives. She was confused by the plastic clip from the heart monitor that was clamped to her forefinger like a laundry pin. She mistook it for the handle of a coffee cup, and repeatedly raised it to her dry lips and sipped as if her favorite instant coffee had recently been served by a polite waitress. "Gracias," she said to the air and slurped her invisible brew.

They just shook their heads.

They had to get Big Angel to her bedside.

This would be a major operation, akin to military maneuvers. Just getting him onto a toilet required strong backs and strong noses. Getting him dressed was a nightmare of clenched teeth and gangly limbs, everybody terrified of some shattered bone or wrenched shoulder blade. Brother had his own problems, pues—they knew better than anyone, they told themselves. Of course everyone told themselves this. That was the funny thing about a lingering death: everybody attached to the spectacle wanted to accrue mastery of the mystery—own it without actually dying. Especially anyone who wiped the afflicted's bottom.

But Big Angel's wife felt that she knew better than anyone. As did his daughter. And his son. And his pastor. Everybody had been worn down by death. Everybody had an opinion.

"Call him."

"You call him."

"No me gusta."

"It's too sad."

"It's creepy calling him."

"You are bad, bad, bad."

"I never said I was good. Don be estupid."

They had presided over Big Angel's last three death scenes, from which he had unexpectedly resurrected and returned home, more arrogant than ever. But now he was carved down to the size of a child and not able to walk more than ten steps, and those while leaning on his walker. True, his son had affixed a bike horn to it and to his wheelchair, so Big Angel could make *ah-oo-gah* sounds to amuse himself. But it was a diminishment of the patriarch, for sure. Only little kids and cholos laughed.

They called Big Angel's house and began the major production of getting that branch of the family to rouse him and clean him and dress him and roll him out.

Big Angel was wheeled into the waiting room by Perla, who wanted to be anywhere but there. Hospitals horrified her; she had been in too many. She didn't like Big Angel's Old Spice, but she had never told him that. In her mind, it mixed with the hospital smells.

He felt he looked excellent. Only Minnie knew enough to think he looked like the guy in his giant suit in the old Talking Heads videos.

The family was all seated, muttering over the insectile buzz of a game show on TV. Coffee in cardboard cups.

He announced, in his new little reedy voice, "I will not let Mamá see me like this."

His hands were shaking. His ankles, where they peeked out from under his trouser cuffs, looked like chicken bones. He was biting down on his own agony.

And he rose from his chair, struggling, grunting with effort, grinning like a maniac with sheer fury, and he refused the aluminum walker. It hurt so much the watchers felt it. They leaned toward him but checked themselves from reaching out to help him. His trousers and white shirt fit him like billowing tents. He wiped the tear out of his eye and staggered into her room under his own power.

A feathery hug for MaryLú. A longer hug for La Gloriosa. He breathed in the scent of her hair. But he didn't look at her. His eyes were on the small creature that was his mother. He walked to her bed and bent to her, as if bowing.

He took her hand and spoke: "Mother, I have come."

"What?" she said.

He talked louder. *"Mother, I have come."*

"Qué?"

"MADRE!" he shouted. "AQUI ESTOY!"

"Ay, Hijo," she scolded. "I never taught you to be so rude! What's the matter with you?"

And then she died.

He had done his duty—had met with his mother's priest ahead of time, slipped him a check for his services. They didn't like each other. Big Angel knew this nasty little priest didn't approve of him. There had been rumors—Big Angel had possibly slept with all his wife's sisters. That's what the gossipers in the parish said. And Big Angel's father may have done the same. And nobody ever went to confession. Rumor had it Big Angel was a Protestant, or a Mormon, or a Freemason. Possibly a Rosicrucian. Or a Jesuit! Or all of the above.

Big Angel didn't approve of the priest's teeth. The other thing he railed against, after "Mexican time" and lame excuses, was bad teeth. Mexicans could not afford bad teeth if they expected gringos to take them seriously. And gold teeth didn't help, though Mexicans thought they looked like rich people with gold in their mouths. This priest had teeth like a rat; they made him whistle a little when he talked. And when he really got going, he sprayed like a little lawn sprinkler.

After slipping Big Angel's check into his pocket, the priest admonished, "Don't be late. I am a busy man."

"Late!" Big Angel said. "How can you suggest such a thing?"

"You know how you Mexicans are." A small rodent's smile. A jocular little punch to the shoulder.

Big Angel rolled out of the sacristy fuming.

Gracias a Dios

1:00 p.m.

He never knew when the memory would intrude. The crunch of the club hitting the man in the side of the head. How it hurt his wrist. He hadn't meant to kill anybody. Sometimes it jerked him from sleep. Sometimes he shook his head violently and said "No" during a TV show or a breakfast, and everybody thought it was just Pops being Pops. He fiercely rubbed his temples now to drive it away. And the smell of the gas on his hands. He was certain the others could smell it. The whoosh of the flames still audible a lifetime later.

"We are late," he announced. Again.

Everybody was getting tired of his bitching. It was his own damn fault. Big Angel knew this. It had started in his bladder at first, and he had told no one about the blood in his urine. If he hadn't passed out one morning, they would not have discovered the tumors. Still, he had beat it back. Minor surgery, snipping the little bastards out like grapes. Sticking a long probe up his urethra. His father had taught him to be stoic. Pain was how a man measured his worth, so he didn't flinch during the probes, and he was asleep for the rest. And suddenly the little grape bundles of tumors were gone.

Until they grew a crop in his belly. X-rays and MRIs and needles and poisons in his arm. Followed by poison pills and pills that smelled like rotten fish and radiation. His reward: spots on his lungs. He cursed every cigarette. Cursed himself. And then his bones withered. The chemicals and the inserted metal going up his urethra and the radiation had shrunk it all. Until it hadn't.

"You won't die of the cancer, per se," Doctor Nagel told him at their last conference. "It'll be a systemic collapse. Kidneys will go. Heart. Or you'll get pneumonia. Your will is strong, but your body is worn out."

"How long?"

"Prediction: a month."

That was three weeks ago. He smiled as if he'd won the lottery when the nurse wheeled him out. Perla with her eyes red and watery with worry. Minnie wringing her hands and twisting the ends of her hair in her fingers, and Lalo stoic and hiding tears of mourning behind his shades. All believed Big Angel's smile because they needed to. Because they had always believed him. Because he was the law.

"Flaco," Perla said. "What did they say?"

"Well," he said, "I'm sick. But we all know that."

"But you're cool, Pops?"

"Of course, Lalo. I told you I was fine."

Minnie hugged him and made him feel like her hair was smothering him.

"It could be worse," he told Perla.

"How?" she cried.

"At least I don't have hemorrhoids."

She would have smacked his arm, but she'd seen how quickly he bruised, and she never smacked him anymore.

He was tired of shouting at what was inside his body. His wrath was spilling out on the toxic landscapes all around him. Somebody had killed him. He thought it was his wife's cooking. He thought it was the coating on the frying pans. He thought it was the trials his family put him through. Salsa. Beef. DDT. He thought it was the mile-high pastrami sandwiches he could not avoid no matter how he tried. He thought it was Mexican Pepsi with salt peanuts in it. The clock—*time, you bastard*. Or God.

He struck the back of the driver's seat, but his punch was too weak for his son to feel.

"Don't get excited, Daddy," Minnie said from behind, rubbing his shoulders.

He jerked out of her grasp.

"Minerva!" he shouted. "You're hurting me! Vultures, all of you!"

She wept silently for the hundredth time. But only one tear. To hell with this.

His wife sighed. His son blew a bubble of chewing gum full of cigarette smoke. He held his ciggie out a crack in the window. Big Angel watched the smoke whip away.

He squeezed his eyes shut and tried to remember the things his friend Dave had told him: gratitude, meditation, prayer, attention to the small things, which were paradoxically eternal. He reminded himself that soul resided in family and relationships, not only in good times but also in bad. The soul—in potting plants and eating breakfast, Dave said. What a bunch of lies, he decided.

"Goddamn it!" he said.

He apologized to God for taking his name in vain.

But really.

The minivan still had miles to go, and the clock never stopped ticking.

⌘

The fam had rented out the Bavarian Chalet of Rest funeral home on the Mile of Cars. Honda and Dodge dealerships in the distance. All the dads in the family arrived at the parlor and craned their necks to look at the candy-colored ranks of Challengers and Chargers sitting in the lots as they drove up. The young-uns and shorties were scoping the Honda lots for *The Fast and the Furious* road rockets. Neither generation wanted to drive the clunkers their elders had driven.

People loitered at the double doors.

They had buried Braulio through this place. And Grandpa Antonio. They had a relationship with it—it was their tradition. They felt oddly at home here and chipper in some inexplicable way. Regular attendees knew where the coffee urns were, and the cardboard cups and whitening powders. It was like their own Disneyland of death.

Outside, on the main drag, a half block from the driveway, a watcher lurked. The legendary Yndio. Alone, dressed all in white. His arms were muscular, and he had a tribal tattoo of hummingbirds and vines on his left biceps. Aladdin Sane on the other. A line of Bowie lyric down that arm: THROW ME TO-MORROW. Across his left collarbone, above his heart, a name he had never explained and had no intention of explaining: SWEET MELISSA. That was the problem with these people, Yndio thought. They didn't ever let anybody have a secret, but they were hiding things from one another every day of their lives.

Little Angel had given him that Bowie record a hundred years ago. From his choker, a single black enameled feather dangled. He slouched in a white Audi A6 with a pearl paint finish. The car's interior was all ebony. His shiny black hair spilled over his shoulders and down his chest. And he crept along the block with Curtis Mayfield's "Pusherman" on the deck, watching them through twelve-hundred-dollar sunglasses.

He hadn't seen many of these people in years. Not since Braulio's funeral. Well, he'd seen his mother. Moms and Minnie. Somebody had to make sure their hair was presentable. He had a good facial man who kept them fresh. Waxed away those sideburns Moms had started growing. It was their secret.

It irritated him that the family kept acting like Braulio had been some teenager when he died. Fucker had already served in the army, for God's sake. He'd been thirty-five! They diminished the boys even in death. He blamed them all for being so stupid.

Damn—there went Tío César, the middle uncle. Dude was tall—he hadn't remembered how tall César was. And his notorious wife—as tall as he was. They seemed like giants among Hobbits. She was some Mexico City chilanga. He'd never really talked to her, so he didn't care who liked her and who didn't. He knew they didn't like her; Minnie had told him. They didn't like outsiders anyway. The family suspected everybody of being an invader. He didn't like most of the family, to be honest. He didn't see either one of the Angels.

"Cabrones," he said aloud.

He revved the engine. It snarled like some jungle cat. Just the way he liked it. He wasn't about to join them. He ripped into a U-turn and vanished north.

*

1:20 p.m.

The big Crown Victoria slouched at the back of the parking lot. The funeral home had a fake Germanic facade and stood across the street from a taco shop, a gas station, and a Starbucks. The street smelled of carne asada. The stained-glass windows were plastic. Pigeons flocked all about the alpine roofline, moving neurotically from palm trees to mortuary to taquería and back again, frantic that one of them might have found an onion ring that had been overlooked by the others. Little Angel got out of the car and walked into the building.

Inside, the family was arranging flower wreaths, some of which looked like displays for championship high school marching-band competitions. Banners with glitter spelling out condolences. Pictures of Mamá América in better years stood on easels around the central altar. "What a babe," one of the grandsons said. They all smiled. The girls had hot-glued white Styrofoam-and-feather doves to the frames of the pictures. It was quite lovely, everyone thought. Little Angel sipped his skinny caramel latte and tried to look comfortable in his sports jacket and black tie. Women he didn't remember hugged him and left smudges of makeup on his lapels.

Love and sorrow wafted across the chapel like perfume.

So did the perfume.

He didn't see Minnie. He watched for La Gloriosa. No sign of his big brother either, whom he was scared to see.

The funeral director hid in his back office, watching golf on his phone. He paused it and stirred himself and came out and plugged in a laptop that started playing a slide show of Mamá's life to a soundtrack of her favorite singer, Pedro Infante. The pictures began to cycle through: Big Angel as a boy, some weird little black dogs, babies, old houses with flower vines on the walls, a desert, Big Angel and MaryLú and César as jug-eared kids with thick eyebrows and skinny bellies, more kids in black-and-white photos taken with a Brownie camera. A motorcycle. A filthy fishing boat. A stack of clam and oyster shells taller than the children. No pictures of Don Antonio.

Mourners started to file in, stunned by the extravagance of the funeral the family had arranged and looking around for Big Angel. Forty-five minutes of embraces and ostentatious arrivals and all the siblings arranging themselves in the front row and the rings of descendants, like shock waves of a meteor strike, radiating back through the room. Paz, the controversial chilanga sister-in-law, cast angelic glares of disdain at everybody she felt was not dressed properly. She watched them as she spread gold lamé sheets over the altar. César's third trophy wife. Dressed in leopard spots, and her hair in a fancy spiky bob with purple tips. Little Angel stepped up to him and they embraced.

"My sexiest brother," César said and reached back to grab Little Angel's ass.

Little Angel looked around to make sure nobody saw that. This seemed inappropriate on so many levels.

Paz sneered.

"Happy to see you too, Carnal," Little Angel said.

Paz stared at him. He had aged, but not enough. He thought he was so special. Living with hippie gringos far away. No troubles at all. Why would he age? Though he had some gray showing at his temples, she was happy to see. And César, squeezing his brother's ass. He'd hit on a hole in the ground if he thought there was a gopher in it.

"Let go of my butt."

César's sad face crinkled into its first smile in seven days. "Did you miss me?" he said.

"Always."

César watched Little Angel as his eyes roamed the crowd. He looked at every face as if he didn't know any of them. He was exactly like Big Angel, César thought: always watching.

Grandchildren were holding obstreperous great-grandchildren on their hips. Americanized teen chicks lurked around the far edges, looking at their cell phones. Everybody had dressed up as best they could, except one old knucklehead in a Hawaiian shirt and shorts.

Big Sister MaryLú came into the room, somber and elegant in her black dress. Little Angel loved her smell—she was all Chanel No. 5. Hugs, air kisses.

"Baby Brother," she said.

Everybody speaking English.

"Is everybody coming?" he asked.

"Pos, chure."

"Even El Yndio?"

They looked at the door as if he'd appear.

"It's complicated," she said.

The awkward pause felt long enough for a dandelion to germinate.

Finally, Little Angel said, "Where's the patriarch?"

She looked at her tiny rectangular watch with utter ferocity. "They must be making him late." There seemed to be a sadistic satisfaction in her smirk, like the face of a teacher who had just caught a kid cheating on his pop quiz.

She took Little Angel's hand and led him to the pew. They formed a little line there, brother-sister-brother. And Paz—

who was MaryLú's greatest enemy on Earth. Each of the women elaborately ignored the other. César nobly constructed a border between them with his body.

MaryLú opened her pocketbook and produced clear mint Life Savers. Little Angel accepted one and a folded Kleenex just in case. He took a small notebook out of his pocket and clicked his pen.

"You're going to *write?*" she said. "*Now?*"

"No." He leaned into her and showed her the pages. "I'm taking notes. I don't know who anybody is. It's my cheat sheet."

"Paz," it said, surrounded by black circles. A squiggly line extended to César. On the facing page, César's exes were in their own circles, with outriders radiating—various kids. A grandkid or two. These were fractal pages.

MaryLú made the family's I-know-what-you-mean face. "Mm-hm," she intoned. "Tell me about it." She tapped the offspring page. "You missed Marco."

"Who's Marco?"

"Satan."

César leaned around his sister and held his fingers straight up from the top of his head. "Hair," he said. "Es mi hijo!"

Little Angel added Marco to the pattern, with erect hair atop the little circle.

Meanwhile, the priest, in full regalia, skulked behind the curtain at the front of the room, like Liberace. He checked his watch. He didn't care if Big Angel was there or not. He burst forth exactly on time, raising his arms and cracking a toothsome grimace. He seemed to lack a theme song. He began shouting straightaway, as though demons were being blown out the back windows. He pointed above the heads of the mourners toward the distant and blessed greeny shires of heaven. He ignored the siblings and their children, firing his evangelical rockets over them. People were shaking their heads and wondering, *Is he yelling at me?*

They had seen this before. Lately, it seemed Mexican funerals were being reimagined as last-ditch chances to terrorize the survivors into converting. It had happened at Don Antonio's service and had disrupted Braulio's funeral as well.

"We mourn Doña América!" he said. "We miss Mamá América! You all claim to love her? Then why have more of your family not come to her service? Nearly a hundred years old, and the rest of you are what? *Watching television?*"

The general thought, among the mourners, was a version of *Oh shit.*

The priest was revved up like some kind of Elysian dragster, about to pull religion wheelies all the way down the track. They were in for it now with no way to get out.

"She gave you nearly one hundred years of *motherly sacrifice!* Good mother, good grandmother, good Catholic, good neighbor! The lines of mourners should be *out the door!* Shame. Shame. Shame."

Well, he wasn't wrong.

❧

Big Angel's minivan was just pulling up outside.

"Ahora, sí," he said. He rubbed his hands.

Lately, his anger often manifested itself in a wicked good mood. The shorter his time on Earth, the more convinced he was that he was invincible. If only everything would comply with his plans. What was it Little Angel had said when he was in college, reading all those European books? "Hell is other people." Meds worked all right, but his own ability to outsmart and outmaneuver everyone and everything—even death—was his secret superpower. *Screw death.*

Dying was for worms and chickens, not angels.

Bone cancer? He had found herbs and minerals that would make bones rebuild like coral reefs! Vitamin C, vitamin D, vitamin A. Chaga tea. Tumors in his organs? Turmeric! Selenium, by golly.

I am invincible, he told himself. *I am not invisible.*

Even in his wheelchair, Big Angel believed he could kick the ass of anything that came at him, and everybody else believed it too. They needed it to be true. Even when the kids thought they were fooling him by lying about some ghastly eruption of malfeasance and moral rot, they secretly relied on his infallibility. Big Angel would always catch them, but he would forgive.

I am the patriarch, he told himself for the thousandth time as they wrestled him out of the minivan and got him folded into his chrome chariot. That made him so mad he smiled at his wife and son and daughter. It scared them all.

He heard the wails coming through the door in florid Spanish: "Mother América wanted nothing more than to keep you out of hell! You generation of vipers!"

What kind of squawking was this?

"Yeesus krites." Big Angel pointed at the double doors of the chapel as if leading a cavalry charge.

He sure as hell had them bang open the doors as loudly as possible. He directed them to roll him down the aisle, front and center. He was taking over. After all, he was named Miguel Angel. Who else in the family was named after the archangel Michael? He wished he had a flaming sword.

Goddamn it. Sorry, God.

His smile grew wider. He was pretty well persuaded that he could outsmart God too.

Perla leaned into the chair and kept him moving. Hungry Man marched behind, bearing the walker. Big Angel made plenty of noise. He coughed. He kicked his footrests a couple of times so they clattered, adding to the percussive cadence.

Poor Minnie stared at the floor and tried not to laugh. Oh no—there was Uncle Little Angel. No way. No way was she gonna look at him. She would pee herself laughing if he looked at her. Everybody was turning around. She avoided Little Angel's eyes.

Big Angel let his left brow rise and gave them his most ironic glare, letting them know that the sheriff was back in town. The kids and grandkids called him Pops, and that magic word flowed down the gathered clan.

"Here comes Pops."

"Pops in da house."

"Check it. Pops is low-riding."

The elder members of the family never failed to marvel at the attitude of the kids, how Big Angel was a rolling laugh riot to them, arbiter of bad jokes, spiritual insight, ice cream money, and shelter when they were bounced out of their houses or were let out of jail or rehab or needed to come in off the streets at midnight.

He nodded to them, making eye contact with every single one of them, and raised one finger at his favorites, which seemed to each person to be her- or himself.

"Go slow, Flaca," he told his wife. "Roll me right down the middle. Go slow."

"Ay, Flaco," she said softly. "Don't make a scene."

"Just watch me, Perla."

She shook her head and smiled at the gathered faces: *I am married to a willful man*, she was telling them all with her eyes.

He was as fierce as a falcon in his chair. He could smell the priest's breath shooting up the aisle like a secret weapon. Big Angel, pointing at his thousand nephews and granddaughters and children. His brothers and sisters were the old generation now. Sitting in a grim line up front. All of them looking at Mamá's urn and realizing the same thing at the same moment: *We are now the oldest generation, and we are the next to die.* They looked back and were shocked at Big Angel's appearance, even though they saw him daily.

Big Angel craned around in his chair to nod at Perla's sisters. There was steadfast Lupita with her American husband, Uncle Jimbo. In shorts! And there she was, La Gloriosa. As tragic and magnificent as he had ever seen her. He couldn't remember her real name, just her nickname. He couldn't remember if he had ever heard her real name. She had always been the Glorious One. Alone. Lost, as always, in the cool meadows of her own thoughts. Shiny black hair with a supernatural silver streak spilling down the left side of her face. Her shades were impenetrably black. He didn't know if she was looking at him or not.

Her hands smelled like warm, sweet spices. He thought of the side of her neck. Orange peel, lemongrass, mint, cinnamon. She nodded slightly. He looked away.

Perla watched this. She had been noting their shenanigans for decades. She squinted at her sister. La Gloriosa made a Qué? face back at her.

Big Angel was excited to see his youngest brother sitting in the front row. The great lost soul. English teacher who had gone off to Seattle and lived in the rain. Big Angel felt like he had built his little brother from some kind of model kit. Little Angel. His namesake.

i broke my little brother's nose and it felt good

⌘

Little Angel sat at the far end of the sibling row and grinned at his big brother.

Big Angel waved at Little Angel—he could raise his hand only a few inches off the armrest, but he held it up as if giving a benediction.

Little Angel whispered to his sister María Luisa, "Hey, Lu-Lu—Big Brother has become the pope of Tijuana."

Everyone still called her MaryLú. It had been so kicky in 1967. When she wore go-go boots and pinned falls in her hairdo. She had never worn jeans or a T-shirt. She used to have a bright pink rattail comb and a jar of some hairstyling phlegm called Dippity-do.

Even seated, brother César was taller than the rest. Everyone joked that Mother must have had a secret lover because nobody could explain his size. His Valkyrie wife sat on his far side, making sour faces. Poor César was utterly crushed by his mother's death. He was sixty-seven, and his mother had still ironed his shirts for him. She had given him a chocolate orange every Christmas. Always had menudo for him and her old Spanish *Reader's Digests*. Being without her made him feel like a child lost in a rainstorm. His hands shook. He could not even consider the details of his big brother's illness. He reached out for Big Angel's hand. Their fingers touched. Big Angel's were as cold as the grave. César clenched his own hands and held them before his lips.

The priest, sensing his grip on the crowd slipping away, suddenly shouted: "Sinners buy ten million condoms for Mardi Gras every year!"

If Mamá América were alive, she would have slapped him for talking about condoms in front of her urn. The two Angels locked eyes and started to laugh. The wheelchair loomed in the aisle between the front pews, about a foot from the priest.

"Aquí estoy," Big Angel announced, settling a little more comfortably in his chair.

The priest stopped and stared at him.

"Carry on," Big Angel said. "I give you permission." He opened and closed his skinny legs and held his hands in his lap. "Go on."

The good father collected himself.

Big Angel smiled like Saint Francis. He gestured impatiently. Tapped his watch.

"You're on Mexican time, Padre. We're working people. Vámonos, pues."

"I . . . gave up television," the priest preached. "For forty days. Not because I had to. But because I wanted to offer it up as a sacrifice!" He was catching his stride again. "Protestants want to take away our saints! Our blessed statues! Our Virgin! And they want to have unmarried sex. Sodomy is the law of the land! And you, the cursed generation, turn from God and the values of your matriarch, who rests before you now! The least you could do is sacrifice! Sí, mi pueblo! Sacrifice TV!"

He held up his hand.

"Our Lord and Savior demands a sacrifice! Sacrifice your favorite television programs."

"Chingado," Big Angel said, looking around at his family. "There goes *Ice Road Truckers*."

They strangled on laughter. Little Angel had to lean on his big sister's shoulder.

"Shh!" she and César said.

MaryLú was still a good Catholic girl. Sort of. She covered her mouth with her hankie and guffawed. "You're bad," she whispered.

Minnie sat behind Little Angel. "Daddy, for the win," she said.

He looked back at her, and the look in his eyes said: *He always wins.* And her look said: *You know it.*

"Amen," the priest finally choked out, and he flew through the fake-satin curtain beside the altar.

Big Angel said, "Now the family will speak for itself."

Nobody was ready to give a eulogy, but el patriarca had commanded them. One by one, they came forward and spoke what poetry each could muster. He sat with his hands folded over his tiny belly, nodding and smiling and laughing, but he never wept.

⊘⟡

3:00 p.m.

"Oh, my mother," Big Angel said.

He had failed her. He knew he had. He had failed in so many ways, at so many things. Mother, Father, Mazatlán and the Bent family, Braulio, Yndio. But it had taken a while to get control of the ship. There had been mistakes. *Captains are not born*, he told himself, *they are made.* He wasn't yet convinced, however.

But Mother. He felt that she had not respected his beloved Perla, and he had let her fade into the background of his life. He liked to think that a Mexican mother would respect a man who stood by his wife; he didn't count on the rules set by this Mexican mother. No dissention, ever. No disobedience. So they had been cordial with each other. Still, when she came for a visit, she would have some terrorist act in her bag of tricks. She would wander into the kitchen and somehow get into the cabinets so she could say in a conversationally mild tone, "You'd think these pots and pans would be brighter. Maybe they're old, not just dingy." Or a helpful note that Perla should scrub coffee cups, not merely rinse them.

Big Angel had not physically cuddled his mother like his brother César had. Hell, even Little Angel had hugged her more than he had. César ended up sleeping on her couch after each marriage ended. She had still done his laundry and packed him lunches for work.

Every son, he told himself, *will suffer after his mother has gone and he realizes how little he thanked her.*

"I am nobody special," he said. "Just a husband, a father. A working man. I wanted to change the world."

There was no one there.

છ૭

Big Angel was turning seventy. It seemed very old to him. At the same time, it felt far too young. He had not intended to leave the party so soon. "I have tried to be good," he told his invisible interviewer.

His mother had made it to the edge of one hundred. He had thought he'd at least make it that far. In his mind, he was still a kid, yearning for laughter and a good book, adventures and one more albóndigas soup cooked by Perla. He wished he had gone to college. He wished he had seen Paris. He wished he had taken the time for a Caribbean cruise, because he secretly wanted to snorkel, and once he got well, he would go do that. He was still planning to go see Seattle. See what kind of life his baby brother had. He suddenly realized he hadn't even gone to the north side of San Diego, to La Jolla, where all the rich gringos went to get suntans and diamonds. He wished he had walked on the beach. Why did he not have sand dollars and shells? A sand dollar suddenly seemed like a very fine thing to have. And he had forgotten to go to Disneyland. He sat back in shock: he had been too busy to even go to the zoo. He could have smacked his own forehead. He didn't care about lions, tigers. He wanted to see a rhinoceros. He resolved to ask Minnie to buy him a good rhino figure. Then wondered where he should put it. By the bed. Damned right. He was a rhino. He'd charge at death and knock the hell out of it. Lalo had tattoos—maybe he'd get one too. When he got better.

People filed out. Cousins hugging cousins. Big abrazos.

He was taking inventory—in his mind, a spreadsheet: he repented of one sin per day, and he moved it to the other column marked PAID. On this day he repented that he had ever loved eating sea turtle soup. Sopa de caguama, how rich it was. With lime and cilantro, fresh rolled corn tortillas with salt in them to catch a bit of broth, and some chile. He didn't like chile, really, but his father had taught him a man ate chile until he broke out in a sweat. It was supposed to prevent cancer. Old Don Antonio had sneezed every time he ate it—sneezed until he turned purple. But he went back for more. Suffering had been his religion. Big Angel shook his head. But his tongue wiggled from just thinking of that soup. Now all he really wanted was to simply swim with the turtles and beg their forgiveness for finding their flippers so delicious for so long.

"Lotta troubles," he said. "Y muchos cabrones."

He observed them all from the short watchtower of his chair.

There were days when he could not recall any sins at all. On these days, he thought he might be through with all his transgressions. Clear. But he was a smart man—too smart to fall for his own tricks. There was always another sin drifting in the shadows, waiting to alight and sting the heart.

When Minnie stopped to check on him, he said: "Mija—a rhino has such thick skin, mosquitoes and flies can't bite him. They bend their beaks on him."

"How nice," she said.

❦

3:30 p.m.

Home for a minute. He had to get his diaper changed before the burial. *Poor Minnie*, he thought. *Having to deal with that. But you do what you have to do. It's family, pues.*

His friend Dave had given him a nice little set of three moleskin notebooks and had told him to write his gratitude in them.

"Gratitude for what?"

"That's up to you. I can't tell you what to be grateful for."

"This is silly."

"Dare to be silly. You take yourself too seriously anyway."

"Gratitude?"

"Try it. Gratitude is prayer. You could always use more prayers."

"Liking mangos and papayas is a prayer?"

"It all depends on you, Angel. Do you mean it? Will you miss it?"

"Claro que sí."

"Well, then. Besides, what's wrong with doing something silly to make yourself happy?"

The notebooks had a title: My *Silly Prayers*. He kept one in his shirt pocket, when he was wearing a shirt with a pocket. Or he kept it tucked under his left buttock in bed or in his wheelchair. He terrorized his daughter with his demands for a steady stream of blue G-2 pens. He refused to write with anything else. Those were the pens he had used at work, and those were the pens he used now.

mangos

was the first entry. And then:

(dave you idiot)

in case his friend ever saw it.

marriage
family
walking
working
books
eating
cilantro

That surprised him. He didn't know where it came from. *Cilantro?* he thought. Then:

my baby brother

Every day, he found his gratitudes more ridiculous. But they were many, and they reproduced like desert wildflowers after rain. He could not stop himself; his daughter had to buy him a second, then a third, set of tiny notebooks.

wildflowers after rain
the heart breaks open and little bright seeds fall out

Before that, he hadn't realized he was a poet, among his many other attributes.

◈

He missed sex, even masturbating. All he could hold now was a soft tenderness that filled him with despair. He had been famous in his bedroom for volume, trajectory, and distance. And these things had faded until even the branch itself faltered and nothing could come from him again.

"Ay, chiquito!" Perla cried when they made love. "Eres tremendo!"

He remembered brown nipples—they floated through his days like strange shadows of delicious little birds that he could not touch. Almost buttery against his tongue. His fingers and palms felt cinnamon bellies and backs even as his hands lay at rest on his quilt. He tasted the sea inside his lover. And her milk.

He missed walking, missed his restless flirtations with Perla's sisters, though he felt repentant about that part. La Gloriosa, especially. Good God—even now, she could stop a truck with a flash of her leg. He hadn't felt a stirring in his palo for ages, but just thinking of La Gloriosa in a colorful dress and some dangerous heels made him remember the swell and pulse of the branch. For a moment, he believed he had been cured and it would bloom. He shook his head ruefully.

Walking, he told himself. Focus on the subject at hand! Strolling in the park, walking to McDonald's, holding hands with Perla and perambulating along Playas de Tijuana, watching the Border Patrol helicopters just north of the rusting border wall, eating fish tacos in the stands by the seaside bullring. The ease and pump of his strong body. Comfortable shoes.

He utterly missed his unbroken body.

Somehow Perla knew when he was thinking these things. Especially when he thought about women. So he cleared his mind. He had been the first in the familia to use computers, and he told himself now: *Reboot. Reboot, cabrón. Control-Alt-Delete. Absolutely, Delete.*

"Es muy sexy, mi Angel," Perla often announced when they were all gathered.

It was hard to feel sexy with all his bones turning to chalk and his legs aching day and night. Wearing a diaper. His brave daughter asked him often, "Daddy, did you pee-pee yet?" Jesus Christ. *Sorry, Lord.* But how did he get smaller than she was?

being taller than my kids

Big Angel had always been their leader. Since Don Antonio had abandoned them to starve in La Paz, his siblings had looked to him as their father figure. And now he was his own daughter's baby. Now she put baby powder on his nalgas. This felt like one of the corny jokes he loved to tell when they were all together.

"You all right, Daddy?" she said.

"I'll never be all right again."

He stared for long stretches, and though she knew there was a lot going on inside him, she had no idea how much.

Minerva—she hated that name. But her homegirls right away had changed it to Minnie, which became La Minnie Mouse. Made it easy to buy her Christmas presents—she had quite a collection. Minnies and Mickeys. Plushies and plastic, hoodies and pillows.

He gestured for two of the gathered peewees to come to him. Grandkids, he thought. Maybe great-grandkids. There were always a couple of them around. His children had all had children, and those children were having children. His nieces and nephews even had children.

They crowded around his chair.

"Yeah, Pops?"

"When I was in the hospital the last time," he said in his delightfully accented English, modeled on Ricardo Montalbán. (Because the peewees could only say "taco" and "tortilla" in Spanish, he spoke English.) "Do you know what happened?"

"No, Pops."

"There was a guy, a very sick guy."

"Sicker'n you, Pops?"

"Ay sí. So sick they had to cut off half of him."

"Gross!"

"Yeah. They cut off the guy's whole left side!"

"What? Like, everything, Pops?"

"Todo. His left arm, his left leg, his left ear. His left nalga."

The kids shouted—they valued random butt references.

"But guess what?"

"What, Pops?"

"He's *all right* now!"

They didn't get it.

Here Comes the Rain Again

hot showers
driving
Perla pulling up her stockings
eggs frying in hot lard
tortillas — corn not flour!
Steve McQueen

Lalo came for him.

"Nice and clean," Big Angel said. "Feeling fresh." He spoke English to his boy. He felt great. He tucked his little book under himself. He was going to beat this. "I am alive."

"Right on."

Lalo had changed out of his uniform. He wasn't going to admit to anyone that it was too tight. And he knew he looked fine in his best suit. His only suit. Big Angel had taken him to the mall and found him a dark blue two-piece with a thin chalk pinstripe. White shirt with a maroon tie. Black wing tips.

Minnie had gone ahead with Perla and Little Angel, who had waited for them in the parking lot. *One more day*, Big Angel thought as Lalo wheeled him across the tarmac and onto the cemetery grass. One more day to go. Till the pachanga.

"Careful, Son."

"Gotcha, Pops."

"Don't dump me out."

"That would be funny, though."

"Have you no respect?"

"Nothin' but! Respect for the OG!"

"OG. Does that mean 'old geezer'?"

"Funny, Pops!"

"I know. Hurry."

❧

The hell was Pops in such a hurry for? Lalo thought the old man needed a major chill pill, like soon. *Dude, what's the rush?* If Lalo was heading for the grave, he'd drag his feet, fire up a few blunts, kick back, and ease into it. Well, that's what he was doing now, because where else was everybody going? Freakin' hole in the dirt. Make it muy suave, homie—ain't no race, so slow your pace.

His left forearm itched like a bitch. His newest tat: an image of his dad in better days, with that old-school Mexican mustache. It said POPS 4EVER. Cost him $260 in San Ysidro. He wanted to scratch it, but he didn't want it to bleed into his new threads.

Lalo was the last of the boys. Life had taken the others. One was here—close to where Grandma was going to rest. It made him feel weepy. *Damn, Braulio*, he thought. The blood stayed on the sidewalk for days—turned brown. It was like some dead lake. He and his homies stood beside it, staring, staring, crying, vowing payback. Flies got at it when it turned to pudding in the sun.

How come nobody thought to rinse it off? Flies—man, he hated flies. Iraq was full of goddamn flies. There, blood got into the dirt, though. Puddles didn't last long. Soaked through the dust and gravel. You could see it, like some shadow, but what you could really do was smell it.

He shook his head.

After the pudding dried, wasps came and tweaked out all over it, shaking and nibbling bits of crust off the edges of the stain. Braulio. It all blended with combat in his mind. His leg scar was burning. He wondered if his own blood was still in the dirt back there or if some dog had dug it up and licked it clean.

And his other brother, his big brother, had gone away and didn't care to come back for a visit. Yndio. *Yeah, okay, your loss. Culero.*

He pushed his dad along. "I'm the good son, Pops," he said.

Big Angel reached his hand as far over his head as he could, and Lalo gave him a soft five, sliding his fingers off his dad's.

"Thank you, mijo," Pops said.

Big Angel was negotiating with God: *Give me one more birthday and I'll make it good. Nobody's ever going to forget the day. They'll be thinking about you forever, God. All those miracles you do. Right? Like me. Like giving me one more day. You got this, God. You can do this.*

His mind burned with random glory. Sunsets over La Paz. The shadows in a ruined Mexican cathedral after the workers had shoveled out the dead pigeons and dung. The infinity of folded shadows between his wife's thighs. The whale he saw in the Sea of Cortez, rising from the water and hanging there in shattered glass skirts of sea water as if the air itself held its impossible bulk aloft, and flying fish as tiny and white as parakeets passing under its arched belly and vanishing in foam.

He looked up. It was still raining. Perla hated rain, but Big Angel knew a signal when he saw it. New life coming. Life carries on. He arched one of those brows at the Lord.

Ahead, Little Angel held an umbrella over Perla. She leaned on him as they walked across the wet grass. He didn't fool Big Angel. He knew his baby brother had always been attracted to his wife. Who wasn't? He wondered if, on one of those party nights, when the tequila was flowing...But, no. No way. Why get suspicious now?

Perla and Little Angel veered to the side, aiming, he knew, for Braulio's grave. But she never made it there. As he expected, she started to collapse. In ten years she had never made it all the way across that lawn. Little Angel held her up and semi-dragged her toward the correct burial. Her wails were small across the space, and muffled. It disturbed him as if he were having some terrible dream. He turned his head, took in the vista—tombs, statues, trees, rain—then looked back at his wife and baby brother.

She had shrunk too. Just like Big Angel had. All short now. Poor Flaca, in her black dress and shawl. Her skin was still beautifully brown, though—too brown for the taste of his own mother. Mamá América had preferred paler hues. But he and Perla had earned their splotches and scars and moles and wrinkles. Her legs were veiny and bowed, but he knew damn well Little Angel had admired those legs when Perla was in her prime. So had his other brother. So had his father. But she had remained his. And he admired her exactly as she was.

She'd had to teach him where to put his tongue when they were young, but once he knew, he never missed.

"I win," he said.

The only other umbrella they could find in the house during their mad scramble to the funeral was a silly child's parasol. Big Angel popped it open. He tried to ignore the picture he must make as he squinted out from under the pink Hello Kitty.

There was just a bit of mistiness in the air, really. Evanescent and funeral appropriate.

Big Angel looked a little harder through the mist, and there he was: the Old Man. Don Antonio's ghost, looking dapper. It was lounging behind the tree, waiting for Mamá América to get done with this gala so they could go dancing on Saturn. Big Angel nodded at his father. His father grinned and moved back behind the tree with his finger over his lips.

"Lalo," Big Angel said, turning back to his son. "Death is not the end."

"Yeah? Huh. I'll study up on that." *Looks pretty final to me, Pops.*

Usually, Lalo spent the day in gym shorts and an old Van Halen tee. But there were times, like today, when the world needed to remember what kind of man he was. Big day demanded big props, and he liked good clothes to demonstrate those props. *Props to Pops,* he said to himself.

But this "There ain't no death" bullshit? Yeah. No.

Death sure was the end for his brother. *Death* sure was the big mother-effer that took out half his boys in that Allahu-Akbar alley. *Death* sure as shit should have taken him instead of them and one of his balls. It just unzipped his leg, used his ball sack like a zipper pull and opened it on up from thigh to knee, around the knee and into his boot. Just to get a look. Like steak inside there. Yndio called him One Ball when he got home. Lalo didn't know why that was so funny, but he'd laughed so hard he cried, telling his brother, "That ain't funny, asshole!"

Death?

It took two hands to count the homies he'd lost right here in town. At McDonald's, at the park, under the off-ramp to 805. And that cop Braulio and Joker had beaten down with chains.

That dude wasn't getting up again. He wasn't gonna dance no more if he ever woke up.

That right there was for real.

Yeah—not a peep from any one of 'em. None of them players ever came back. That mystical Pops brujo stuff was just some cosmic old Mexican bullshit. Death not the end? Maybe so, if you counted nightmares. There were lots of chatty dead dudes in nightmares. Pops knew things, sure, but he hadn't seen no brains on no sidewalk. Like all vatos, Hungry Man was a philosopher. Damn, his leg ached; he was hoping to get a little taste of something to ease it.

And Big Angel was thinking: *These children are so stupid; they think they are the first to discover the world.*

❧

Lalo knew he was a sharp-dressed man in that new pinstriped suit. He was taking the raindrop hits on his semi-shaved head like a boss. It was bare to the elements since he'd taken off his beret. He imagined his face looked carved from dark wood. All Chichimeca warrior, cabrones. Firme.

His 'stache drooped a little, and the soul patch under his lower lip looked bandido as hell. His black shades revealed nothing. Though he was always glancing back and forth— watching for knuckleheads from La Mara or El Hoyo Maravilla. Them gangbangers was always looking for trouble. You couldn't be from the wrong neighborhood.

He was furthermore engaged in watching for the damn Border Patrol. And government drones. Peeping the brown man, count on that.

Migra! For some reason his TJ homies called the Border

Patrol the "Little Star of the Sea." WTF, Lalo wanted to know. But he couldn't go back to TJ to ask nobody. Not right now.

The Border Patrol had been sneaky lately—he heard peeps talking about BP agents staking out PTA meetings and grabbing brown parents on their way out. Later with that! He wasn't about to have some migra em-effer grab a tío or tía. Not today.

Or himself, for that matter.

No cops. Which he called "chota," or "placa," in the language his father did not understand. Braulio and Yndio had taught him. Though Yndio was scarier than the other boys. So tall, so dark, and, man—those muscles. He wasn't really what he seemed. That boy was the best of all of them. Braulio had them fooled. He was hilarious. He could pour honey on Moms and Pops. Nobody had any idea but Minnie. Wasn't Yndio who ever got arrested. It was Lalo.

He'd already been in jail a couple of times. It was bad, the last time—feds and everything. But the worst part was making Pops look bad. Pops had warned him over and over. If he kept getting in trouble, not only would it make the family look bad but the cops would figure out he was illegal and kick his ass out of the USA. "Don't worry, Pops. I'm a wounded veteran." Yeah.

And he had never asked them to carry him as a baby across the Tijuana River. But there it was. Lalo just born, in 1975, and Pops decided it was time to drag them across the border to San Diego, where he'd been hiding out and working, illegal as hell. Camping out at Grandpa's house. "Building a better life for them," as he liked to say on weekends when he came creeping back to Mexico. Lalo was feeling sorry for himself—Dude grows up in Dago, thinking he's a Viva La Raza American vato, and finds out all of a sudden he has to hide from the Border Patrol. Ain't that the shits.

"Why is it always me?" he said.

"What?" Big Angel replied.

Lalo was glad he'd said something, because the way Pops was slumped in his chair, Lalo was starting to think he was asleep or dead. *Better not be dead, Pops. Not on my watch.*

ↀ

Lalo forced himself to look across the wet grass at Braulio's stone. So painful. It was all he could do at the moment. "Hey, bro," he whispered. It would have to be enough.

It was Braulio who thought he'd figured out the immigration thing. Minnie didn't have to worry about it. What a gringa. Homegirl was all borned up in National City, like a real American. She didn't have to deal with these things. She could vote.

Maybe Braulio had even wanted to be good. Do good. Who knows? Get some meaning into his life along with his papers. Lalo had learned anything was possible.

Braulio, when he got kicked out of school for fighting, had stayed away from the house more and more to avoid Big Angel and Perla's disappointment. Until 1991—when he was twenty years old. On one of those prowling days, he ran into some army recruiters. They had a small booth at the mall, like those earnest characters who hawked "magic-vision" 3-D posters and small plastic helicopters that zoomed around like alarming insects.

Braulio liked to take Lalo to the mall with him, cruise the chicks, hit up the cookies at Mrs. Fields. They usually mall-crawled with Joker, Braulio's junior gangsta homeslice, but this day they were flying solo, just the two of them. Braulio was looking for some skinny jeans, and Joker, being a traditional vato, didn't go for that emo shit. He would have mocked

Braulio all day long for going all gabacho and trying to look like some white boy.

So they had just exited The Gap, with Security keeping a cyborg-sharp eye on them. They were snickering and trying to say dashing things to the Filipina girlies in their tiny shorts. "Damn!" was about the best they could come up with. But what mattered was how you said it. "Dayum!" Like it was made out of caramel and would stick to their lips. "Dayum, gurrrl," with a little corner-of-the-mouth *chk!* and a slight shake of the head. "For reals." Maybe a hand briefly upon the dick. Poor Lalo—he thought this was slick business.

Then Braulio saw the tank.

The Army booth had a plastic M14 mounted to the back wall and a tank on its seven-foot-tall poster, rampant in mid-launch off some distant and foreign sand dune. A young blond soldier was greatly in evidence in the foreground of this action shot, lit up like the Pet of the Month. He was giving the world a giddy thumbs-up. The blocky-headed sarge at the desk had a pen made out of a .50-caliber bullet. His teeth were as brilliant as white plastic. There was a small crowd of boys milling around the booth. From behind these boys, Braulio and Lalo heard such utterances of awe as the following popped from the boys' lips: "Dude"; "Firme, vato"; and (for hodads too lax to say "bro") "Brah."

Drawn in as if by a tractor beam, Braulio rolled right out of the '80s and into some tech future of metal and engines. Lalo felt his brother slip out of the family in the fifty steps it took to be drawn into the U.S. Army. He never understood the alchemy of that transition.

By the time Lalo caught up to him—that walk for him was a mile—Braulio had pushed through the bros and football players and was sitting at the desk, already spooling his line of barrio bullshit to the sarge.

"Like, I ain't gonna lie, sir."

"Don't call me 'sir.' I work for a living."

Braulio didn't know it was a cliché, and he found it profoundly badass.

"I got some beefs," he said.

"By 'beef,' I don't assume you mean prime rib!" Ha-ha-ha-*hah*, he very precisely broadcast. "By 'beef,' I am gonna assume you're telling me you have some *gang-related* issues, what with you being *Hispanic* and all." Ha-ha-ha-*hah*. "Lookit." He aimed his bullet pen at Braulio's skinny face. "Best boys I ever served with were goddamned taco benders, Son. No offense."

"Well, I got some immig—"

"Say no more." A massive palm formed a miniature border fence in Braulio's face. "Don't even say the word. I don't give a shit if you're wet or dry, if you get my meaning. *Wet* or *dry* don't matter shit to me. And it don't matter to Uncle Sam."

"For reals?"

Lalo watched the sarge grimace—he wasn't deeply into vato English, apparently.

"If you are willing to fight for your nation," Sarge lied, "your nation is ready to fight for you. *No greater gift*, and all that. Fighting for the USA. Son, you join up, we handle your papers. Hell, when you muster out, bingo, you're American. Automatic-o."

Braulio looked up at Lalo with real emotion in his face.

"Least we can do," Sarge said and shook Braulio's hand.

Braulio put in two years, most of it in Germany, never saw combat, and came back with heroin in his veins.

Papers. Right. That was some major b.s. right there, but Lalo didn't know it, and Braulio didn't live long enough to find out. Lots of homeboys fell for it, and later they were all squatting in veteran bunkers in Tijuana, wondering how they got kicked out of the country.

Lalo remembered the sarge when he got in trouble years later. It wasn't no thing—just some minor "gang-related" shenanigans—but he wanted to stop it before things got any worse. At twenty-six, he felt too old to be a soldier, but the government was desperate and they were taking almost anybody. He knew, too, that a dude almost thirty would face much more trouble for petty crimes than a stupid kid. A little weed, a knife in the pocket, a street fight. He wanted to be as good as Pops. He could never be that, but he could at least be as good as his bro. The army would make him a man, something he seemed to be struggling to do for himself. So he went looking for the booth. He didn't think there'd actually be a war. In some place he'd never even heard of.

And he didn't expect to get blown up on his first tour in that alley smelling of burned meat. But once Pops came for him at the VA—he was walking with a cane for a while—he felt large and in charge. He was a citizen. They told him his military ID was all he needed. They were right, he believed, until he really stepped in it and was suddenly in serious trouble. And found out he'd been lied to. The recruiters, the army—everybody had said what they needed to say to get one more body on the firing line.

Even though he considered himself an American now, he still went down to Tijuana to hang with some of his friends. In 2012, he was all bold, talking himself up to his Tijuana boys. There was a dude in Colonia Independencia who wanted to get to San Diego—he had a promise of work at the Del Mar race-track, hot-walking the race horses. He said he'd cut Lalo in, get him some cabbage if he helped him. Maybe a full-time job, depending on what the boss said. Firme! Lalo was down with that.

He became an instant expert in schooling the undocumented immigrant.

"You're a Chicano, from Barrio Logan," he instructed his pupil. "None of that Mexican shit. Just say that, homie. Let me do the talking." He gave the kid a Padres cap and a pair of Vuarnet surfer shades. "When they ask you where you were born, say Detroit, Michigan."

"Porqué?"

"It's like, American, güey. Like, real far from TJ. "

"Órale. I got it."

"Say it!"

"Chicano! Logan! Detroit, Michigan. I got it! USA all de way!"

"Say 'Detroit, man.' Like that. Sound American."

"Detroit, meng."

"Not 'meng'! *Man!*"

"Mang."

"Forget it! Stick to saying 'Chicano.' And 'Detroit.' A'ight?"

"A'ight."

"I got the rest. I'm American as hell."

In those ancient days, they didn't need passports to return to the U.S. Lalo drove his '67 Impala convertible. Dropped to floor level, low 'n' slow, in custom Candy Apple blue with white trim. He still owed Big Angel for that. He would get a job, he told himself. Any day now.

He chose the longest line of cars, figuring the border agent would be tired and easy to get by. He had his Raiders cap on his head, his Mountain Dew in his lap, had the radio tuned to oldies, had a little American flag on his antenna. When they pulled up to the booth, the guy turned out to be a woman, and she was giving Lalo the gas face before he even smiled at her.

"Citizenship?" she said.

"U.S., ma'am." Flashed his army ID. "Purple Heart."

"Uh-huh." She curled one lip to warn him to mind his p's and q's. "What was your business in Méjico?"

"Tacos el Paisano. And, you know, shopping."

She leaned down and stared at his homie, sucked her teeth. "You, sir? Citizenship?"

"Chicano, meng."

"I see."

"USA. All the güey!"

She nodded and fingered her radio.

Lalo was getting nervous. "We good?" he said, smiling like Pops to disarm her.

"Sir?" she said to his homie. "Where were you born?"

"Detroit!" he said.

She nodded and withdrew. Lalo was about to drop it into gear and book out of there when the menso beside him decided to add to it.

"Detroit," he called. "Michoacán!"

Daaang.

They were accompanied to the secondary inspection area and cuffed forthwith. He didn't see Moms and Pops until his trial for alien smuggling. He was as surprised as everyone else to find that, well, he was not actually a U.S. citizen. In spite of his best efforts, he brought more shame to the family when he was summarily deported.

And now he was living in his father's garage after creeping and running across the Tijuana River in the dark like some friggin' wetback. Things were okay in TJ, but he needed to get back to take care of Pops. As soon as Yndio came down to tell him Big Angel was sick, Lalo headed north. Getting it together. Saving a little money. He had, like, kids now. Shit to take care of. Couldn't take another fall.

"Chále!" he said out loud.

"What?" said Big Angel.

"Nothin', Pops."

"Are you talking like a gangster again?"

"I was saying 'No way.' That's chále. It's, like, no."

"No to what?"

"To death."

"Then why don't you speak Spanish? Why don't you say no, like a human being?"

"Don't be no racist now."

"A Mexican can't be racist to a Mexican."

"I don't know about that." Lalo was looking around to see if his kids were there. "I'm a Chicano. I'm talkin' Chicano."

"Didn't I tell you that the word 'Chicano' came from 'chicanery'?"

Bullshit, Lalo thought. "Here we are, Pops," he said, parking his father. Freakin' culture clash up in here.

✑

Lalo smiled as they beheld the tent top, erected to keep rain off the mourners: the rule was that everybody see Big Angel was the captain and his soldiers *were hopping to*. Why the hell not? Life was good. He was proud to wheel his father across the lawn.

"The eagle has landed," he said.

He hit the little brake lever with his foot so Pops wouldn't roll around.

Big Angel craned around and looked at his son's nice slacks. His jacket. It was too bad about the tattoos. That damned cholo cross thing on his hand.

He had thought this about his son's new suit: *I want the boy to look good at my funeral. I want Lalo to look at the pictures and feel proud that he was dressed to the nines. Know he dressed like a Mexicano, not a vato. And know that his old man picked that suit out, that the old man had set the dress code for his own burial. And he will feel awe.*

That was all Big Angel ever wanted—to inspire awe.

The grave was a small open shaft among flat headstones laid out like a mosaic in the lawn. Big Angel's siblings gathered, along with those others who had stuck around to pay their respects to the familia. MaryLú, César, Little Angel.

Various feuds and internecine scandals were held in abeyance for the day. It kept them busy, otherwise, shaking their heads over one another's minor atrocities. Gathering in clandestine kitchen meetings to scissor their victims in absentia. Their victims were as tattered as abused coats when they were done. Allegiances shifted like the seasons. Rhetorical weapons ever at the ready.

Minerva was standing over her brother's stone, wiping the rain and the leaves off it. As if she could protect him now. In emerald light, beneath the melancholy leaves of the maple. Her hair gleamed with a thousand small diamonds of rain.

Little Angel stood next to her and bent his head.

"Minnie," he said.

"My big bro, Tío."

The stone said: BRAULIO DE LA CRUZ, 1971–2006.

"It's almost ten years, Tío."

She sniffled. He handed her MaryLú's Kleenex from the funeral.

"I come over here sometimes to talk to him. He was such a brat." She wiped her nose. "I used to eat standing up, right? Breakfast. When I was still going to school. He'd sneak in and scream in my ear and make me throw Cheerios all over the kitchen." She laughed. "Fool," she told the stone.

"Sorry I wasn't here," Little Angel said.

"I'm glad you weren't here. It was bad." She looked around. "You don't need this stuff. It's better you have your world far away from here." She thought for a moment. "Sorry I drunk texted you."

He patted her back. "Made me feel special."

Little Angel had been terrified of Braulio. The kid had been skinny, but muscled like Bruce Lee. Sometimes he'd had a look like a Doberman, trembling before it attacked.

"Is it nice up there where you live?" Minnie asked.

"It's beautiful, yeah," he said. "And Bigfoot lives there."

"You crack me up, Tío." She hugged him with one arm. "I hate this town sometimes," she said.

"Come to Seattle."

"Nah. This is home. I belong here."

They turned away.

"Who's gonna run things if I go?" she said.

"There is that."

"Tell you what, though," she said. "I wish my big bro was here. The biggest bro. He and Daddy don't like each other right now."

Little Angel looked at her.

"Yndio," she said. "He made...lifestyle choices."

"I see." But he didn't, not really. Little Angel forgave himself for not remembering the details, if he'd ever heard them. He didn't want to hear them.

But apparently Minnie wasn't done with him. She produced her cell phone. "Check out his Facebook, Tío," she said. She opened the profile page. The photo was a picture of Marilyn Manson from a few years back in his full cross-dressing outfit with a pair of rubber breasts. The name listed was Yndio Geronimo. Not sure how to respond, Little Angel said, "Uh, wow."

"Right?" said Minnie. "But read what it says."

Non-cisgendered, non-heteronormative cultural liberation warrior.

"That's my bro."

"Minnie, I'm not even sure what all that means. But I can see why your father can't deal with it."

"You think Dad has problems with it? You should ask my mom. She acts like he's dead to her. She makes believe she doesn't even miss him. Then we sneak out to eat pancakes with him so Daddy don't know."

He tried to come up with avuncular wisdom and ended up making a *whee* sound, then clearing his throat.

Frankly, Little Angel had barely registered Yndio's presence. Neither of those two boys had seemed like real family to him. And when Yndio drifted in and out of the mix over the years, Little Angel had barely noticed. *Bad uncle*, he thought.

He watched Minnie walk over to her man and take his arm. He didn't remember if they were married or not.

Little Angel went to the back of the crowd and assumed his position. El Yndio, he thought. Some kind of actor, or model. Hair to his ass, that much Little Angel remembered. He had given the kid Bowie records. Big Angel and Perla hadn't liked that. He suddenly wondered if he had been a catalyst for this sexual revolution. And if he had been, was it a good thing or a bad thing?

A family inheritance, he thought. Endless drama. This was why he lived in Seattle. Family. It was all too complicated.

☙

Big Angel whispered to his mother, "Forgive me if I have no tears to spare for you, Mother. I am down to my last ones. I know you understand."

rain

Most mourners were jammed under the tent. They pressed forward to lay a hand on the blue vase of ashes, sitting on a small folding platform. Beautiful wreaths surrounded the open hole. More were coming—husbands of the various ladies trudged along carrying the flowers from the Bavarian chapel. A UPS man hauled out wreaths delivered from Mexico. No priest, though.

There was a small blue tarp over the raw dirt pile. La Minnie came to it, wiping away tears. She was as beautiful as the Angels had ever seen her. Her dude stood awkwardly behind her, hands clasped in front of his zipper as if he needed to pee.

Little Angel saw it even if they didn't: she was the new backbone of the family. She was wearing a black and blue outfit, and her hair was a cascade of curls and waves, and her nails were two-toned. She was saying "Dios te bendiga, Grandma" to the urn. Her guy stared at her like he'd been hit with a chair in a wrestling match. The Look of Love.

Big Angel watched. He couldn't remember the guy's name. What the hell? He'd known that guy for years. Then he realized he couldn't remember the name of the guy on TV either. That black guy on the nightly news. With the glasses. And he couldn't remember the name of Perla's sister Lupita's pinche Americano husband in the fuchsia shirt. Christ. *Sorry, Lord.*

He cast about, surveilling the crowd. The girls had mostly come in high heels. They were sinking into the mud, picking up fallen leaves with their heels like groundskeepers in parks with spike sticks. Lupita unwittingly displayed three leaves mounted at fetching angles upon her left shoe.

He noticed some of the women were standing on the flat headstones to keep from sinking into the lawn. He shook his head. He imagined dead men lying beneath them, looking up their skirts.

La Gloriosa stood far back under her own umbrella in reasonable flats and a black Burberry overcoat. Huge French sunglasses. Slightly angry. Weeping softly. She wept for them all. Wept for herself. There was a grave about a hundred yards from this family plot that she dared not visit. She didn't even look in that direction. Yes, Braulio was a great tragedy, but he wasn't the only one to die that night. She turned her back to that other grave. Then withstood the full assault of guilt and shame at her cowardice. She watched Little Angel. She had always thought he was a pretty boy. Mexican women, she reminded herself, women of a certain age, could not resist blue eyes. She curled her lip. Estúpida, she thought. It was only her broken heart wanting what it didn't need.

He was flirting with her, she thought. *Todavía lo tienes,* she told herself. She tugged the coat tighter—old curves, maybe, but still curves. Whenever she glanced at him, she caught his eyes turning away, like she'd interrupted his staring. What a child. Any real man would lock eyes with her and make her blush. And once she'd blushed, he'd come stand beside her.

She wanted him to claim her. Just for the afternoon. Not leave her out here alone and wet like some bedraggled puppy.

There was a time when they all would have been at her feet. She could have kicked each one away. The least he could do now was to offer her his arm and accompany her. She shook out her hair. In case he looked again.

≈

Middle brother Julio César and his djinn of a wife, Paz, stood beside sister MaryLú—César standing guard between the warring women. A one-man DMZ. His siblings never stopped calling him Donald Duck—it was an old joke. He couldn't help the sound of his voice.

It was a toss-up whether the women could make it through the burial ceremony without fighting. Whenever Paz leaned over to cast a poisonous glance at César's big sister, César gallantly moved forward and blocked the eye punch with his chin. His exquisite second ex-wife stood apart with his sons and didn't look at him. The first wife? On a ranch somewhere in Durango. Big Angel saw all this, and he saw his brother's thoughts etched on his face: *What the hell was I thinking? Too bad for you,* Big Angel thought. *I stayed with my Flaca the whole time.* He held his chin up.

He had already bought a double plot not far from Mamá's. On the other side of the little maple tree shading her. Beside Braulio. He and Perla would lie together. So, no peeking up skirts for him. FLAQUITO Y FLAQUITA the stone would say, with their names and dates beneath. Perla intended, however, to lie about her birth date when they did her stone.

They would spend forever side by side. And the rest of his fallen children would one day slumber around them all, a constellation of extinguished stars.

❧

Lalo stepped over to Little Angel. "S'up, Tío?" he whispered.

"Doing my duty."

"I hear that."

"She was good to me. Your grandma used to tell me 'I am your mother number two.'"

Lalo did a little Snagglepuss laugh from the side of his mouth, tiny ratchets of appreciation: *skitch-skitch-skitch.*

"I didn't ever meet your moms, did I?"

"Ah no."

"She white."

"As can be. So, you all right?"

"Yeah, Tío. Large and in charge."

"That's what I'm talkin' 'bout," Little Angel enthused with imagined barrio brio.

"Yo, Tío. Where's your wife at?"

"Gone."

"Like *gone* gone? Or dead?"

"Gone. Her and all my furniture."

"Dang. She white."

"Yes."

"Son," said Lalo, "go brown next time. Don't be no race traitor." *Skitch-skitch-skitch.* "Down and brown!" Lalo nudged him with his elbow.

"Órale," Little Angel said, for what else could he say?

Lalo laughed softly and knocked knuckles with him. He pulled up his sleeve and showed him the POPS tattoo.

Little Angel nodded sagely. "I should get one of those," he said.

"Yours will say 'bro.'"

They watched the sad crowd.

"This family," Little Angel noted, "sure does talk a lot. I can't keep track of what they're saying. Or who they are." He showed Lalo his notebook, which greatly amused his nephew.

"Talk, yeah," he finally said to his uncle. "Talk's all we got." With that, Lalo went back to his bodyguard position behind the wheelchair.

❧

There came a little bustle, the crowd parted, and poor Ookie Contreras stumbled out. He still played with Barbie dolls, most of them naked and some beheaded. Ookie was in a huge suit jacket somebody had given him. A brown fedora from some ancient tío, cocked against the rain. He could have been thirteen, and he could have been seventy. His eyes were crossed. Little scraggly pubic chin beard. They called him Ookie because he could never say "cookie." And that homie loved a cookie. But he was infamous in the neighborhood for creeping into people's houses, looking for Legos to steal. Ookie loved Legos more than he loved Oreos or headless Barbies.

He stepped up to the urn. "Gramma," he said. "You be the greatest gramma anybody ever seen." He looked around at the crowd. "Right?" he said.

"Right!" homies shouted.

"Did I do good?"

"Good job, Ookie!" Big Angel called. "We are proud of you, mijo!"

Inspired, Ookie took off his hat. "Big Angel," he cried. "You the best Big Angel I ever seen. Sorry you got to die!"

Stunned silence. A cough.

"We all have to die, Ookie," Big Angel said. "But not today."

Ookie smiled. "Was she my gramma?" he said.

"No, Ookie," said La Minnie.

"Am I your cousin?"

"Neighbors, Ookie."

Ookie pumped his fist one time. Then remembered to wipe a pretend tear from his face before he wandered off.

"Foxy lady," he said. "Purple haze."

Little Angel allowed himself to breathe. Another disaster averted. Family was too much responsibility. That thousand-mile buffer zone was the only thing that worked.

An actual grandson urged his fourteen-year-old daughter forward, and she played a song on her violin. The vida loca faction could not believe a homegirl played violin. They approved. That was badass right there. Her dad had pushed her into it because he wanted her to join a mariachi group. But she wanted to play classical and had managed to get into her school's orchestra. Debussy gave her tingles, not Selena. The vatos would kill for her. It was the college kids, all ironic and hipster, who snickered at every sour note.

"Beautiful, mija," Minnie called.

They clapped.

A group of men from the family stepped up and sang a tremulous ballad that made everybody choke up. They all had to look away. They all stared at the rain. They held one another's hands.

"Shit's *grim*," noted Lalo, who did not enjoy crying.

Big Angel looked behind him, trying to find his baby brother.

Lots of the youngsters were in the New American Pose: heads bowed, hands at mid chest, looking like monks at prayer, texting their asses off on their smartphones. They snuck selfies and posted them to their social media: ME, AT MY ABUELA'S FUNERAL. People with names like La Wera and Viejo Bear were saying things like SO FUKN SORRY, MIJA!:-(

Big Angel found Little Angel. He was also texting.

♂♀

4:48 p.m.

Back at the house. How could you end a whole era and bury a century of life and be home before suppertime? Big Angel could not reconcile himself to this dirty deal they had all been dealt. Death. What a ridiculous practical joke. Every old person gets the punch line that the kids are too blind to see. All the striving, lusting, dreaming, suffering, working, hoping, yearning, mourning, suddenly revealed itself to be an accelerating countdown to nightfall.

When you had seventy years ahead of you, nothing mattered, though you thought it all mattered greatly. But you didn't really feel the pressing need to do anything about it. Suddenly, though, there comes a birthday when you think: *I have twenty years at best*. And those years slide into the dark until you think: *I have fifteen. I have ten. I have five*. And your wife tells you, "Live, don't fret. You could be hit by a bus tomorrow! Nobody knows when the end comes."

But you know she lies in the dark beside you counting the years she has left, even if she won't admit it. Wondering if every twinge in her left shoulder is the final heart attack. And then you find that you have no years left. You have days.

That is the prize: to realize, at the end, that every minute was worth fighting for with every ounce of blood and fire. And the majority of them poured down the toilet, unheeded. He had seen only sixty-nine Christmas mornings. Goddamn it! *Sorry, Lord.* Not enough. Not nearly enough.

So you fill your hours with hubbub. Like now. The house seemed to be bulging elastically like an old cartoon—music and dust flying out through the gaping junctures of the bouncing, jiving walls.

Big Angel surveyed his domain.

✣

The kids had paid for a tent of their own: a wedding reception company was spreading a white vinyl roof over Big Angel's porch and part of his backyard on tall aluminum legs. They were setting up long folding tables. Folding chairs. In the open far back, a small stage with amps for various testimonials or impromptu song recitals. Under blue plastic tarps.

Cars were jammed all down the block, but there were always families gathering in the hood, so it was hard to tell who was there for Big Angel's house and who was hanging down the block watching NFL highlights or having a tamale fest. The minivan was parked half in the driveway. They'd wheeled Big Angel in through the garage—Lalo didn't like it because when they hit the remote, the whole front wall of his bedroom rose and exposed his bed and personal stuff to the street. There were usually a couple of trucks in the driveway, so nobody really saw his small empire. But his Chargers posters fell down.

It was a classic Southern California ranch-style house, built in 1958. In a Mexican neighborhood south of San Diego, between National City and Chula Vista. Lomas Doradas. It used to be a sailor's neighborhood—old Anglo swabs from various wars, and dockworkers from the National City boatyards. Basque tuna fishermen. Gradually, Filipinos moved in, and they gave way to the raza.

All the houses had bars on the windows, which scared outsiders but which nobody from there even saw. None of the grannies on the street wanted some imagined pachuco to break in and steal their Franklin Mint collector plates. John Wayne and angels defending little blond kids with flaming swords hung on kitchen walls all down the street.

Palm trees. Beige walls with bits of brick trim. Asphalt-and-gravel shingles on the roofs. Each house, 1,250 square feet. Five models, each turned at a different angle on its slab for variety. Lantana and geraniums, depressed birds of paradise, cacti. A Joshua tree leaned forward in front of Big Angel's in a small circle of stones in a slim lawn.

All the houses had four bedrooms and a living room, two bathrooms and a nice kitchen-dining area by the sliding door to the quarter-acre backyard. And myriad garage kingdoms developed as unemployed children came home to Mamá.

América, pues.

At Big Angel's, a concrete patio faced the backyard, which swooped up a bank taller than the house. Drought-slaughtered ivy and patches of pickleweed and one psychotic nopal cactus that was well on its way to growing into some prehistoric tree. If you went up there above the cactus, you could look south and watch the lights on the Tijuana radio towers blink. In the dark, even Tijuana looked like a scatter of diamonds.

Big Angel had paid for it all.

There was a second building back there, the size and shape of another one-car garage. It was known as Big Angel's workshop, but nobody had messed with it for years. It had a padlock on the door. They had occasionally raised chickens in the backyard, and the back wall of the workshop was the wall of the coop where they had mounted the sleeping and laying boxes with their straw nests. Fresh eggs every day. And Perla was happy to behead chickens for her pot without blinking. Until the neighbors complained, and the city came along and removed the coops.

Lalo called the neighbors "chicken snitches."

Perla sat at a table on the patio and rubbed her aching knees. Her small flock of doggies was scuttling around like animated empanadas on meth. "Ay, qué perritos," she said. They were Chiweenies. Chihuahua/wiener-dog mixes. La Minnie called them "naked mole rats" since she took her kids to the zoo often and knew these things. Minnie had even been to the art museum.

Perla watched the dogs occasionally leave the earth and pogo around the legs of the workers.

She was not going to think about that cemetery for the rest of the weekend.

"Mija," she called to dear Minnie. "Minerva! Café, sí? Por favor, mi amor."

Minerva, thought La Minnie. Why did she have to have the weird name?

"You got it, Ma!" she called. "Comin' right up!"

"Qué?"

Perla had only lived in the United States for forty-one years—she couldn't be expected to learn English overnight.

"Gracias, mija."

For example, when she tried to call her daughter "honey," she still made it into Spanish. She called her "la honis." In her mind, "honey" started with a Mexican *j* and ended in a long *e*. *La jo-nees*.

Perla sent a slow sigh upward to Our Lady of Guadalupe. She knew that real prayers, women's prayers, didn't even need words. What mother didn't understand her daughter's sighs? Her prayer said: *This party is too much pressure*. The Virgin would just nod. She knew all about complicated males.

Perla's sisters were helping, of course. Lupita, Gloriosa. They were always with her and Big Angel. For holidays, funerals, weddings, births, baptisms, birthdays. For coffee. After divorces. Sitting in at supper or breakfast or cracking a fresh bottle or playing dominoes.

She was watching the bustle, and she watched the little kids run around the yard with the Chiweenie mole rats. Lupita ran the kitchen. La Gloriosa was late—it was her task to lead the children in their mad dashes and to keep the flow moving. Gloriosa was the directora de eventos. It was all a dance. She was always late. La Gloriosa—when you were glorious, you did what you had to do. The world could wait.

Perla lit a cigarette. She had been quitting smoking for fifty years. She shrugged. Even La Gloriosa still smoked sometimes.

Perla squinted.

Who were these little kids? Grandchildren. Great-grandchildren. Nieces. Grand-nieces. Neighbors. There was a tall black kid lounging in a corner.

She called Lalo. "Mijo! Juan! No, Tonio! No! Digo, Tato.

Cómo te llames, pues. Ven!" She couldn't remember anybody's name anymore, and she didn't particularly care.

Lalo was in his garage, watching Big Angel's old VHS tapes. There was, like, a whole library in cardboard boxes. He was in the middle of the '80s monster movie *C.H.U.D.* He paused it. Rolled out of his garage and ambled over. He had shed his suit and was in his Chargers jersey and giant gangsta shorts. Black Chuck Taylors, no socks. He told a little fat boy, "Yo, mijo, don't be a chud!"

He towered over Perla.

"It's Lalo, Ma. Not Tato. Whazzup?" He kissed her head.

Minnie brought out the coffee, said, "Move, huevo head."

"I ain't got no huevo head. Check yourself, puppet!"

"It's like a soft-boiled egg," Minnie noted.

"I'ma kick you."

In Spanish, Perla said, "Who is that negro?"

Lalo said, "That's your nephew, Ma."

"What's he got on his head?"

"Padres hat."

"What's his name?"

"Rodney."

Minnie put the cup of coffee down before her. "Move, cue ball," Minnie told Lalo and rubbed his shaved head.

"Puppet," he said, "be careful nobody don't cut your strings."

"Shut up, boy. Damn."

"Life is wonderful, Minerva," Perla told her. "Full of many wonders. I see ghosts."

"Cool, Ma." La Minnie went back inside to slave in the kitchen. Slightly baffled, but that was what the old-timers did to you. Bad enough Daddy was talking crazy, but now Moms was doing it.

"Don't be no chudhole, Minnie!" Lalo called. He kept scratching at his POPS 4EVER tattoo.

"Pobre Rodney," Perla said. "Is he uncomfortable?"

"'Bout what?" Lalo said. "He's, like, freakin' Rodney. He's always been here, Ma."

"I was never white enough for your father's family," Perla told him. "I mean, she was never white, Mamá América. Brown, como café con leche. But she was whiter than me. O sí, mijito. I heard her calling me an India. I wasn't deaf, you know!" She sipped her coffee. "Too hot," she noted. "Who made this? Anyway. Your grandmother never approved of me. She thought I was low class. She called me a prostitute."

He didn't know what to say to that. "Dang," he said, then went back to his movie in the garage.

He was trying to just shut it all out. His son had called him an hour before. They knew who did it.

"Did what?" Lalo had asked.

"Offed Tío Braulio."

"No shit?"

"Word, Pops," his son said. "So whatchu gon' do about it?"

And Lalo said, *"Me?"*

❧

5:00 p.m.

Little Angel parked down the block. The neighborhood was damp in the gutters but habitually sun flogged and dusty looking. The grass was yellow, and the walls looked faded. He had grown up on the white side of town. The kids in school had thought his family was French.

But his house could have been here: 1,200-square-foot box. Bougainvillea. Big Wheels and scooters abandoned in driveways. Basketball hoops over the garage doors. *Similar class stratum*, the professor inside him lectured. Music was different, though.

He walked up the street. Felt like a camera was watching him. Like eyes were at all the windows. Locals peeping the Crown Vic, thinking: *Pigs!* He hung his head and slumped his shoulders, as if he could become shorter and somehow invisible.

Who's that gabacho?

Oh, it's the gringo-Mex.

Dude looks like a narc.

He always felt self-conscious just walking in the front door of Big Angel and Perla's house like everybody else. As if he hadn't earned a membership yet to their club. But whenever he knocked or rang the bell, they all scolded him. What kind of brother knocks? So he manned up and opened the heavy steel-mesh security grate and stepped inside. People lounged around the big table set up in the living room. Baseball caps with straight bills. Cigarettes.

La Gloriosa had just gotten there and stood in the bright dining alcove, backlit, hands on hips. Her Spanx were killing her. Her skirt was golden and flared off her brown legs. He saw the shadows of those legs through the fabric. Her hair, piling on her shoulders, was electric with highlights, like glitters on a sea of ink.

She eyed him. He grinned. She was as magnificent as a velvet painting of an Aztec goddess in a taco shop. She had muscles.

"Mi amor," he said.

"Ay, tú." La Gloriosa had no time for foolishness. She tipped her head back, dismissing him with her chin. Ringlets flew: a rebuke.

He answered with a quick bounce of his eyebrows.

Her head tipped down, ringlets cascading over her shoulders: a possible reconciliation. She looked up under her brows like a she-wolf. He flushed, made his eyes dewy.

Her left eyebrow rose slowly and lodged. He looked at her collarbone. Down, but not indecently. Eyes rose slowly to meet hers. He smiled with one side of his mouth.

"Don't be naughty," she said.

Perla came in from the backyard, looking for more coffee. "Es mi baby!" she cried, staggering over to Little Angel and petting his face. She looked back and forth between them. "Not this again," she said.

La Gloriosa made a moochy-lip mouth gesture at him that crinkled her nose, then she vanished behind the pantry to rattle things in the sink. In mock irritation. If he had been born with a crest, his feathers would have risen and he would have flown out to find her a pretty twig.

"Tu hermano está en su cama," Perla said, gesturing to the back room where Big Angel rested. "Always in bed."

Little Angel said, "He must be exhausted."

"Siempre. Pobre Flaco."

She was looking around, her empty coffee cup hanging off her finger. He took it from her and led her to the little aluminum table and sat her down. "I'll get it," he said.

"Tenk yous," she said. "Leche, please. Y azúcar."

"Sí."

"Sugar—lots of sugar."

La Gloriosa's back was to him as she scrubbed last night's pots. He stepped up to her and caught a sweet sniff as he leaned around her to get to the coffee pot on the counter. She felt him leaning in, and she got a blue bolt of electricity right up her neck, but she showed nothing.

"Excuse me," he said, putting a hand on her back.

She jumped. "I am sixty years old," she whispered.

"Sixty's the new forty," he said. "And I'm almost fifty. So you're younger than I am."

She had to think about that one.

The coffeepot said, *Gloop*.

She squinted at him. "Don't play with me," she said.

He stood there, coffee steaming. She was close enough that he could feel her body heat. She smelled like almonds and vanilla.

He could tell she did not remember that once, when they were both many years younger, she had drunk too much Thunderbird at a rare gathering at his parents' house. She had been showing his mother Latin dance moves. La cumbia. Rumba. Cha-cha. She was hilariously pickled by the end of the night, and she had found him in the hall outside the bedroom used for coats and had leaned on him and said, "Kiss me good night, you bad boy."

He gave her a teenage peck.

"That is not how you kiss a woman," she said. And *kissed* him on the mouth. "That's how you kiss a woman." And grabbed her coat and was gone like some apparition from beyond.

"I am not playing," he said now.

"You think it's so easy!"

"It is easy."

"O sí, cabrón? And what do you want from me?" She blew hair out of her face. *What a pendejo!*

"Do you want me to stop?" he said.

She banged a pot in the sink. Stared out the kitchen window at the vatos standing around in the driveway. She shook out her curls. Sighed. "No," she said.

He took the coffee and the Carnation milk can and the sugar to Perla.

"Instant?" she said.

"No. Coffeepot."

She made a face. These old-timers, they lived for instant coffee.

Perla didn't even look at him. Simply gestured at Gloriosa with her eyebrows. "Picaflor," she said.

"Me?"

She blew on her coffee.

He thought about how he'd explain that to his students. One of those Mexican phrases. Honeybee? No. Bumblebee? Nope. Hummingbird? A creature who goes from flower to flower, sampling the nectar.

He cleared his throat. "I—"

"Go talk to your brother," Perla said.

⚶

First, he stopped in the living room and inspected Big Angel's citizenship papers. Big Angel kept them in a little frame on the wall for everyone to admire. Miniature American flags tucked in the corners. A faded picture of the kids—Yndio and Braulio. Little Angel squinted; he had been beautiful, that Braulio. Cherubic. And little Lalo all cheeky and curly. Minnie, apparently, hadn't been born yet.

The family portrait hung beside that. It was in a huge white frame with gold filigree vines carved into the wood. A color photo from Sears. Mamá América holding a photograph of Dad. And Big Angel, MaryLú, and César gathered around her. There it was. They hadn't thought to invite him. There was no slight intended. Which made it feel worse somehow.

Minnie came up beside him and looked at it.

"The whole family, Tío," she said.

"Most of it."

She looked at him, back at the picture, at him, at the picture. "Oh," she said.

"Yeah."

"Oops," she said.

"A minor oversight," he said with chipper self-pity.

"You got an identity crisis, huh?"

"Secret's out."

"You ain't alone, feeling alone like that. Some of us know what that feels like." She went out the front door and wandered down the street.

He walked the fourteen steps back to the bedroom door.

&

It terrified him.

Little Angel was certain his brother would be dead. Or he would be in some gruesome medical crisis. Or would smell somehow, some embarrassing stink that would upset them both.

But none of these things were true. Big Angel was sitting up, with his back against a pile of pillows. He wore a bright white undershirt and comfy pajama pants. Thick white gym socks on his feet. He smelled like baby powder and a little sweat.

Big Angel was addressing a small clutch of ninth graders,

who stood at the foot of his bed, looking awkward. Each of the girls had one arm folded across her belly and clamped to her ribs with the other arm dangling as if lifeless. The boys had the ends of their fingers stuffed into their pants pockets.

Big Angel was saying: "A panda bear walked into a restaurant."

"Yeah, Pops?"

"Sí. And he sat at the counter and asked for food and a Pepsi."

"So what happened, Pops?"

"He ate, drank, pulled out a pistol, and shot the cook."

"What!"

"As he left, he shouted, 'Look it up on Google!'" Big Angel was grinning like a mad street person, eyes glittering and feral.

The kids looked at one another.

"Did they look it up, Pops?"

"Of course. Do you know what it said?"

They shook their heads.

"It said, 'Panda bear. A vegetarian mammal that eats shoots and leaves.'" He laughed.

They looked at one another again.

"I get it," said one fat boy.

"Out, mocosos," Little Angel said.

They shuffled out.

"I ain't got boogers, Tío," the fat boy protested.

Newspapers were scattered all over the bed. Big Angel had circled an infamous picture about a hundred times. A dead toddler facedown in European surf. Drowned and cast off like a little bag of unwanted clothes. Big Angel saw Little Angel looking at it. He picked up the paper, folded it carefully, and set it on his bedside table.

"Nobody wants the immigrant," Big Angel said. "He drowned, that boy."

"I know."

"Trying to get a new life."

"I know."

"Our people look like that," Big Angel said. "In the desert."

Our people. "I'll have to think about that one," Little Angel said. It occurred to him that maybe Big Angel wasn't a Republican after all. He realized he knew very little about his big brother. "Seems like we've been here a really long time," he said. "Seems there are very few de La Cruz bodies in the desert." He couldn't stop himself, though his brother's face darkened. "We're pretty much Americans now, right? I mean, this is a post-immigration family. By what, almost fifty years?"

"Yeesus."

"I'm still Mexican," Little Angel said. "Mexican-American? But let's face it, I don't live in, what, Sinaloa."

Big Angel wiped his lips. He had thought they were wet, but they were chapped. "Must be nice, Carnal," he said. "To choose who you are."

Little Angel looked off into a fascinating corner of the room. "Let's not get into this today."

"What?"

"Your 'I'm more Mexican than you are' games."

"I thought you just said you were a gringo."

"Eat me," Little Angel muttered.

"Culero."

They were suddenly eleven.

"Okay." Big Angel shrugged one shoulder. "I'll be dead tomorrow, so no problem."

Jeezuz Jiminy Jumpin' Christ. Little Angel smiled warmly.

Big Angel patted the bed. "Sit."

Apparently the ethnic civil war had passed like one of the tardy little rain clouds speeding east to collapse against the Cuyamaca Mountains.

"Carnal!" Big Angel said, eyes suddenly as bright as little black campfires. "Remember how my father peeled oranges?"

Little Angel nodded. "I remember our father, yeah."

Big Angel took the hint. "Our father. Put chile powder on oranges."

"And salt."

"Tajín!"

They found this funny for some reason.

"He peeled oranges in one long strip," Big Angel shouted. "He made snakes out of the peel. Every time."

They laughed some more. It felt good to laugh. Mindless. Safe.

"He told me they were tapeworms," Little Angel said.

"Did I ever tell you about—" Big Angel blurted, and he was off on a binge of storytelling. Jokes and sorrows. Strange tales of their ancestors. Questions about Seattle. When he began a detailed tour of the many medicine bottles on his table, and doses and times of administering them, Little Angel gave up standing there awkwardly and climbed into bed beside his brother.

silence
good talk
oysters
a day without pain

The Night Before the Party

10:00 p.m.

Big Angel was asleep when Perla finally came into the room. Her days seemed endless. So much work to do, so much organizing, so much praying. She felt like she was carrying the tumors sometimes. But she dared not acknowledge that terrible thought. She did not deserve self-pity, she told herself. There would be time for that soon enough.

Most everybody had gone home. La Gloriosa had ushered Little Angel out as if he were a stray cat. It was a wonder she hadn't hit him with a broom. Now she could finally leave. She put on her coat and hurried to her car with her keys in her fist, sticking out between her clenched fingers, in case any pendejo stepped up. She had Mace in her purse. And a Taser she'd bought in Tijuana. She was in no mood.

La Minnie went to Dunkin' Donuts and bought a box of donuts for her men. El Tigre. He could get behind some donut action for sure. She couldn't figure out how he kept his six-pack eating all the bad crap he ate. It cost her a fortune to do hot wraps to try to sweat it off.

Minnie's oldest son was a sailor and told her that in Portland there was some kind of voodoo donut shop. Like, you could buy a coffin full of donuts. Crazy hippies. The boys on his ship were all tweaked about bacon-wrapped maple bars. She wished she could get some of those. Her man would love them.

Back at the house, diehards muttered in the living room. Video games bleeped and yowled behind the locked garage door. A pile of peewees snored and snuffled in the back room, layered with dogs.

Perla went into the bathroom, brushed her teeth, and undressed in the dark. She didn't like to look at herself in the mirror. Now she wore big white grandmother underpants. And her bra held back a flood of flesh. Well, the hills are old, but they still have flowers on them. Seventy was difficult for a woman who imagined herself as a thirty-five-year-old with a slightly bad hip but otherwise in good shape.

She pulled on her nightgown and crawled into bed very slowly. It took real control to get in without bouncing the mattress. Big Angel was sweet and friendly all day long...unless you bounced him unexpectedly or bumped into him. Then he'd snap. Everyone cried a little when he shouted, "You idiot!"

Her jaws hurt from clenching her teeth. One knee, then the other. Popping. She grimaced.

She got her bottom settled and laid her head down very slowly. She slept on the left side of the bed. He was on the side with the little table—all his pill bottles there within reach, looking like the model of a futuristic city. Plastic skyscrapers loaded with colorful pills. Tomorrow, she was thinking. Diosito lindo, *get me through tomorrow.*

When her head sank to her pillow, he said, "Flaca, has everyone gone home?"

Damn it!

"Flaco! I thought you were asleep."

"I am asleep," he said. "But I watch you even when I'm dreaming."

He had been saying strange things for a while now. He'd always said them. He was a genius. Geniuses said crazy things. But he was even stranger now, carrying on like some brujo out in the wilderness. He had told Minnie, "Rivers believe in God." What the hell was that supposed to mean? He had told poor Lalo, "Birds have always known the language of the dead."

Over breakfast one morning, he had looked at her and said, "Flaca, the universe can fit inside an egg." Mildly, because she didn't know how to handle these outbursts without inflaming them, she'd said, "Oh really, Flaco?" "Yes. But the hen that sits on this egg must be so big we can't see her. I wonder what will hatch when the universe cracks open." She'd replied, "How nice," while silently crying out to God and the Virgin to help her.

"Flaca," he said brightly, as if they were at lunch on a summer's day.

"Sí?"

"Do you remember when we met?"

"How could I forget? Go to sleep."

"And then I didn't see you for a year."

"Yes."

"But then I saw you at the movies."

"I know, Flaco. I was there. Go to sleep."

"It was that nasty little theater we called 'Las Pulgas.'"

"Yes. You got fleas in there. It was filthy."

"We saw that doll people movie. You were in the row in front of me."

"Puppet people, Flaco. I still have nightmares."

"I bought you a Pepsi-Cola."

"A 7UP, Flaco. You called it 'un siete-oop.'"

They laughed.

"And then," he said.

"Stop."

"On the beach."

"Cochino!" She put her hands over her face and groaned.

"You had a white dress. And you lay on the sand. And I rubbed your back."

"Oye, Angel! Enough!"

"You were lying on my jacket. And as I rubbed your back, your skirt rose."

"Dios!"

"You shook. I saw your hands dig into the sand."

"Ay."

He'd been seventeen, and she sixteen.

That night, the moon was a curl of God's fingernail. A group of kids from the secundaria had lit a bonfire a quarter kilometer away. The water was black, with glowing white foam and a long highway of silver coins tossed across the swells by the light above. It started with a kiss. Her tongue invaded his mouth. It was slender and cold and tasted of the strawberry juice they had just bought on the malecón. Big Angel understood right away: this tongue thing. She knew about the world.

At first, he knelt beside her. Water was coming out of the sand and soaking his trouser knees. He had not put his hands on a girl's back before. He was hypnotized by the feeling of her tight shoulders and the way they relaxed under his hands. And her sighs. How her ribs could be felt through the exquisite pliancy of her flesh. Her heat radiating through the cotton. The straps of her brassiere, crossing her back. And the slight swellings on the sides, where her breasts began. He trembled just slightly, as if he had carried very heavy bundles down a long road.

And he suddenly found himself straddling the backs of her legs without quite knowing how he got there. He leaned into her. Smelling her hair and her perfume. Feeling the alarming heat of her thighs through the legs of his pants. And then, that white dress, all one piece, rising farther. Was that another scent? His throat hurt and his jaw ached from clenching it so tightly. He looked down and watched the skirt creep up the backs of her legs. He could not stop. He leaned forward and stared. She knew he was looking—her thighs tightened and she shivered—and he knew without knowing what was happening between them. Then, the double curve of her bare bottom had peeked at him.

"And I saw your nalgas."

She laughed, deep in her throat. Her nasty laugh.

And his hands had slid up her thighs and encountered her. She jumped and sighed, and he drew breath. Carefully moved his fingers into that wet heat, afraid he might overstep his bounds, face burning, hands shaking. She was like an ocean there.

"I have a little fountain," she said. "For you."

His own pants were drenched. He didn't know what was happening. Did this happen to men? He was worried about hiding it. Then he forgot to care.

For the rest of his life, that would remain his favorite moment.

They lay there, at once in their bed and upon that old warm beach. She put her head close to his shoulder.

"And then what?" she said.

"You were my first."

"Ay! What an angel."

He touched her face. "I kissed your bottom!"

Proud of himself, he crossed his arms behind his head. The cool tremble of her cinnamon curve. The dangerous shadow between her nalgas. The sweet scent of her back and skin. The tang of her like liquor swimming in his limbs and head. His shaking hands. He wanted to smoke a Pall Mall.

After a while, she said, "That wasn't all you did."

That comfortable old silence spread between them, as warm and luxurious as a well-fed cat.

"I am tired," he said.

She patted him softly. "Go to sleep," she said.

"I astral project," he told her. "So I don't get any rest."

"Ah, cabrón!" she said.

"I can leave my body and walk around."

"Que qué!" she said. It was as if she could hear him smiling in the dark.

"I don't need a wheelchair for doing that, Flaca."

"What are you talking about? You've gone crazy. First my nalgas? Then leaving your body? Stop talking crazy."

"Kissing your nalgas made me leave my body," he said.

"I'm warning you . . ."

"Little Angel got to MaryLú's house all right. I saw him just now. He's going to sleep on her couch."

"You scare me."

"I'm not crazy," he said. "Just looking around so I can see what's going on. So I'll know where my soul will go when I'm finished here."

The breath she took shuddered in her chest. "Well, don't look in my sister's bathroom."

He chuckled. "I can't visit La Gloriosa in the bubble bath?"

"No!" she said.

They lay on their backs, a hundred foggy scenes in the dark hovering over them.

"A good life," he said.

She took his hand. "Because of you, Angel."

"Because of you, Perla."

"We did it together."

He yawned. "Eso sí," he said and turned to her in the dark. "But I am tired now."

"Sleep," she said.

"More tired than that."

There was a long pause. "Flaco, no."

"It might be time, mi amor."

"No. No."

"My work is done, Flaca. Our children are grown. I think I am done."

"Angel. No digas eso." She scolded him like his mother used to. "You're talking like a crazy man again. We have grandchildren! Your work is not done! What about me?"

He sighed, squeezed her hand.

"Don't make me mad," she said.

"Or what?"

"I'll spank you with my slipper." La chancla.

"That might be nice," he said.

He smiled; she felt it.

After a moment, she said, "Flaco? You can't really see my sister naked, can you?"

But he was already snoring.

ঙ্কপ

10:30 p.m.

Little Angel was stretched out on MaryLú's couch. She wouldn't hear of him sleeping at the hotel. Even though he'd left all his stuff in his perfectly good, air-conditioned room. She had given him a toothbrush of his own and a towel. She had even bought him a package of boxers and a nice Bob Dylan T-shirt at Target. Amphetamine 1965 Dylan, with a harmonica, Wayfarers, and shock hair. She thought he needed a haircut.

Her kids were in L.A. Going to college. Starting businesses. Giving her grandchildren. Spreading the seed.

Her couch wasn't so bad. Well, it wasn't really her couch—it was her mother's couch. That astounding América. Little Angel thought of her often and started to laugh almost every time. Nobody else thought she was all that funny. But they hadn't seen what he and Big Angel had seen.

Sometimes, when thing were dull, one or the other of them would say, "Parrot." The others could not understand what was so damned funny. They asked over and over, and neither brother would tell. It had become some kind of sacred secret, this memory. Only for them. Little Angel actually considered telling MaryLú about it but decided this was not the time. Later.

But he was busting to tell it now. Everything was shifting. Delineations of a new paradigm in transborder familial dynamics: a theorem.

❧

MaryLú had been living with the old woman for three years, caring for her. After her divorce, she hadn't really been able to afford her own place. Yes, it was embarrassing at sixty-nine to camp out at Mamá's house. But nobody else had been free to do it. God truly had his own ways of arranging things.

"Hermanita," Little Angel said.

She loved to be treated by him as if she were a young girl, fresh in her teens.

"Brrotherr," she replied.

"How is this situation all going to work out?" He opened his hands in the air.

She sat on a kitchen chair and ate peanut M&M's from a small bowl in her lap. La Gloriosa kept trying to get her to come to the gym with her. She had been on a diet for forty years. Well, Gloriosa wasn't here right now. She ate another. They were just two pale souls in the dark of the world, quiet in their refuge. As if everything was well. As if the night held no terror. And the stars circled silent and icy all around them.

They always spoke English, except for little bursts of Spanish.

If you looked at Little Angel, you'd never know he was Mexican. Unless you looked really close. His sister-in-law Paz called him "Apache nose"—nariz de Apache—when she wasn't hissing insults at him. She didn't know the semi-handsome crook in that nose had come from one of Big Angel's punches.

MaryLú watched him from the kitchenette. Little gringo. His mother was an American, after all. It made the others mad, Papá Antonio leaving them behind for a gringa. Big Angel called it "buying a Cadillac." She smiled a little. Then she shook her head.

"Ay Dios," she said, as had every generation of Mexican women back through time.

She and Little Angel were intimate strangers. They hadn't even met until he was ten. Little freckle-nosed pudge.

"Y tú," she'd asked, "cómo te llamas?"

"Angel."

"How are you named Angel? Angel is standing right over there!" she cried, pointing at her big brother.

He'd shrugged. "Papá forgot he already used that name, I guess."

This struck everybody as hilarious. It was so true. Even now it made her grin. Then her grin slid away and she ate more chocolate.

Frankly, Little Angel didn't like the crunching. Having been raised in isolation, he didn't enjoy the sound of others chewing. The rest of the clan seemed to take comfort in it.

"Baby Brother," she said. "You know Angel can't last much longer."

"I know."

"He wanted a birthday, pues. A last birthday."

She hove to her feet—back hurting—and brought forth a plate of Mexican pan dulce. He couldn't resist the pig-shaped gingerbread cookies. Marranitos. She liked the sticky rainbow-colored stuff with shaved coconut on it. She set a glass of milk on the coffee table for him. He sat up and reached for it.

"Everybody knows he won't see another one, right?" he said.

"Most of them. Sure." She shrugged, bit her pastry. "Some people aren't so smart."

"Leave it to Big Angel," Little Angel said, "to attend his own funeral."

He sipped his milk. He was thinking about Lalo telling him, "Talk's all we got." They watched Jimmy Fallon before going to bed, Little Angel thinking: *Is that it? Life just ends? And we watch TV?*

Little Angel lay on the pull-out couch, thinking. He was covered in those multicolored Tijuana blankets tourists liked to buy. *I am a cliché*, he thought. *Where's my sombrero?*

His girlfriend in Seattle didn't know about the name they knew him by—he wasn't "Angel" to her. He used his middle name up north. Gabriel. It was so romantic.

Don Antonio, their Great Father, had been called Angel by his mother, the legendary Mamá Meche, grandmother to the tribe. He was her baby, what they called chiqueado. Spoiled, in the far weaker American term. A boy coddled and carried, whose mother's spit healed his every scratch, who could do no wrong. It wasn't lost on Big Angel and his sisters that this pitiless old lady was named Mercy.

The siblings thought of their father as First Angel—El Primer Angel. It was like some South American novel—every man in the family with the same name. At least they had been spared a sister named Angela, though one of the grandnieces was named Angelita.

It was a swirl. He caught small flashes of family history like shreds of colored paper spinning in the wind. Until massive assaults of revelations and confessions came out of nowhere and destroyed whatever drinking party they threw.

He put his hands behind his head.

Little Angel Gabriel was the Third Angel, after Big Angel and Don Antonio, El Primer Angel. He had hung like a moth in the spider web of his parents' marriage. Don Antonio, strangely truculent and guarded in one corner of their apartment, fuming over racial slights at the hands of the gringos cabrones in his diminished immigrant life. He oozed cigarette smoke from his mouth and nostrils like a burning barn, his broken teeth like the shattered boards of the barn door. Teeth worn down to painful stubs from their nightly grinding. Night-mares of guilt and regret for his many sins made him embrace the endless pain in his mouth. Those without pain infuriated him. And those who feared pain, who did not suffer as bravely as his victims did, were to be reviled, not pitied.

Don Antonio had seen men beaten with bats who made less fuss than his boys did when they fell down and split their knees. To hurt his children was to prepare them for life. He stared at Little Angel with disdain and fear. He didn't enjoy hurting him, but it was his duty. "I don't know," Don Antonio had confessed to Big Angel, "if he is a genius or a psychopath."

"He's American," Big Angel said.

"Chingado."

Don Antonio, full of rage over Little Angel's mother—so American. Betty. He had looked for the ultimate Americana, and he'd found her. All Indiana milk and honey. Cornflower-blue eyes. Thought herself so superior. Turning his son into some American faggot. Buying him comic books and hippie records. Yet asking Antonio to wield the belt when the boy transgressed. There were better punishments than belts. Better ways to love him into manhood. He had smoked and glared and thought, *Tough little bastard, though*—Little Angel had stayed that way no matter what Don Antonio did.

Dad. Dead and more unreachable than ever. And now Big Angel was going to die.

His brother had always had a rich voice—not a basso voice, but a rich lower baritone. Strong. Perhaps the most shocking thing about his condition now was not his skeletal thinness or his diminished physical stature. But his voice. A weird, reedy alto. A voice that sounded like the big brother of the family had inhaled helium. Or had somehow reversed age as the body collapsed—he had his Baby Angel voice back. That six-year-old's voice and six-year-old's eyes. That ravaged face held two ardent coals—his black eyes shone with mad light, hunger for the world, amusement and excitement. They raged with delight in everything.

Little Angel had never seen his big brother look more excited. He seemed so keyed up with energy that if his legs could hold him, he would leap from his wheelchair and play hopscotch with his grandchildren. In spite of his obvious pain, he had a smile on his face at all times. One of his uncles had raised his eyebrows at Little Angel and spun his finger around beside his head, but Little Angel thought his brother was anything but crazy.

He had asked, in the sick bed as they shared his pillows, "What are you teaching, Carnal?"

"Reynolds Price."

"Who is that?"

"Novelist, poet."

"Tell me a line."

"'I am waiting for Jesus in a room made of salt.'"

Big Angel had thought about that. "That's good," he said. "That's me."

"He says if he cries, the room will dissolve."

Big Angel rubbed his eyes. "Yes," he said.

"He's dead now," Little Angel said.

"I know that from the poem."

Big Angel's thick, dark hair was now a white post-chemo flattop. Little moles visible on his scalp. But that too made him look alarmingly young. Don Antonio had kept his boys in crew cuts. Little Angel had been the first to grow freak hair and disgrace them all by having his ear pierced. It hadn't taken long, though, for time to roll over them all until the nephews discovered Van Halen and grew mullets and got tattoos. Another generation ruined.

Big Angel and his father had forced Spanish on Little Angel with brutal force. Still, he was an English speaker. It was the language he used to speak to his mother, after all. They had wrestled to a draw.

"I gave you books," Big Angel noted. "Don't forget."

"I never forget. But then I gave you books too."

"Travis McGee mysteries."

Little Angel smiled.

"Perla threw them away because they had girls on the covers."

There had been nothing to add to that.

◊◊

1:00 a.m.

La Minnie finally crawled onto the couch. Her man was asleep in their bedroom. She didn't feel it was mean of her to wait till he was snoring. She was too tired to snuggle with him. She sipped her wine. Snoring. Somehow it put her to sleep. So no touching right now, but later, maybe.

She was tired from a lot of things. She just sat in the dark living room, smoking and thinking and listening to some John Legend and Prince down low. A glass of white wine. One slice of a peach in it. She painted her nails in three shades of purple. Dark, light, and palest lavender. A slender gold bracelet loosely circled her left wrist. It said "Mouse" in old-school cursive script.

She put "Little Red Corvette" on repeat. La Minnie did not

cry. But some nights she wanted nothing but the darkness on her skin.

⌘

2:00 a.m.

The pain awoke him, as it often did.

Perla was making soft noises in her sleep. She made soft *pew* sounds with her lips. He reached out in the dark, felt for the codeine pills, and swallowed two with gulps of tepid water. He realized he hated the taste of chlorine. That was one thing he would not miss.

"Too cheap to buy bottled water," he said.

"*Pew,*" said Perla.

He listened to the sounds of his house. He would miss it, that was for sure. It was a bit worn down now, true. Needed paint. Needed new carpets and better furniture. Curtains. He was recently surprised to see a sheet thumbtacked over one of the back windows. There were nail holes and scuffs and dings all over the walls. The ceiling in Braulio's old bedroom was still stained brown over one corner from a leak in the roof.

Big Angel remembered how he had climbed up there in a storm with a pot of tar and a spackling knife. Back when he could climb. He had hopped up onto the outside water softener and onto the roof of the tiny water heater closet attached to the back of the kitchen. And up top in the rain, filling the hole in the tar-paper shingles until he had been sure the dripping was remedied. He could smell it, lying there in the dark—the scent of California rain, carrying the perfume of wet dirt over the roof, and the smell of the shingles, and the smell of the tar.

For a moment, he wasn't in his bed but up there again. Reliving the astonishment of standing astraddle his roof and seeing the world from on high. Seeing the lightning striking the hills of Tijuana. Seeing everything laid before him, nothing but possibilities and opportunities.

Oh, this humble house had seemed such a palace then. It still felt that way. Every day, in the weariest corner of the house, he could remember that he had snuck north from Tijuana once. And now he owned an American home.

Silently, he rose out of himself and left the bed. He walked down the hall. The breeze was wonderfully refreshing as it moved through him. It knew to find the tumors and cool them. Such relief. Like fresh water on a sunburn. Very good. Gracias.

He saw the two couches side by side in the living room. One had been bought long ago on layaway from Montgomery Ward's, and nobody but he and Perla knew that Minnie had been made there. He knew it was true for the simple reason that they hadn't had enough beds for everyone in those days, and he and his waifa had shared the couch so Braulio could sleep in a bed so he'd do well in school. But of course he had been kicked out of school. So they had taken their bed back. And now Minnie slept on that couch when she stayed with them. Her body an echo of its own creation.

The second couch was in bad shape, but that made Big Angel like it more. They had gone to collect it from his father's sad apartment after he'd died. It had cigarette burns in the arms. They had brought it home to find an old 1967 nudie magazine under one of the pillows. Perla threw it away, but Big Angel rescued it and hid it out in his workshop. He was thirteen again every time he looked through it. Astonished to see white women bared to the world. Tired women on piano benches grimacing up at cameras as if they had forgotten what smiles looked like. Women playing volleyball nude on some scrap of beach, caught forever in mid-levitation, their breasts seeming to yearn for flight. It was a gallery of sorrows. And he had found his father's thumbprint smeared in the cheap print of the single "Naughty Nightcap" erotic story.

He liked to sit on the couch and rub the cigarette burns with his fingertips. The back of the couch, along the tops of the pillows, had stains from his father's hair pomade. Big Angel remembered the brand: Dixie Peach.

"I remember everything," he said aloud.

Like the ornamental iron railing along the edge of the living room, where it dropped a step to the entryway of the house. A useless little fence. He laid his hand on it, and he remembered El Yndio chasing Braulio and poor Lalo through the house, how small they were, and how Lalo had run smack into the railing and split his eyebrow. Oh, the wailing! Blood everywhere. Lalo's caterwauling had started Minnie crying. The drive with Perla holding paper towels to Lalo's head. It had been only the first of Big Angel's many drives to Paradise Valley Hospital's emergency room. Two stitches, which gave Lalo a devilish split eyebrow he later used as a weapon on the muchachas. And now Lalo drove him there, every time he thought he was dying.

The patriarch patted the couch. When Little Angel's American mother threw their father out for sleeping with her best friend in their bed, he had come here. They had sat at that same kitchen table. Drinking coffee and staring at each other.

Big Angel stood, drifted to the middle of the room, and invited every memory to come to him and clothe him in beauty.

Then
(En Aquel Entonces)

Big Angel was still a boy when he first saw Perla. Barely sixteen. He wore American black jeans and a ridiculous yellow checkered blazer his Tía Cuca had sent from Mazatlán. It came by fishing boat, something that seemed altogether normal in La Paz but would assume mythical proportions later, in San Diego. "Check it, dawg—Pops got his threads off a fishin' boat, no lie!" The same jacket he would christen on the beach within a year.

His father always made Angel dress up when he came to the police station with him. "Un caballero," he told his son, "always dresses well and is always clean-shaven except for his mustache, and that has to be trimmed carefully. And fingernails always short and clean. Otherwise, he's no gentleman." He also made Angel call the shoeshine man—with the rag tied on his head and an ugly little wooden box with the footrest on top—"Maestro."

Angel was already too old to ride behind his father on the massive police motorcycle. But he no longer had any physical intimacy with him, and Angel took advantage of the rare days when his father felt disposed to allow him to cling as they sped along. Some days were like that. Inexplicable days of grace.

It was a huge thrill to ride across La Paz with his father. The police uniform was of course intensely dramatic—the shiny badge in bronze and ceramic with its eagle and cactus centerpiece. The mirror-bright black knee boots. The immense pistola in a creaking leather oil-scented holster. And the inscrutable twin pools of nothing when the aviator shades covered his father's eyes.

But being perched behind the vast oaken back of his father, the Harley thrumming beneath them as they slanted in and out of traffic—that was the greatest thrill of his days. He watched people slow and pull aside, fearing Don Antonio, seeing the Jefe de Patrullas Motociclistas roaring down the road. His thought, beaming it out to the world like a lighthouse beacon: My father, my father.

He would shout into the wind, "Siren!"

And his father would hit the button with his thumb. And the shiny silver klaxon mounted on the front fender would yawp hideously, frightening people and animals for a block. These two burning through the city like furious gods.

Angel might get permission if he had curried favor, but Little Pato and María Luisa were forbidden from even touching the big machine. They all called César El Pato Donald because his rusty voice sounded like Donald Duck, and when he got mad, they laughed until they cried. Their laughter enraged him, so his squawk became more frantic, and they laughed harder. It was his misfortune that, as he grew, his voice lowered into a deep mallard's squonk, and the name never left him.

But not even Donald Duck could touch the Harley. Don Antonio kept it spotless, polished. Like many houses in La Paz in those days, theirs had a rickety wooden gate that hid a dirt courtyard with a ciruelo and a coconut palm, a woven palm-frond palapa, and a hammock. The motorcycle rested beneath the palapa and a rainproof tarp like some mythical beast that slept standing, that might awaken and eat any of them at the slightest provocation.

In the early mornings—when Mamá América was cooking breakfast in the open kitchen, smoke billowing from the wood-burning stove, tortillas heating on the sheet-iron comal over flames, the green parrot and the mourning doves in their wooden cages—the children would pause outside the small chicken coop and watch the Harley sleep. Their father's snores were loud, even out here, so they knew it was safe to approach his steed.

He called it El Caballo Mayor.

Mother was aware of their curiosity but kept her back to them. She feigned deep interest in boiling frijoles and chopping tomatoes and onions. She melted a pond of lard in the huge skillet and dropped beans and soup into it with a savage roaring of fat and a vivid white cloud of steam and smell. The parrot gripped his guano-caked perch and flew in place inside his cage, maniacally beating his wings until the cage wobbled on its nail, shrieking warnings to the world that the fire was out of control. She ignored it.

She mashed the beans into the lard, spooning the hot lard back over the beans until it had all fried into a viscous mass. The children were on their own. They had chores to do before school: sweeping, feeding the animals, tending the laundry or taking it down. They were also expected to collect the eggs their three hens offered up. She knew they would waste time before school, looking for iguanas or teasing the idiotic turkey, La Chichona.

They had a fatal interest in the forbidden motorcycle. So she didn't watch them, and she let them peek. She observed them nonetheless with the supernatural powers of the Mexican mother. Ears that could hear the change in a child's footstep. That could hear an intake of breath. Or worse, whispering. Her slipper could come off in less than a second, and the dreaded chancla would be flailing at their behinds if they were found misbehaving.

Angel was skinny. Dark. He was already too old to spank, but that wouldn't stop the chancla. He looked angry all the time because he had inherited his father's flagrant eyebrows—a jungle on his brow ridge that grew together above his nose. He had combed his hair into an Elvis pomp, though he couldn't manage sideburns yet.

With his finger over his lips, he led the two chiquitos on tiptoes under the palapa and lifted the edge of the tarp so they could see the motorcycle's great front tire angled jauntily as if it were the foreleg of a steed, hoof tipped in sleep. And the fat fender above it. They sighed.

"¡Muchachos!" Mamá said, and they scattered.

The big motorcycle was as loud as a summer storm. Cops in their finned patrol cars with the single red light bubble on top lifted a finger at them or held a hand out the window. Don Antonio merely nodded, his cap at an angle on his head, his hair heavy and plastic with Dixie Peach, imported from Los Angeles or some other exotic gringo place where he had aunts. That Germanic-looking police cap never budged, tipped slightly over his right eye, high peaked, just touching with its gleaming black bill the top of his inscrutable aviator glasses.

For Angel, La Paz was mostly light and smell.

The sunlight, bouncing off the sea and the backs of whales,

silvered by marlins and waves and sand, ricocheted from bare rock spires and desert shimmers, was as saturating as a flood. Yellow, blue, clear, white, everywhere vibrating, everywhere frank and blunt and without nuance. Red flowers, yellow, blue as plastic. *Light*. In cataracts.

Angel also loved the rainy days, when shadows made their mysterious ways around corners and across alleys. And everyone loved sunsets. The light lost its sanity as it fell over the hills and into the Pacific—it went red and deeper red, orange, and even green. The skies seemed to melt, like lava eating black rock into great bite marks of burning. Sometimes all the town stopped and stared west. Shopkeepers came from their rooms to stand in the street. Families brought out their invalids on pallets and in wheelbarrows to wave their bent wrists at the madness consuming their sky. Swirls of gulls and pelicans like God's own confetti snowed across those sky riots.

Angel was afraid of falling off the machine. He wrapped his arms around his father's grand torso, laid his cheek to his back, and only then let his eyelids drop. If he held tight to his father, he would not fall. Even though, with his eyes closed, he almost believed his father had levitated them above the earth and was trying to make him tumble through clouds to the desert below. He believed Father would hold him aloft.

He breathed deep—for he could really smell the world if he was focused. Utterly focused. He had already formulated many theories, which is why Don Antonio sometimes called him El Filósofo, for his philosophy was already in place. And this was one of his theorems: to know the world in each of its parts, a seeker must shut out the unnecessary senses and focus on the target.

Today, the day he was destined to meet Perla Castro Trasviña in the Centro police station at eight thirty in the morning in the magical year of 1963, the world was all scents.

It began with his father's back. Redolent of cigarette smoke and leather, the wool of his tunic, and the bay rum and shaving soap blowing back from his cheeks. The smell of wind and sun in his uniform, and Mamá's lye soap. And even a hint of her.

Behind these smells, and all around them, the sea—the relentless sea. Salt and seaweed and shrimp and distance. The bitter stench of beached dolphins turning to gray swamps on the rocks. The scent of mysterious Sinaloa somehow coming across the gulf. The choking reek of guano, and the delicious scent of a million miles' worth of clean, rushing wind.

"Siren!"

"Mijo! Como chingas!"

And the smells of the smoke—everywhere, smoke. The world was made of smoke. The sky collected all the burned offerings and built palaces of scents above and around them.

Cooking smoke was the best. Carne asada. Carnitas. Roasted corn with lime and cheese. Fried fish. Tortillas. Diced nopales in scrambled eggs on a cloud of melted lard. Yeasty bread smoke from the bakeries. Sugar smoke. Shrimp tacos crisp in the breeze.

Trash fires. Incense from the shops and the old women's houses and the churches. Cigars.

And dust.

If the rain came, the creeping smell of the desert going wet. And diesel and exhaust, especially the big belching trucks and ancient buses. From alleys, the stench of sewage and rotten fruit. Flowers, yes. Flowers. They were not just colorful—but their scents colored the air. There came scents then of onion and tomato, chiles and the faintly soapy strange smell of cilantro. Mint leaves. Charcoal. Perfume and rank old beer in the tepid squalls of air billowing from cantinas.

Somewhere in that vast tapestry of interwoven odors, Angel was sure he could smell the dead. Not their bodies, but their souls. His newest theory was that the dead came as ghosts in sudden finger-thin wafts of perfume or cigarette or hair's sweet soap scents when it was drying in the sun...

※

And then they were just past the center of town with its drooping wires festooned with lights left over from Christmas. Tubas were playing in the plaza—Angel opened his eyes when trumpets sounded a nationalistic fanfare. And the engine's blat and rip grew massive and reverberant as they went between walls and up the narrower street to the station—bucking as Don Antonio slowed, cobbles and fractured chunks of concrete in the street, and they stopped before the jail and police station complex. Smells of urine escaped from the barred windows in back. Hopeless, flat human voices came from the barred and wired high windows. Don Antonio revved the engine and cut its noise, mid-shriek. They sat as though stunned by their own silence.

"You will learn," he said to his son, as if he had been thinking this during the whole trip, "that pink nipples are more intoxicating than brown."

Angel looked up to him, his father's face just a shadow now against the sun, and he thought: *What?*

And Don Antonio's big shiny boot lifted and went over Big Angel's head as he ducked, and his father stood tall, setting his belt, checking his cap. He pinched his balls through the trousers and shifted his lariat to the left. He looked at the boy and pulled off his dark glasses.

He winked.

✧

Inside the station, the usual tumult. The stinging smell of ammonia and pine cleaner. Brash echoes off pitiless tiles. Young cops deferred to Don Antonio with shy glances and slightly sideward motions. Their shoes squealed on the floor. Old cops slapped Father's back and fake-punched Big Angel. He flinched. It infuriated Don Antonio. Flinching! His dark gnome of a son. Didn't play guitar or baseball. Brooded like some...poet. Yes, he was hard on the boy. That was love. Look at this world.

He remembered flogging his son. It seemed just yesterday. It had been over a year, but his remorse made it seem fresh, even though he refused to admit to himself that he felt anything but righteousness about it. He was a man, pues. Making a man. He had forced Angel to stand naked in the back room.

"Bend over," he'd said.

"No, Papá!"

The belt hung from Don Antonio's fist.

"All right, mijo. Defy me. Make it worse."

As he lay twenty-five stripes across his boy's ass and back, he ordered him: "Do. Not. Cry. Cabrón." One syllable per blow. Don't. Cry. Ca. Brón. The whistle, and the snap when it hit. The boy's hands trying to block the blows. "Raise your hands again, pendejo. Raise them to me. That tells me you want to fight me. And I will add twenty-five to this. Yes? It's what you want. Does that make you happy?"

And he looked to see, for he knew that when he whipped naked men in the jail they sometimes became hard, rising like small branches as they screamed. His boy covered himself with his hand. Don Antonio suddenly lost his strength. His will drained out. His arm fell, and he stared at the network of red X's all over Angel's body as if they had appeared miraculously, like the face of Jesus in a cloud.

He looked at his son now. Regretting it a little. He gripped Angel's shoulder and smiled at him.

"I touch your shoulder," he said grandly, "for good luck!"

"Thank you, Father."

He rubbed Angel's head. "Mijo!" he said.

Honestly, Angel didn't know what to think. He was pretty sure his father didn't care for him much. He leaned around Don Antonio and stared at the suspect's bench. Father turned and looked over there too.

And there they were: the Castro family, bedraggled in the no-man's-land between the front lobby and the dreaded cell-blocks in back. Nobody had yet handcuffed them to the gouged wood of the bench. A skinny young man, dripping blood in slow, fat, greasy drops from a gashed chin, held his hands together between shivering thighs. He had a black eye. Beside him sat a girl—Perla—with skinny, knobby gray knees and cuts on her face still sparkling with bits of glass. No more than fifteen. She had huge eyes, filled with fear, and she clutched the hand of a smaller girl. This would turn out to be the young Gloriosa, playing with a naked doll, twisting its arms as if trying to dismember it.

"What is this?" Don Antonio called.

"Car wreck," the deskman said.

"Anybody die?"

"No."

Don Antonio snapped his fingers. "Reporte," he shouted.

There was no report.

"What do you mean there is no report?"

Shrugs. "It is early, Jefe. This just happened."

The kids on the bench stared at the floor.

A cop stepped up and spoke: "This pendejo," he said, pointing to the bloodied boy, "ran into a pickup truck full of ranch hands."

Una pee-kah.

"Ah, cabrón," said Don Antonio, looking down at them.

Perla started to cry.

"Sorry," the boy said.

"Where are the cowboys?"

"They ran away."

"But you didn't run."

"No, señor. They stopped right in front of me—I didn't have the chance to stop."

"You couldn't stop."

"I couldn't stop."

Even Angel knew that in the matter of car wrecks on the peninsula, everyone was arrested and investigated. Even the injured. Guilty until proven innocent.

"You didn't know enough to run away too?" he said.

"Yes, sir. But I could not leave my father's truck."

Angel watched the skinny girl in the middle weep. She was inconsolate. He was immediately in love. He rose into gallantry as if he knew it was demanded of him, pulling his handkerchief out of his back pocket and stepping over to her. He extended his hand. She stared at the white square and then looked at his eyes. He nodded. She took it.

A young cop mocked them in almost-English. "Everybody goin' to jail!" He laughed, saying *yail*.

"Ya pues," Don Antonio said, watching his boy seduce the girl.

Angel was in a swoon. She was a bit younger than he was— Don Antonio saw that right away. And wanton. She had that look about her. She already knew how it felt to have a man. He might have gone after her himself.

He glanced again at his son. Angel was thinking with his little pistola, Don Antonio saw. He took an inventory of the girl. Her eyes were as huge as a deer's. Her wild hair still dropped pebbles of glass. Her nose was big.

Angel reached over and took some glass out of her short black hair. She stared up at him. He smiled at her. She smiled back.

Don Antonio thought: *He can't even see the smoke coming out of her.*

"Can I pay a fine?" the wounded boy on the bench said.

Don Antonio rose in height and inflated his chest. "What are you suggesting?"

"I—"

"Shut your hole."

"Yes, sir."

"Are you suggesting that we accept bribes here?" He used the classic term: la mordida.

"No, sir."

"Are we dogs that bite?"

"No, sir."

"Is that what you're calling me? Do I look like a dog to you, pendejo?"

"No. Never."

Angel glanced up at his father. His father stared back. Christ. He was smitten. He was imploring his father with his eyes. Don Antonio chuckled, looked over at the deskman. They both laughed. The girl had taken her big brother's hand. She was willing to protect him. Don Antonio liked that.

"Está enamorado," the other cop at the desk noted. "Tu hijo."

"You," snapped Don Antonio, pointing at the girl. "Cómo te llamas?"

"Perla Castro Trasviña."

"You could go to jail right now."

She covered her face with her hands. The others continued to stare at the floor. Portrait of a family trying to discover the gift of invisibility. His idiot son pushed into this bedraggled family group and put his arm over her bony shoulders. As if he could defend her.

"Perla," Don Antonio finally said. "What does your family do?"

"Restaurant, sir."

"What's it called?"

"La Paloma del Sur."

"If we come to see you, I expect good food. You cook it for us."

"Yes."

She was leaning against Angel! Ah, cabrón!

Don Antonio put his hands on his hips. "This is your lucky day," he said. "Take your brother to a doctor."

They goggled at him. So did the other cops.

"Go on," he said. "Get out."

They scrambled away.

"I like shrimp tacos!" he called as the door slammed shut behind them.

The police all laughed.

Don Antonio put his hands into his pockets and jangled his change and keys. "Mijo," he said, "I am the law. Never forget."

"I will remember," Big Angel promised.

☙

The last time Big Angel saw his father in La Paz was at his own farewell party.

They had conspired behind his back to be done with him.

Parents were mysterious creatures, full of plots and plans and secrets. Angel tried to be the guide for Pato and María Luisa through the strange landscapes of their parents' marriage. But sometimes even his brilliance was bested by their weirdness. All families were strange, Angel already knew. He didn't like to visit other families, because he was always ill at ease. The Basque family down at the end of their alley put bizarre sauces on their food, for example. And the hallelujah Christian converts kept saying "Gloria a Dios" and "Amén" all the time. They kept trying to give him Bibles. He palled around with El Fuma (for "Fu Manchu" due to his attempted mustache), but he steered clear of Fuma's family. They said grace before they ate, and he didn't know the words. Don Antonio would just take his place at the head of the table and await Mamá América's food with a rolled-up corn tortilla in his left hand and his elbow on the table. Tortilla raised beside his ear like some weapon about to fall.

After his erotic night on the beach with Perla, however, Angel saw her and her family every day. Don Antonio could have locked him in one of the rebar-fronted cells at the station and he would have tunneled out. He barely completed his classes every day in high school before he was first out and hustling across five alleys and four main streets and one dusted plazuela to arrive at the front door of La Paloma del Sur. Then he tried to act very casual, as if he had happened to wander by on his way home. Hands in pockets, looking up and down the street. Then turning, looking up at the restaurant's front window, as if startled that he had ended up before it. Squinting in. Elaborate performances of nonchalance contorting his features. And the whole while, the Castro family inside, watching him and laughing.

Perla didn't go to school. La Paloma was her school. Her father had drowned in a fishing boat accident, and her brother had signed on to the big tuna boats and gone into the Pacific. So it was her and her sisters, Lupita and Gloriosa. Watched over and kept busy by their terrifying mother, Chela. She of the relentless flyswatter who could find a leg even as the girls ran to escape. She whose voice sounded like a frog and whose squat body looked like a clenched fist. She of the prematurely white hair and the most exquisite frijoles fried in lard of all La Paz.

Big Angel would mosey in, blushing like a red electric sign, and the females would ignore him in the elaborate fashion of Mexican women who are watching a man quite carefully. Except for Perla, who fluttered and flushed and rushed to place Pepsis and limes in front of him, and to waste tortilla chips on him. Chela told her and told her and told her: "Make men pay. They come in here to look at you; make them pay for it. Once you give a cabrón anything for free, he'll be all over you and never think of buying you a ring. Look at him—he's pole-vaulting across the room every time he sees you."

"Ay, Mamá!"

In back, there was a small courtyard and a shaky metal stairway that led up to one of those improvised concrete-block apartments found everywhere in Mexico. An outside sink with yellow water, and inside, two rooms and a toilet. Angel never got upstairs to see it. Chela would have broken his legs.

But Chela knew a good thing when she saw it: the policeman's son. Yes. *Mucho dinero,* she thought. She could get her girl in that crowd and manage things nicely. It was a terrible fate to have a house full of daughters, she thought, but she had been raised to be a ranchera, and she could trade stock and move breeding heifers around to everyone's advantage. So she allowed this simpering romance.

Still, she wasn't going to smile at the horny little bastard.

✑

Perla wasn't even there when the world changed for Angel. It would take years to see her again. And it would be in Tijuana.

His aunt Cuca had married a pirate. Well, that's what Don Antonio called him. He was half Sinaloan, from the legendary town of Chametla. Chametla! Where Cortez allegedly sat on a rock on a day so hot the stone was melting, and his nalga cheeks had left a permanent impression. And he was half something else, from one of the many Anglo-Celtic incursions into Sinaloa in pursuit of mining jobs. Vicente, or "Chente." Chente Bent.

Chente Bent! Skipper of the heinous fishing boat *El Guatabampo*! It clanged and farted into La Paz's docks in a miasmic galaxy of stench, attended by hysterias of seabirds engaged in air battles over Chente Bent's offal. Don Antonio called Chente Bent's family "los cochinos," which made the children giggle, while Mamá América scowled; Chente Bent had whisked off her younger sister, and she was *not* dirty. Her sister was now Cuca Bent. Just like that—the whole name, for Chente Bent announced himself thusly every time he spoke of himself. He made of the name a kind of brand, all run together: Chentebent. He could have been selling nasal sprays or a new model Chevy. The all new Chentebent.

Cucabent, as much as she suffered under the toxic attentions of the pirate, deserved more respect than to be called dirty by Don Antonio. And their daughter was Tikibent. They had a German shepherd named Capitán Bent. Capibent.

More than a name, the Bent surname was a pronouncement.

"Los Pinches Bent," Don Antonio complained.

❦

El Guatabampo sailed across the Sea of Cortez twice a year, in search of sweet La Paz abalone and little rock lobsters. It was a regular celebration when the boat arrived at the La Paz docks. Chentebent brought flounder and shrimp and sea urchins (whose orange meat made Angel vomit) and octopi and long steaks of oily marlin. Don Antonio would send off for a goat to be shot, and he roasted it in a bed of coals under the ground. They ate and drank beer and belched and gossiped for several days.

Tía Cucabent and the frizzy-haired cousin, Tikibent, some-times hitched rides on the old boat, and they came into the family's little courtyard smelling of spoiled fish and perfume. It wasn't especially agreeable to Angel, though Tikibent showed an alarming interest in him on that last visit, and whenever the adults weren't watching, she snuck him beers and pressed against him. She had a black eye.

"Son, you have real impact on your cousin," Don Antonio whispered.

"She smells like Chentebent."

"Ah, cabrón!" Don Antonio pulled him aside. "Put Vicks in your nose."

It worked.

They danced.

❦

That day, Cucabent and Tikibent joined Mamá América in cornering Angel. They herded him into his parents' bedroom like a recalcitrant yearling bull. He didn't like all the women closing in on him. "Your eyebrows!" Tikibent cried. "You look like a crow is stuck to your face."

The torture began: tweezers wielded mercilessly, the women clearing the scrub off his brows and pinching him or insulting him when he squirmed or cried out. They harried his poor face until they had sculpted this extravagant hedge into two surprised-looking Rita Hayworth arches. Forever after, he would make this ritual part of his secret life with Perla. No one would ever know.

❦

Don Antonio and Mamá América sat him down after his Spanish Inquisition eyebrow experience and informed him that he was going to Mazatlán on *El Guatabampo*. He cried out in outrage tinged with delight. He didn't want to leave Perla! Yet he didn't mind missing school. And he had never taken a long boat ride. Or seen far Mazatlán. The big city! Where all the sophisticates lived.

They thought he was stupid, as parents often do. Well, he

was stupid, as children often are. He had no idea he was being moved aside to facilitate the dissolution of their marriage.

Don Antonio had for years engaged in mysterious visits to the northern border on "police work." Mamá América knew he was visiting a cousin—a "secret" lover of his in Tijuana. But he really had his eye on the other side. In those days, Mexican men wanted two things: American cars and American women.

He had told her that very week he was leaving her for the other woman. But she knew what the other woman didn't know: Antonio would leave that woman too.

She never let out one word of this betrayal to the kids. She was not about to beg him to stay or to let her horror show. She knew, however, that she could not deal with Angel's stormy emotions once the betrayal hit. The little ones would be hard enough. She and Don Antonio would have to move Angel out of the house before the world collapsed around them. Hence the idea for him to leave with Chentebent.

Sometimes she imagined poisoning Don Antonio. A little rat poison in his coffee...

The plan was for Don Antonio to board the long-haul bus as soon as Angel the Sailor set out to sea. By the time their son found out, the damage would already be done and time would have passed. Letters were slow. Don Antonio demanded only one thing of his wife and her sister: that his son never be known as Angelbent.

Mamá América thought of Don Antonio's old gray upright piano, which sat in a corner of the house. He had bought it from a rotten cantina on the outskirts of town, where desert rats slumped in the dark, drinking pulque and mezcal. The owner had sold it to him for a hundred U.S. dollars. It was covered in cigarette burns and stains. But he loved it. He played it for the family every day. He played a few Agustín Lara tunes now, for the party. After he was gone, América decided, she would chop it up for firewood.

All through that smoky last supper with the Bents crowding the small table under the plum tree, América never dropped her faint smile. The Harley was parked beside the back wall of the garden, exuding malevolent energies from beneath its shroud. She was smiling because she planned to roll it into the sea as soon as her bastard of a husband was settled in his bus seat.

Chentebent was telling appalling jokes that made Mamá América send the smaller children to their beds. Angel was hypnotized by these nights, when his father drank liquor— Chentebent was a notorious carouser, along with his many other attributes, and he caused Don Antonio to drink tequila. An astonishment. And Don Antonio transformed from a carved pillar of righteous strength to a fluid, dancing creature of many voices and filthy uproars. For the rest of his life, Angel would long to reduce a house full of people to a choking, bellowing mess like these men did.

"Ay, Chente!" the women would cry. "Ay, Tonio!" Whether red-faced from laughing or embarrassment, Angel could never tell.

"And then," Chentebent shouted, "the elephant stuck the peanut up Pancho's ass!"

Guffawing, Cucabent fell out of her chair, and Don Antonio jumped up and goose-stepped around the courtyard, holding his stomach and trying to breathe through laughing. The parrot screamed in its cage, as if it understood the joke as well.

"Listen, listen!" his father said when he caught his breath.

Their hilarity died down. The meat still crackled in its red-hot pit. Shrimp heads lay all over the table, staring with their black pencil-tip eyes. And Tikibent grinned ferally at Angel with a shiny wet mouth he knew would taste of lime and salt and fish oil. Beer cans and tequila bottles and several glasses covered the table and the ground beneath it. Mamá América thinking all the while of sharp knives and testicles.

"Listen," Don Antonio repeated, unsteady in the middle of his wobbling shadow, pushed jaggedly across the flagstones by lamps hung in the tree. "I have a joke for you! So. Little Pepe was playing in the garden."

"Pepe who?" said Chentebent.

"Pepe, pues. Any Pepe!"

Chentebent crossed his arms. "I don't know who you're talking about."

"I'm talking about Pepe! Oye, cabrón! It's a joke! There is no Pepe!"

"If there is no Pepe, why are you talking about him?"

"Damn you, pinche Chente!"

"You are imagining things," Chentebent said, draining his beer and belching softly with a luxuriousness that only a liter of shrimp gas could create.

"Listen, you bastard!" cried Don Antonio.

This exchange lived on for Angel as the most deeply amusing moment of the night. It was better than the jokes. He discovered at that moment that he was an absurdist—it came to him as a Zen enlightenment. He fell back in his chair. Tikibent ruined the spell by widening her legs for an instant and allowing him full view of her bloomers.

"Little Pepe," Don Antonio resumed, "was playing in his yard."

"Where did he live?"

"Go to hell, pendejo. And his grandfather came along and sat on a bench and watched him playing. He called Pepe over and said, 'Look at this earthworm on the ground. He just came out of a hole.'"

Chentebent raised a finger. "Excuse me," he said. "What was the grandfather's name?"

"Who cares! It's a goddamned joke! Stop interrupting!"

Angel and the women were snickering.

Wounded, Chentebent said, "It seemed important to you that everybody had a name in this story." He expressed his sense of futility with his lower lip and the shrug of one shoulder.

Don Antonio released a cry of cosmic protest to the heavens and said, "Carlos! Grandpa is named Carlos! All right? Is everybody happy now?"

"I am happy, Father," Angel said.

Chentebent yawned.

"Grandpa Carlos showed Pepe there was a damned worm on the ground, wiggling around beside its hole. And he said to the boy, 'Pepe, I will pay you a peso if you can put that worm back in its hole.'"

"Cheapskate," Chentebent noted, using the infuriating Mexican term "codo duro"—he of the hard elbow—which Angel never quite understood.

Wisely, Don Antonio ignored Chentebent, which silenced him. "So Pepe thought about it," Don Antonio continued, "and ran inside. He came out with his mother's hair spray. He picked up the worm and sprayed it until it was stiff, then he slipped it down the hole. His grandfather gave him his peso and hurried away. The next day, Pepe was outside playing again. His grandfather came out of the house and gave him a peso. 'But, Abuelito,' Pepe said. 'You already paid me yesterday!'

Grandfather Carlos said, 'No, Pepe. That peso is from your grandmother!'"

Don Antonio stood there with his arms raised.

Suddenly the women burst into cackles, even Mamá América.

"Ay, Tonio!" Cucabent shouted.

After a pause, Chentebent said, "I don't understand a word you said."

This exact moment was when hell came through their gate, and Don Antonio showed Angel that he was a madman and a Pancho Villa. As they all laughed, the gate flew open, and a drunk fisherman staggered into the courtyard with a huge knife, one meant for gutting sharks and tunas, clutched in his fist.

"Chentebent!" he shouted.

One of the myriad enemies of the odiferous Bent corporation, come to call.

"I slice you open like a pinche fish, cabrón!"

The knife swung back and forth, held low like a real knife fighter would hold it.

"You slept with my wife!"

The women cried out.

Tikibent jumped behind Angel and wailed like a police siren.

Don Antonio still stood with his arms stretched wide. He wasn't in uniform, so he didn't have his pistola on his hip. He was sorely disappointed when he reached for it to blow this asshole back out of the gate.

For his part, Chentebent downed a tequila shot and turned his watery red eyes on his assailant. He didn't seem inclined to rise to his own defense. He didn't know this pendejo, nor could he imagine which of his various paramours might be attached to him.

"She wasn't any good anyway," he said. Then belched.

Mamá América rushed to shield Angel with her body. And Tikibent moved her aside so she could see the fight. The green parrot in his cage began trying to fly, shaking the cage so badly that seeds rained out on them.

Don Antonio turned to the deadly sailor.

"You shit," he said.

"What?"

"You vermin. You pig."

"Watch yourself."

"You son of a whore. You come into my home and threaten my guests? You dare wave a knife at me? I will kill you and your entire family. I will kill your children, and I will kill your grandchildren. And I will dig up your ancestors and shit in their mouths."

"Hey."

Don Antonio tore his own shirt open. "Stab me, chingado. If you think you can kill me, stab me now. Right in my heart. But be sure I'm dead. Because I am about to unleash all of my wrath on you, you fucking dog."

The sailor stared at him with true terror on his face. He had no idea who this maniac was, but he was clearly the one man in La Paz the sailor did not want to fight. The sailor didn't even pause to muster his dignity. He spun around, ran into the street, and charged as fast as he could toward the sea, upending trash cans as he fled.

For the rest of his life, no matter what he thought of his father, no matter what hardships or sorrows, what humiliations or horrors befell him, Big Angel remembered that moment as the single most heroic thing he would ever witness. He thought he would never be able to be a man like his father.

Even Chentebent clapped his hands, albeit softly.

The next day, Angel boarded *El Guatabampo* and sailed into the hazy blue. He had no chance to bid farewell to his Perla. And her family did not have the technological miracle of a telephone. He tore himself away from the land, choking back tears. Chentebent hooted the steam whistle incessantly, in spite of his own hangover. Life was pain, after all. Leaving Perla, Angel was sure, would be the worst of it for him.

The last thing his father said to him was "We need to know—did you sleep with Tikibent?"

"Qué?"

"Did you *sleep* with her?"

"Father! No! She is my cousin!"

"Idiot," his father replied. "You could have done anything you wanted with her!"

As soon as the boat was out of sight, Don Antonio and his little family walked home. He collected his two bags, gave the two children formal hugs, and—oddly, it seemed to everyone—shook Mamá América's hand.

"If you could have produced more sons," he said, "I would not be forced to leave you."

She had a completely still face, thinking: *You vermin.*

"Take care of my motorcycle until I send for it" was the last thing he said. He trudged away toward the center of town. Whistling.

América had been planning to murder that damned motorcycle, but she wasn't stupid. She strode over to the machine and ripped the drop cloth off it. "Play," she told the children, who had no idea their world had just ended. And later that day, while her older son vomited operatically into the Sea of Cortez, she sold the motorcycle to a doctor from Cabo San Lucas, for she knew she would have to feed the household. But even that money would eventually run out. She and these two would go hungry. They would even eat the doves in the patio cages, and regret that they couldn't bring themselves to kill and cook the parrot.

⌁

Meanwhile, far across the sea, Angel worked every day and saved his centavos for when he could escape the hell he had unwittingly entered. Chentebent barely paid him. Cucabent did his laundry and cooked for him, and, by God, that was generous enough in their opinion. Where Angel had imagined nightly gatherings and uproar as he had known during the Bents' invasions of his home, he instead found himself in the outer dark. Alone. Miserable. Hungry. Under siege.

At first, he slept in a little lean-to in the family's small huerta—tucked in among bananas and two mango trees. A date palm full of iguanas. Giant spiders that terrified him. And the washhouse-toilet, where he showered in cold water. Mazatlán was almost always warm enough for a cold shower, and so it wasn't the water that bothered him as much as the huge roaches that flew out of the drain.

One of his duties was to mop out the evil little toilet room— he had to empty out the tin toilet paper can since the pipes would not swallow soiled paper. It disgusted him. He held his breath. Chentebent wadded up giant knots of awful paper while allowing Big Angel five sheets a day. "Scrub your culo with a sponge!" his uncle said.

Angel started to sense something was wrong when he learned that the neighbors did not like the Bent clan and tended to shun them. Chentebent's behavior was unacceptable to good Mazatlecos. People on the street were even wary of saying "Good morning" or "Good afternoon," which was rare in Sinaloa. Rudeness was a real sin to them. He told himself the beatings weren't so bad—Don Antonio could hit harder than Bent could. At least they weren't every day. And Tikibent got hit more than he did.

He did toilet duty every morning and night, and he raked the huerta, and he swept the house, and he scraped and painted and mopped and hauled nets on the boat. He was hungry all the time. His growling stomach wouldn't let him sleep at night. Cucabent and Tikibent filled the little toilet bucket with "los secretos"—things that were best kept secret, in his opinion. And then he realized that Tikibent left him other things: underpants draped casually over the edge of the sink. Or the door left half open as she showered. He missed his mother and father, and he wept at night thinking of Perla.

He didn't know why it took him so long to write to her. Perhaps it was shyness. Or shame. He could not find the words for her. And it was suddenly six months later, and he borrowed some paper and an envelope from Tía Cucabent. And he bent to it like some monkey transcribing scripture, agonizing over each line and crumpling drafts until he was down to his last sheet and had to let the letter go.

"Mi Dulce Perlita," he wrote, then tried a fresh opening added to this one:

Perla of Great Price—

> *I miss you like a caged bird misses the sky. I am in a cage. But I will be free. And I will come for you because I know*

you miss me as much as I miss you. And we will make a new world!

He went on in this vein for a few more lines and ended with tears and great kisses and exhalations of fervor. He trembled when he took the letter to the mailbox by the docks. In those days, of course, there was only the somnambulistic Mexican postal service to deliver messages. And his ten-centavo letter took almost two weeks to arrive in La Paz. And his response was tardy in the writing, followed by its glacial delivery. So he didn't hear from her for over a month. A month spent fretting and waiting. It was the epitome of romance in his mind—somehow noble. He felt elevated every day by his suffering for her—a suffering of greater depth and quality than these squalid days as Chentebent's scut boy. But like many lovers before him, awaiting some imagined billet-doux full of brace, he received the letter all dreamers fear most.

Esteemed Angel.

Oh hell no, he thought. He knew already. Say no more. Life had already ended with those two anemic words of greeting. It could have just as easily said, "Hello, Loser."

He scanned the bad handwriting for the three lines it took for her to confess: "But you never wrote to me, and I have found another." Angel immediately burned Perla's letter. And he crept to Tiki, against his will—he sinned. It was like his little pole dragged him, the most powerful magnet on Earth. Just the sight of Tiki made it start to bounce. Like some band conductor's baton, counting out the beats of his broken heart. He thought if Tikibent saw this bouncing, she would flee from him. So he wore his shirts untucked. When she saw his shirt-tails, Tikibent thought he was flying a battle flag to announce his intentions. She took that jumpy twig in hand and strangled it until it relaxed.

He was embarrassed to be alive. His hands shook. And he was sure that God would strike him down. His life was shame. Betrayed and abandoned by everything and everyone.

But before God could be stirred to wrath, Chentebent struck first.

He crept out to Angel's hut, reeking of spoiled shrimp and rum. He fell on top of him. Breathed in his face. "Are you hard?" he kept saying. "Are you hard? Do you beat it? Do you?" He scrabbled for the front of Angel's pants. "Let's see that meat. Let's see what you're giving to my girl." Chentebent, laughing and blowing reek in his face, fat and crushing, no matter how Angel kicked.

Angel kept thinking: *I thought you were a good man. I thought you were funny.*

Chentebent collapsed into thunderous snores atop him.

He took his first revenge on the pirate the next day.

When no one was looking, he scooped huge globs of lard out of Cucabent's red cans. Lard being saved for frying beans. And he smeared it inside the legs of Chentebent's favorite canvas pants. When the outraged howling began, Chentebent coming at him with his legs splayed, waddling, red in the face and squishing with every step, Angel stood up to the blows and smiled at Tikibent, who watched from her window, ripping at her hair and laughing. He lost a tooth that day.

Chentebent dragged him roughly to *El Guatabampo*, his great callused fingers leaving livid purple imprints on Angel's arms, as if he had tattooed dark lilies upon them.

"Earn your keep, you goddamn freeloader," he said. "I'll teach you."

Angel had blood on his face, in his mouth.

"Oh, you'll learn your lesson. You little prick."

All Angel had to do was wait. He could outlast anything. He outlasted Chentebent's beatings. He outlasted his uncle's grunting visits at night.

Only when he was alone did Angel weep, snot all over his face. He slept on a pallet of old blankets in the poxy galley, tucked under the sink. And he scraped and painted and scrubbed and gutted, fished and crabbed and mended nets and served as insomniac watchdog all night, alone. He sometimes had to take gaff in hand and beat back bandits and drunken sailors from foreign ships, who crept to the foul boat along the docks. He listened to the drinking and fighting on other boats, the music coming from the shore, the laughter of whores and lovers, and the barking of dogs. When the church bells rang, he felt that the world he knew was in some other land. Was too far away to ever be found again. He would show Perla the depth of her mistake. "I am worthy, I am worthy," he recited as if in prayer.

He was cut across the chest by a skinny old sailor, who took the gaff to the face and vanished overboard among the oil slicks and dead fish. He bled, watching the old man drag himself up a ladder at the next berth, slimy and wobbly as he stumbled into the night. Fat blood drops splashed at his feet. Angel never said a word, but he remembered the moment. Kept it inside him.

He wrapped his chest in rags and taped it over, and the fever turned his front red and made him shiver as if snow were falling, but he never told. He stole rum from the galley and dripped it screaming hot into the pus-drooling wound. He bit his lips and cried and kicked his feet.

He carried on in shock and terror for days out there, waiting for God's wrath or the sailor's comrades—neither of which came. He suspected this entire life was a turn of God's displeasure. He hid his meager pay in a coffee can behind the galley sink, and he found Chentebent's chest of oily pesos—his operating budget for their fishing expeditions—locked in a cabinet in the wheelhouse. Chentebent began to charge him for beans and tortillas.

He preferred to go hungry. He ate only what was in the boat, even raw bait sardines. He saved every centavo he could. Those nights when he ate, and his guts twisted and groaned inside him, and Perla was so far away, and he feared his mother and brother and sister might be hungry and abandoned across the sea, were the darkest of all.

The next time Chentebent came for him, he had the gaff ready. The pirate had come aboard and already opened his filthy dungarees, and Angel swung the gaff with his eyes closed. Blind, flailing. He never really thought he'd connect with the side of Chentebent's head. The hideous crunch of the club hitting the skull. The startled grunt, and the immediate scent of feces. The crippling spike of pain up his own arm when he hit the big man. And the splash.

By the time he opened his eyes—for he had kept them clenched for just a moment, in the hopes that what he had just done had not really happened—the big man was sinking into the oily water, his undone pants around his knees.

Angel waited for him to surface. But he did not.

The rest of that night came in a panic. His memory was never clear. For he was still just a boy, and although he was terrified of what he'd done, he was even more afraid of getting in trouble for it. A thousand lies pulsed through his head. Some part of him believed the fisherman would climb a ladder over at the next mooring and curse at him. He ran back and forth, but there was no magical portal on the *Guatabampo* that opened to some fresh new world where things were beautiful again.

The coffee can of pesos went into his mochila with his two extra pairs of dungarees, his shorts and socks, and his three shirts. He got the box of fishing money out from the main cabin. The boat's extra fuel cans were difficult to lift, but he was strong in his panic. It was all he could imagine now: a fraudulent accident. He saw himself being interviewed by police— perhaps his own father. *No, no! He was drunk. He threw me off the boat and told me to never come back. I took my severance pay and bought a bus ticket. I don't know what happened after I left. I saw nothing. I wanted to join my father.*

Mamá América had finally confided to him in a terse letter that his father had gone north. And that she and his siblings would probably follow. He would confront his father for abandoning his family if it was the last thing he did.

So he took a bus north. Express to Tijuana. It would be twenty-seven hours sitting there, smelling of gasoline. He couldn't sleep. He kept thinking about the throbbing bloom of orange flame visible from the window as the bus had pulled away into the night.

It was 1965, and he felt he had already lived a hundred years. For decades, he told his mother that he had run away. That

he had no idea what happened to *El Guatabampo* or Tío
Chente. He repeated his lie so many times that he almost convinced himself: he had gotten fed up with the work and the
bullying, and had saved up his money and caught the bus. He
assumed that Chentebent discovered his escape and got drunk
and somehow set fire to the boat.

He had thought it was over. But the guilt and the lie burned
steadily through all of his life.

✐

Big Angel stood in the shadows of the living room, buffeted
by stories of the past, things he remembered and things he had
learned. Or maybe things he had dreamed. He could no longer
tell the difference. The stories flew in like wind through an
open window and whirled around him. He could feel them almost pull him off his feet. They seemed to come by their own
volition, leaping over years, ignoring the decades. Big Angel
found himself in a time storm. He saw it all as if the past were
a movie in the Las Pulgas theater.

✐

Little Angel was born in 1967.

Big Angel lived with his mother and siblings in Colonia
Obrera in Tijuana until he snuck across the border to join his
father after one of the old man's infrequent visits to their house.
It seemed easy to him. People either crept through the shal-
low brown Tijuana River down near the coast or joined the
crowds running out of Colonia Libertad in Otay to the east.
There were regular corridors in those days, and day workers

often commuted through the dirt canyons. Big Angel refused to see any other girls. He sent postcards to Perla, which she never answered.

Yndio was born in 1970. By then, Big Angel was camping out at his father's house and working as a donut cooker on night shift with payments made strictly under the table. One of his first American phrases: "under the table." It seemed so elegant.

Braulio was born in 1971. Big Angel didn't know any of this, but he wrote Perla a letter that same year, begging her to come north. Though the letter was later lost, they both remembered the line "Come to me while we still have life and we can wrestle with destiny." It was the noblest thing Perla had ever heard. And she came, throwing everything away to join him.

Braulio grew up fast. He had them all fooled. Minnie was just a dumb kid—she worshipped all three of her brothers. But El Yndio knew, and Lalo knew what the deal was. And as she got older, Minnie made believe she didn't know. Mamá Perla—well, Braulio was her angel. Pops took his standard noble route. Sometimes the boys laughed at him when he wasn't around—so snooty, nose in the air. Making a big show of claiming Yndio and Braulio as his sons. The wisest man in the world, by his own estimation, remained blind to these two. Pinche Braulio—his nickname, Snickers, should have said it all.

Yndio could not stand Big Angel. He was the one who remembered his birth father. Braulio had been too young. Their father had dived for pearls. He shucked oysters with a fat, curved blade and slurped them down with lime juice and red hot sauce. He laughed loud, and when he laughed, his gold tooth shone. And one day, he dove into the waters east of La Paz and never surfaced. Yndio remembered that.

This Angel appeared one day as if he'd always been there.

Yndio was so shocked that his mother had some romantic secret. Some filthy little past life. He wrestled with rage—thinking *Whore* some days when he looked at her.

Not Braulio. He was a prankster. And when he hooked up with Gloriosa's boy, Guillermo, it was some kind of perfection. They were the same age, the same size. They could have been twins. And the girlies called Guillermo "Joker." There was a clear theme. Snickers and Joker, down por vida homies. 4LIFE. When poor Lalo came along, he never could penetrate their society of two.

Things weren't always middle class for the family. They didn't always live in Lomas Doradas, in the happy barrios of Dago town. And in those years of struggle, when Big Angel would not allow anyone to get government help—no welfare, no food stamps—there were lots of boiled beans and fried beans and bean soups. Braulio's favorite breakfast was cold fried beans smeared on a slice of Wonder Bread. Eaten while standing in the sad, tiny kitchen of their first apartment behind a garage in San Ysidro, not fifty yards from the border's barbed wire. Pretty ballsy, since Ma and Pops were both illegal as hell back then.

Nights filled with helicopters and sirens and running feet and break-ins. Days watching out for gangbangers and stealthy Mexican bandits who snuck into the country to steal what little that immigrants like Angel and Perla had. They beat people and stole their watches and were reabsorbed by Tijuana before anybody noticed.

The kids all walked down to Oscar's Drive-In and pooled their pennies to buy a chocolate malt and share it. Snickers, Yndio, Lalo, and Li'l Mouse. She was funny—no front teeth back then. Yndio mocked her, calling her "Moush." She chewed the paper straws with her gums and wrecked them, and the boys smacked her on the head.

Later, Snickers came through for her, getting Minnie to school in Pops's old station wagon. Braulio liked to drive her. He knew he could stab any culero who stepped up to her in a disrespectful way. Everybody was afraid of him, except his family. It felt good for Minnie. No matter where she went in her school, she got respect, because they all believed Braulio would come and set them on fire if they talked shit to the cutie.

Everybody said he had done that very thing to some Mexican outlaw on Otay Mesa. Minnie didn't believe those stories. Not at first.

◌◌

In those days, when Big Angel worked two jobs, sometimes three, poor Perla suffered in that dim apartment. She wanted only to return to Mexico. She did not understand his obsession with the U.S. This was not a better life. At home, at least, there was community, laughter. Even hope. In Tijuana, if you wanted to party, you could build a bonfire in the middle of the street.

Here, she found loneliness and worse hunger than in Mexico—worse, because all around her people were rolling like pigs in huge piles of food and clothes and liquor and nice underwear and cigarettes and money and chocolate and fruit. And she struggled to find new ways to stretch a thin chicken and a handful of rice to feed three growing boys and her man. Minnie? She could go hungry like Perla. It wouldn't do to be a fat Mexican girl anyway.

Snickers and Joker rescued her days. They were wild, hilarious. Joker flirted with her most inappropriately—when she was feeling fat and sagging and old. He'd get up behind her and whisper-growl in her ear. "Tía, me tienes tan caliente!" She laughed and smacked him, but she also felt the hot tickles when he was against her. Oh no. Bad boy. Though she might have pushed back on him once or twice with her bottom.

The boys charged into that place as if it were some palace, blasted the TV too loud, lounged on the couches, and shouted compliments. They always had cigarettes for her. Then chocolates. Then money, which she'd hide from Angel. When Braulio turned sixteen and had gas money, he dragged her out to the car and drove her around. She couldn't understand where they kept getting so many cigarettes.

*

Yndio was different. He was always stoic. Iron faced and strict with the little ones. He was always furious with Big Angel for some reason. He never understood his stepfather's indulgence of the young ones, because Big Angel had been so hard on him. Big Angel tried to be Don Antonio at first—what else did he know? And he had used the belt on Yndio's back. Yndio was already as tall as he was, and the second time Big Angel thought a whipping was in order, Yndio punched him in the face.

"I am your father!" Angel shouted.

"You sleep with my mother, old man. I don't have a father."

When Angel grabbed his arm, Yndio spit in his face.

*

When Big Angel rented the house in Lomas Doradas, it was a surprise for Perla. He told her he needed to go for a drive to pick something up from his boss. He was working day shifts pushing a broom, and night shifts he learned to sell real estate. One of his million jobs. She didn't like to leave the apartment, but he cajoled until she agreed to ride with him. The kids were inside the house, waiting for them. When she realized what was happening, she collapsed. The boys had to drag her to a chair and hold her up.

"Ay Dios! Flaco! Ay Dios!"

It didn't take long for Yndio to spend more time away with "friends."

Then Gloriosa and Joker moved in with them. And Lalo began to learn what Snickers and Joker were really like. First they had tattoos. Then they had money. Then they hid guns in the bedroom. They liked to catch him and stuff him in the cabinet under the sink and stick a broom handle through the door pulls to leave him trapped. They filled socks with glue and breathed the vapors.

All the boys were skinny except for Yndio. He was born with that body. But he never missed a chance to build strength. He had arms that anyone would kill for. He did two hundred sit-ups a day. Push-ups when he came for weekend visits, with Minnie kneeling on his back.

The house started to feel impossible. There were so many bodies crammed in there, they could hardly breathe. There didn't seem to be any air. They had no idea how busy the little house would always be. When Big Angel came home from his jobs, he sat on the slumpy couch with Lalo and Braulio. Minnie sat on the floor between his bare feet, rubbing Quinsana powder between his toes. Gloriosa sat in the used easy chair. The only place left was in the corner, on the floor with the dog that Snickers had rescued in the rail yards. So Yndio sat there and just stared at the TV, never looking at Big Angel. Joker tended to hang in the back room, reading comic books. Perla stood in the kitchen, leaning against a counter. Drinking instant coffee. Fretting and smoking. They all smoked, except Minnie. But she would learn fast.

Big Angel grew dark, brooding, as he worked extra hours. He worked now in a bakery up in National City, so he was able to bring home stale donuts. The kids thought donuts made them rich. Snickers and Joker had never tasted jelly donuts before. As soon as he had changed his bakery uniform, Angel was out the door to clean business buildings in downtown San Diego. He came home and studied to sell term life insurance. And then came night classes in computer programming. He crawled into bed after midnight, to the sound of his wife and daughter snoring, then was up again before 6:00 a.m. to make more donuts.

But he bought the house for $18,000 through the real estate brokers he used to work for.

And that's when Grandpa Antonio moved in, thrown out of his own house by Little Angel's mother, Betty. Big Angel never thought he would end up making peace with his father and certainly never thought he would give him shelter. But once Gramps was installed, Yndio never came back. Perla and Minnie had to meet him at the Pancake House when they wanted to see him. His hair! He had an earring.

One day Perla took his hands in hers across the table and said, "My son. Are you a queer?"

He and Minnie stared at each other and fell over laughing.

ↂ

Angel and Don Antonio spent many tense hours at the kitchen table, elaborately ignoring each other and sipping black coffee. In Don Antonio's view, coffee with cream and sugar was dessert, not a drink for men. Angel felt superior at last to his father. He knew the old man had been thrown out for sleeping with American women in his wife's bed.

"I loved your mother," Don Antonio said, though whenever América came over, he hid in the back room.

"Why did you leave us, then?"

"I don't know."

Another cigarette lit. Perla keeping out of it. Fearing the old man. Fearing he'd come for her one night, and she would be afraid to fight him off because she didn't want her Flaco to suffer another heartbreak. She kept Minnie out of his reach.

"Son, the more I learn, the less I know."

"Oh?"

"I thought getting old made you wise. You only find out how pendejo you are. But when I get too pendejo to drive, put me in my grave."

"Padre, it isn't that bad."

"Well, mijo, I can still get upstairs to a lady's apartment. But my pecker won't stand up to do anything about it."

"I see," Angel replied.

But he would not really see until he was dying, and he'd replay this chat in his bed when he couldn't sleep. *I am just learning how stupid I am.*

ↂ

Easing back into his body.

She snored beside him. Flung across the mattress as if she were running downhill, arms and legs akimbo. He patted her rump. He liked the edge of the sheet over his lips. All tucked in. Tight. Safe.

Early morning before dawn was best, when he didn't remember he was dying. For a moment, he thought he had a future. And he savored his past.

Today, it tasted of butterscotch.

Celebration Day

The Morning of the Party

8:00 a.m.

It was time to get ready.

Little Angel lay on the couch, watching morning light creep across MaryLú's living room. Everything smelled of sweet, powdery perfume.

The sibs all thought Little Angel was cheating the system somehow. A culture thief. A fake Mexican. More gringo than anything. He knew that. He had heard his sister call him a "gringo-Mex." As if being any kind of Mexican had scored him points in the Grand Game. As if being any kind of Mexican in California was a ride in the Rose Parade. But what was he going to say? Tell them all the times he had been called "taco bender" or "wetback"? "Burrito breath"? They would laugh at him. Should he make lists of the Mexican girls he dated when he was a kid? Show them poems he'd written in Spanish?

Spanish! His family didn't even like speaking Spanish to him. He tried, and they insisted on answering him in English. Though they knew perfectly well that he spoke Spanish as well as they did and better than their children did. Each side had something to prove, and none of them knew what it was.

They didn't like his ease with that world of fancy pale bastards up north.

They thought he had it made, growing up with English and Spanish together. And he didn't have an accent in either one. And was probably rich. Everything had come so easily to him. Anything he wanted. Including their father.

They imagined his Christmas mornings as orgies of bright toys and radios and bicycles.

They had seen his class lectures on YouTube. Talking about Chicano authors they'd never heard of. They knew he mocked their accents. They found him disrespectful of their father. Well, perhaps calling him "The Sperm Donor" in his Fatherhood in Latina/o Literature course was ill-advised. He owned that.

He believed he was celebrating them when he shared stories of their foibles. He felt the burden of being their living witness. Somehow the silliest details of their days were, to him, sacred. And he believed that if only the dominant culture could see these small moments, they would see their own human lives reflected in the other.

Unbeknownst to him, across town, Big Angel had again reentered his body after visiting their father's grave in Tijuana and a visit to their family home in La Paz—fallen now and full of tumbleweeds. And a voyeuristic moment in La Gloriosa's bedroom to watch her dream.

⌘

La Gloriosa was up early. She didn't know why everybody thought she was late to everything. Cabrones. She was usually up before almost everybody else. It took time to be this fine— you didn't just jump out of bed looking like the living legend of the family. Ay no. So maybe she didn't get where she was supposed to go when they wanted her there, but she made sure they would remember forever the moment she arrived.

Even though she slept alone, she always wore beautiful things to bed. This morning, she was in a red teddy with black lace trim. All silk and soft. So tender that she loved to run her hands over her own ribs.

Her hair was a mess, and she liked it messy. But she had taken off her face last night, like she did every night, and she didn't like the look of herself without her makeup and eyes put back in place. They looked puffy and small without her attentions. Her skin was splotchy in the morning light. And her lips vanished every night. It took two levels of lipstick to bring out their ravishing power. The delicious center of her kiss and the suggestive darker edges. Men should feel like they were going to topple into her mouth.

"El lippi-sticky."

She knew that her own beauty was aided yet not diminished by artifice. The *Mona Lisa* was in a beautiful frame, qué no? The true nature of her face was enhanced when she allowed the artifice to focus the viewer's eye. And her beauty would show them the pure gold inside her.

A touch of copper on the eyelids and some precise eyeliner craft really worked their magic on her eyes. The nearly invisible blue line above the black. And that eyelash thickener. That was her real secret weapon. Aside from her general wonderfulness. It was hard, some days, to get started. It would be fun to just tie a scarf over her hair, put on sunglasses, and run free along the seashore.

"Buenota," she told herself, for she found herself very good. It was her job to tell herself. She stretched. Her biceps were beautiful—but that floppy back of the arm stuff made her crazy.

"All righty," she said en inglés, though she rolled the r. *Rr-rrighty*.

Before her makeup session, of course, her long shower. Sorry about the drought. But the shower had to be long and hot. Leg razor, French shampoo, L'Occitane conditioning cream, clear bar of peach-almond soap, bottle of milky face cleanser. No soap on the face! Exfoliant and moisture scrub. She wasn't going to look old like those other family girls. She may be aging, but she was going to make sure everyone remembered she was the youngest of the sisters.

When she was a kid, they called cute girls "mangos." She was still juicy. Who wouldn't love fresh mango on their tongue?

After the shower, she planned to deploy her ointments. La Gloriosa never went into the day without lotion on every inch of her body and gentle secret potions sunk into her face and neck before the makeup. Touches of the darkest perfume in her secret spots. Her top beauty secret: Preparation H under her chin and eyes at bedtime. One sacrificed for perfection.

The young girls were going in for waxing, they told her. Waxing? They were crazy. La Minnie, for example, went to the Pretty Kitty Salon in Chula Vista. The Pretty Kitty! Was that what she thought it was? There was a limit. Even though Minnie had given her a ten-dollar discount certificate, there was no way some Filipina was going to pour wax all over her "kitty."

"Eso sí que no!" she said out loud.

She let the hot water run down her back. Everything hurt. Nobody told her this when she was growing up, that you get rusty and aches appear in the unlikeliest places. Her hips hurt. Her head hurt. She breathed in the steam. The headaches frightened her. And the pain behind her left chi-chi. Among her ribs. She was so afraid of these small aches that she didn't mention them to anyone, and barely admitted them even to herself. Even to God.

She ignored a small flicker of a thought about Little Angel. Lifting her breasts from behind. Easing the pain out of her ribs. *No.*

She ran her hand over the scar of her son's birth across her lower belly. She felt self-conscious at the thought of anyone ever seeing her naked because of it. Her poor son. Her only son. She wept in the comfort of the hot water.

Guillermo. Ay, Guillermito. Strangers had shot him five times. Why? It had been ten years now, and every morning she still whispered to him, cried for him. Always her baby boy, never mind how old he was. Why? They had shot him and left him on the sidewalk. And he might have survived—that's how strong he was. He might have survived. But the shooter came back and shot him in his beautiful face. Why, why...

He and Braulio died in the same swamp of blood, black in the streetlights. Braulio staring into the street, and Guillermo without eyes or a face. People took pictures on their phones, videos. The boys' fingers almost touching.

La Gloriosa covered her face with her hands and knelt as if in prayer, letting the sobs come.

❧

8:30 a.m.

Little Angel was surprised, when he got out of the shower, that María Luisa had gone out for a couple of go-cups of good coffee. She'd brought scones too. He came out with a towel around his waist and gave her a hug.

"Ooh," she said, delighted. "You go to hell for flirting with your sister."

He sat. It was a long-standing joke with them. When he first met her, at ten, it was at the beach south of Tijuana. Don Antonio had packed him in the car in San Diego and driven him south, across the border, and down the coast. He had this beach he loved—Medio Camino—halfway down the highway between Tijuana and Ensenada. Little Angel had long believed they owned this beach since Don Antonio always called it his. Roadrunners charged along the highway. And grim dark cowboys often rode along the beach and took them for gallops at ten or twenty pesos each.

One day, Big Angel and some of the other siblings were there with their aunt. There was also this pale girl who was older and taller than he. She was resplendent in a black one-piece bathing suit, with long white legs and black hair. And developed. Little Angel was becoming very aware of chi-chis at ten. He was in love...until he found out the ghastly news that this siren was his big sister. Where had they kept her? What a dirty trick.

The family had laughed at him for decades.

She had watched as Don Antonio dragged him to the surf with Big Angel. Little Angel couldn't swim. And he was afraid of the waves. Antonio held his arms. His brother had his legs. They swung him and threw him into the waves. He cried. So they caught him when he washed up and did it again. And again.

"Learn to swim, and this will end," his father told him.

His brother laughed the whole time.

So did MaryLú—at first. But by the end of it, she had her hands clamped over her mouth.

When he crawled out of the water and tried to run, they chased him down yet again. And again.

Little Angel shook his head to clear the memory of that day and smiled. He ate; he drank. "Man, I love coffee."

"Real coffee, maybe," she replied.

She smirked. The whole family had inherited the bizarre belief system of Antonio and América: instant coffee was some kind of miracle. Mexicans of that generation liked to stir a spoonful of coffee powder into a cup of hot water and tinkle it around with a spoon. As if something highly sophisticated and magical were happening. Nescafé. Café Combate. Then they poured Carnation canned milk into it. They thought they were in some James Bond movie, living ahead of the cultural curve. Or maybe they were just sick of coffeepots and grounds.

"I think I'll take real coffee to Brother's birthday," he said. "I'll get a box at Starbucks."

She ate a second scone: to hell with calories. "Are you going to put some clothes on?" she said.

"Nah. I thought I'd go naked."

She went into the kitchenette. "Don't let Paz see you," she said.

He leaned into her breakfast counter and did a bunch of forty-five-degree elevation push-ups, feeling fatuous and Californian.

"Paz," she continued. "That bruja."

Not this again.

"We can't even look at each other," MaryLú said.

Little Angel nodded, backed off the counter, and sipped his coffee. "I know," he intoned like an empathetic talk show host.

"Did you notice her refusing to come near me at the funeral?" she said.

"No."

"You see? How she snubs me?"

They all stayed away from Paz. Her code name was Pazuzu, the demon from *The Exorcist*. Add tequila, and her head would rotate and someone would be assaulted. Vomit eruptions were not entirely out of the question.

"And," María Luisa added, "she hates poor Leo."

Here we go again. Leo. The Lion. The Dude. "Oh?" Little Angel said mildly.

Poor Leo. MaryLú's ex-husband. The fam kept him in the loop out of some nostalgia for better times that had never actually happened. Or for the opportunity to scissor him behind his back. Each was equally gratifying.

Even after their divorce, Leo took MaryLú dancing. And he survived the family's most notorious New Year's Eve party. It had ended with a drunken Pazuzu slapping him repeatedly and shrieking, "Eres una mierda!" And MaryLú, running to his rescue, bellowing, "He is *not* chit!"

"What was that crap on New Year's Eve all about?" Little Angel said.

"She said Leo exposed his organ to her! In the kitchen!"

"Okay—mistake asking about that."

"You know which one I'm talking about, right?"

"Stop," he said.

"His organ."

"Yes. Not his pancreas."

"Angel, I'm being serious. Leo has a very tiny penis."

"Oh my God!"

She held up her thumb and forefinger about an inch apart. "Like that."

"Stop it."

"Like an acorn."

"Stop!"

"He doesn't even like to show it to me. No way he's going to show it to that woman."

Little Angel fell back in his chair and let out a groan of utter despair.

❦

7:00 a.m.

Minerva Esmeralda La Minnie Mouse de La Cruz Castro lay in bed, dreading the start of the day. It was all going to fall on her. She wanted it to be perfect. Daddy's last birthday.

El Tigre was sprawled naked beside her, with the pillow over the top half of his face. He had some stripes tatted on his right shoulder, swooping down onto his chest and surrounding his nipple. She lifted the sheet and studied his sad little critter. All flopped over like it was drunk.

"Hey, Big Man," she said. "You awake?" She poked him there with one purple fingernail. It moved. Well, Big Boy wasn't dead after all. "Tiger."

He snuffled.

She leaned up on her elbow and flicked his nipple with one of her nails until it stood up.

"Dude," he said. "You gon' give me wood, you don't watch out."

She bent to the nipple and circled it hotly with her tongue.

"Whoa, girl."

She bit it.

"Hey!"

"Well?" she said. "I'm right here." She suckled on him. "Nice titties, fat boy," she said.

"Best be careful what you wish for," he said.

"Boy, you going to talk all day or do something about it?"

"Girl," he said. "You're so fine."

"You know it."

"Watch out, here it comes."

He rolled to her.

Afterward, she made coffee. Then she slipped out while he showered.

*

She lived about five miles from Big Angel and Perla, and she was the one they called every time there was a medical crisis. She had spent countless nights sitting in emergency rooms and waiting rooms. She kept an overnight bag packed and sitting by the front door. She drove, singing as loud as she could to Katy Perry on the radio. Last minutes of peace. Maybe forever. She had to be strong. How was she to know how strong God wanted her to be? If she had known beforehand, she would have checked out. Now she was in the middle of it.

Inside, she was still that girl who had run away at fourteen. *What was I thinking? I know every crazy thing anybody does seems like a good idea at the time. But that's no excuse. I have a grandchild now.*

How did that happen?

*

7:50 a.m.

Julio César El Pato de La Cruz was at his ex-wife's condo, picking up his boy. César was tall, not like the cartoon Donald Duck at all. More like a hungover six-foot-three goose with bags under his sad black eyes. He couldn't do anything about his voice, and he was a little hunched from trying to stop being taller than everybody else.

His son was named Marco Antonio—continuing the theme of Roman emperors that Don Antonio had begun with César. Marco was tall like he was. Pato's ex, Marco's mother, was named Vero, and he still couldn't understand how he had cheated on her with Paz and ruined his life. He wanted to come back to Vero, but she would laugh in his face. He had been texting a lonely Filipina woman in Manila. She had as yet resisted his endless requests for a picture of her breasts.

He didn't think about the first wife he had cheated on with Vero. He hoped there wouldn't be another wife. Four wives would be too much. Perhaps a nice Tijuana divorce, then a series of girlfriends. He thought he could still pass for thirty-seven. The hair dye on his eyebrows did not help.

"Hi, Dad," said his boy.

El Pato stared at him—this alien creature who had replaced his nice Mexican child.

His kid was a singer. Or he called himself a singer. César had never heard anything like the "music" his son played. He had a faux Norwegian black-metal band called Satanic Hispanic. They had a home-recorded CD called *Human Tacos—Taste the Flesh!* He wore a T-shirt that announced: KILLING JOKE.

When he sang, Marco barked guttural shrieks that sounded

like the Cookie Monster possessed by Beelzebub, but unbeliev-
ably loud. So loud, his father expected him to spit blood. It was
the utmost evolution of being El Pato, he decided.

His son roared "EXTREME!" at him in his finest hell voice.

His hair was brushed straight up off his head, in the fashion
of Wayne Static from Static-X. He didn't know the singer
was dead. He had made tattoos on his arms and neck with a
Sharpie. He was extremely happy.

"Mijo," César said mildly. "Listo para la fiesta?"

"*Party at pancake house!* BREAKFAAAAAST, BITCHES!"

"Okay, mijo. Sure."

"I HATE GOD!"

"Okay, mijo."

"I AM DEATH! I TAKE YOUR LAST BREATH!
MOTHERF—"

"Yes, let's go eat *pan-kekis*."

They got into the Hyundai.

"Do you ever sing in Spanish?" César asked, carefully pulling
out and driving at his standard forty miles an hour.

"Spanish is for PUSSIES!"

César forced a smile. He quacked a little Dad chuckle, just
to show his son how tolerant he was. Not square. He had a fear
of being square. Even when Little Angel was a kid and El Pato
got to visit him for a weekend, he wore Beatle boots and taught
the kid to sing "Help!"

He had things on his mind. Women. That was what was
on his mind. Always. Who wouldn't think of women, married
to Paz? He thought about them so much he often drove past
his turnoffs on the freeway and found himself in strange parts
of town as if just awakening from a trance. He wanted to
know how some guys got women to give them their underwear.

Like Tom Jones. He shifted uncomfortably in his seat. He bet
Satanic Hispanic got panties all the time.

He glanced at Marco Antonio. He suddenly noticed his son
had a ring in his nose, hanging off his septum. Like some bull.

"Did you always have that?"

"What?"

"In your nose."

The Satanic Hispanic threw up devil horns. "I was born with
it, Dad."

"Okay, mijo," he said.

"RIDE THE LIGHTNING!"

They pulled into the IHOP parking lot.

"No screaming, okay?"

"Okay, Dad."

César had once attended his baby brother's birthday party at
Mission Bay. Little Angel had had cake and a bonfire and beer.
And lots of American girls. The American girls had made his
cake. How had he arranged that? César was sure Little Angel also
collected their underpants. César had never seen so many American girls in his life. His little brother never knew that César had
lured his girlfriend away for a walk that night and received oral
sex from her behind the slide in the playground. He was shocked
and sad for his little brother that she said, "Yum, yum" as she went
in for the kill. He had steered Little Angel away from marrying
her as often as he could. It was his duty as a loving big brother.

"Ay, Marco," he sighed. "Life is so strange."

"Dad, you worry too much."

"I do?"

"WAFFLES WITH A SIDE OF HUMAN!"

César got out of the car and walked the wrong way, and the
Cookie Monster retrieved him and led him inside.

8:45 a.m.

Little Angel came up the street, carrying a cardboard coffee suitcase from the barista. A half gallon of good Colombian. The box had a white plastic spout with a twist-off cap. He had stolen about twenty Truvia packets to bring to the party.

Minnie was sitting in the driveway on a lawn chair. She wore shades in the morning sun. She had skinny jeans and red sandals and a kind of peasant blouse that came off her shoulders and revealed her collarbones. There was a nice warmth in her belly. She grinned, took a puff of her Marlboro.

Little Angel noticed that each toenail was a different color. And her fingernails were purple rainbows.

"Hi, Tío."

"Nice toes."

"Aw, I feel so special! Thanks for noticing."

She held out her hand for him to admire, as well. She extended her cigarette to the side so he could bend down and hug her. He held the coffee box behind him.

"Love you, Tío."

"Love you, girl."

"Mucho, mucho."

"Sí, sí! Mucho!"

From his lair inside the garage, Lalo pressed his lips to the gap between the garage door and its frame and said, "Hey, Tío. Watch out for chudholes."

"What?"

But Lalo was gone.

Minnie said, "Better not to ask."

"That's our family in a nutshell."

"You got that right."

One hundred forty-nine children and dogs ran between them and vanished into the yard.

"Still wish Yndio was here," Minnie said, flicking some ash and looking down the street, as if her brother might appear at any second.

"You'd think. I mean, right? For this? Yeah."

She took a puff, blew it away from him. "We got a disaster, Tío," she said.

"What happened?" he asked. "And by the way—if only one disaster happens today, it'll be a miracle."

"Yeahright?" she said, like that, a single two-syllable word. *Diphthong*, the professor thought. "We forgot to get the birthday cake." And then: *Is not the word* diphthong *actually a diphthong itself?*

From the cavern, Lalo's voice declaimed: "What a chud!"

"Eh?" said Little Angel.

"I'll chud you, pendejo!" she snapped over her shoulder.

Little Angel patted his back pocket. "I've got plastic right here in my wallet. I can get it."

"Really?"

"Sure, honey. Let me handle it. I'd like that."

"There's a Target across the freeway," she said. "Like a big yuppie Target. Couple of miles, across the bridge that way. They got a bakery. Make them write something fancy on it."

"Okay." He made a muscle. "Never fear, Tío's here."

"You so cute, Tío," she said.

"Shucks."

"Honestly? I was running out of money. So you're my hero."

She grinned. "They got sushi, even." She smiled up at him, and he saw her through time, and she was ten years old.

"Do you want sushi?" he said.

"Ay, Tío. I'd feel selfish."

"But you'd like some."

She nodded and smiled up at him over the rims of her shades.

He said, "Minnie, what you're doing today? All this? Be selfish."

"I always knew I liked you," she said.

"I'm your favorite."

"And the handsomest too."

Lalo hissed: "Sushi's for puppets!"

"Lalo," Little Angel called. "What do you want from Target?"

"Captain Morgan, Tío!" the lips announced. "For reals!"

"Okeydokey."

Minnie shook her head. Mouthed, *No.*

"And get some red-hot Takis, homes."

"Right."

"And ice cream."

"Damn," Minnie said. "You too fat already."

"Look who's talking, Godzilla butt."

"Hold up," she shouted. "I'm coming in there as soon as I get up, and I'ma whup your culo."

"Take you like an hour to get up," Lalo said. "I ain't scared."

Little Angel went inside to deliver his coffee.

morning coffee with pan dulce
all my women all around me

a good job
a garden full of chiles and tomatoes

Little Angel went back to see his brother. And there he was, still in his pajama pants, terrifyingly, ferociously awake. Big Angel didn't speak, just beamed like some small lighthouse. He patted the bed beside himself again. Little Angel climbed on.

Their little raft going down the big river.

"Can you smell the cancer?" Big Angel asked.

"I. No. Not really, Carnal."

"I can smell it coming out of my bones."

"Damn."

"I don't like it."

"Yeah, no, I mean, I see how you wouldn't."

Big Angel settled himself and grimaced as he sank against his pillows. "It hurts."

"Bad?"

He looked at his little brother. "What do you think?"

"Stupid question."

"Hurts enough so I get the message."

For some reason, this made them grin at each other.

Big Angel pulled out his bent and disfigured notebooks. "This," he said, "is for Minnie and Lalo after I'm gone. Sí?"

Little Angel nodded.

"Got it?"

"Got it."

"Don't forget."

"I won't."

"When I'm dead, get in here and pick them up. Don't let anybody else get them."

"Jeez, Angel."

"Don't give them to the kids right away. Wait a while. You can't forget."

"I won't." *Crazy old man.* "What are they?"

Big Angel hid them again. "Me," he said.

They listened to the sounds in the distance of the house and the yard. The way-back bedroom already had kids of indistinct provenance crowded in the gloom, playing video games. The doglets were barking—though sometimes they sounded like birds chirping. Perla was ordering Lalo around.

"How come," Big Angel said, "we never kissed?"

"Kissed?"

"Don't families kiss?"

"Like, *brothers?* Kissing?"

"Why not?"

They pondered this ghastly new possibility.

"Carnal, do you want a kiss?" Little Angel said.

"Not really," Big Angel said and shrugged. "You know."

"There you go!" Little Angel crowed, as if some appealing aperçu had been launched and had brought down the house. "You were just saying!"

"Sure, by golly."

They lay side by side, arms crossed, listening to the holy idiocy of the family banging around. Lalo shouted "Chud!" at somebody.

Big Angel asked, "Qué es eso, Carnal?"

"Lalo," one or both of them muttered. It was a cosmic explanation for everything.

Minnie shouted, "Get out of the flowers! Ma! The dogs are pooping in the flowers!"

The brothers nodded wisely. They were like a pair of magpies on a phone line, letting the morning warm them.

"Do gringos kiss?" Big Angel asked.

"Some," Little Angel said. "I know guys. Kiss their dads."

"Everybody kisses moms, though."

"Kissing moms doesn't count. It's required."

"Right, right. If you don't kiss your mom, forget it, man."

"Right? You don't get to heaven if you don't kiss your mom." After a minute, Little Angel sensed his big brother staring at him. He turned his head. Big Angel was smiling at him.

"Actually, yes," he said.

"What."

"Yeah." Big Angel nodded. "I would like it."

Little Angel rose up on one elbow and kissed his brother's burning forehead.

"Not so bad," Big Angel said.

"No. It was okay."

They had to change the subject.

"Big day," Little Angel said.

"My last day."

"Oh, come on."

"Angel," Big Angel said, grabbing his little brother's arm. "When you leave tonight, don't say good-bye."

"I won't."

"*Never* say good-bye to me."

"I won't." Little Angel looked away. "They forgot to get you a cake," he said.

Big Angel guffawed.

"I have to go buy one now."

"Carnal," Big Angel said. "Get me two cakes."

"Why not? What kind?"

"One white and one chocolate. Put my name on both. But

don't get joke candles. I can't keep blowing out candles that light back up."

"I guess you don't have to watch your weight now," Little Angel said.

A moment of silence, then Big Angel said, "Asshole!"

a kiss from my brother

César El Pato and Marco the Satanic Hispanic pulled up as Little Angel was getting in his rental car for the Target expedition. César jumped out of his little red ride and waved him down and climbed in.

"Wow," he said. "Big car." But in Spanish: *Guau. Qué carrote.*

Mr. Death Metal dragged over a lawn chair and joined La Minnie in the driveway and immediately bummed a cigarette from her.

"I love my family," Minnie said.

"Whatever," he said.

Little Angel fired up the big Detroit engine. Guau was right. It was no little Japanese four cylinder. This was a locomotive.

"Adónde vamos?" César asked.

"Buying the birthday cake."

"Ah! Qué bueno! Un keki!"

They chuckled. They liked using folksy Spanglish. So amusing. Bikes were baikas. Wives were waifas. Trucks were trokas, and pickups were pee-kahs.

Waffles were, of course, two-syllable words, Little Angel's beloved diphthongs: waff-less.

Don Antonio had hated Spanglish. They all got scolded,

even as adults, if they said some bastardized border word. They didn't realize it was funny till after he was dead that he hated that word troka. Because he believed the correct word was una trok. Oh, Father.

"How are you, Carnal?" Little Angel asked.

"Sad."

"Me too."

"No me gusta."

"No."

El Pato let escape one low, long quack of sorrow. He was nearly erased by all the tragedy falling upon him. His Mamá had still ironed his shirts until she was taken ill. Everything on Earth was filled with sorrow. Little yellow weeds that broke through the tarmac made him feel weepy. The moon, like some pale paper cutout in the morning sky, overwhelmed him.

They drove to Target together through the metallic drought light. All traces of yesterday's rain had burned away. Punk-ass little Chicanitos with lowrider bikes and skateboards assembled on a dusty basketball court down by the McDonald's. The bridge over the 805 was as empty as a zombie movie, though the freeway below was clogged. It was too early for anybody to be out in the hood except those poor suckers going in to work and the skater vatos skipping church.

"This all reminds me of when our father died," said César and made a face.

Little Angel loved that expression. Though it denoted distaste and displeasure, it was one of the great family faces. A squinchy little monkey expression. It had vestiges of Mamá América in it. The old matriarch asserting herself in the faces of her children. All men had women inside them—they just could not admit it.

"That was a bad time," Little Angel said.

"Yes."

"But we knew it was coming."

"Yes."

"He was hard on himself."

"Chit. He was hard on everybody, Carnal." El Pato shrugged one shoulder. Moved his hands upward in a double-flip gesture that denoted forever and the far distance and *Anyway, there's nothing you can do about it.* "He kicked Grandma's dog down the steps."

"Why?"

"Because."

They drove the mile to the bridge and across the 805. As they passed over the congested traffic, pigeons launched from the bridge and scattered over the roofs of the cars. They looked like doves for a second, diving off a pale cliff. All this gleaming Mississippi of Americans in their cars, rushing past the invisible barrio, unaware of the lives up here, the little houses, all these unknowable stories.

But Little Angel reeled it back in and focused on his brother. "He didn't take care of himself," he said.

"Taking care was not what he did, Carnal." El Pato reached over and squeezed his knee. It seemed like the most beautiful gesture ever. "Were you sad, Angelito?" he asked.

"Of course. He was my dad."

"I don't know how I felt," Pato said. "Very sad. But a little…glad? Is that bad?"

"No."

"I mean, my poor mamá."

"I understand."

"Your poor mamá."

"Thank you."

"He wasn't like other fathers. You know how Mexican fathers are. Wanna be good. Wanna be great." He wobbled his head back and forth. "Some fathers."

"You're like that."

El Pato quacked with pleasure. "Gracias, Carnalito."

They smiled. Keeping it noncommittal.

"Hard. Hard." Pato ran a finger along his chin, making little sandpaper sounds on his stubble. "A hard man."

It was only three more miles to Target, but it felt like ten.

"Then," said Little Angel. "He was sweet. All of a sudden. You'd come home and he'd have made a big supper."

Pato pursed his lips.

"Supper. Really? What did Father cook?"

"Spaghetti with hard-boiled eggs."

They laughed.

"He put the eggs in there instead of meatballs."

They parked, but César wasn't ready to get out of the car.

"Were you close to Papá?" he asked Little Angel in Spanish. "I mean, I know. You were close. Right? He lived with you."

"Close?" Little Angel didn't know what to say. Yes. No. Too close. Abandoned. What. "Sure," he said at last.

"Sabes, Carnal? After he left us and came to Tijuana? We followed him. Angel found us later. Can you believe that? He came all the way on a bus and found us. We were living in the hills. In Colonia Obrera. It was rough. The boys there used to beat me up. Angel hit them with a pipe."

Little Angel did not know this.

"He and I had to go out and walk around Tijuana looking for food. Mamá had nothing to feed us. Do you know how hot it was? MaryLú cried all day long."

Little Angel suddenly felt guilty about his spaghetti.

"We didn't steal," Pato said. "Mamá would never forgive us for stealing anything. But we looked for dandelions. You ever eat those?"

Little Angel shook his head.

"We filled our pockets and shirts with dandelions. You can't eat the puffs. But you can boil the plants and the flowers. Or fry them. If you have lard. Sometimes Mamá fried them."

Little Angel turned and stared at his brother.

"So Angel came to Tijuana when I was a kid. Maybe twelve? He was already planning to marry Perla. He knew where my father...our father, perdón...was. At our abuela's house. He went there every week."

"I know."

"She was the first one to move to Tijuana."

"Yes."

"She liked *The Perry Como Show*."

They chuckled.

"She had to live on the border, pues. Just to watch it."

"That and Lawrence Welk," Little Angel said.

"Well, Angel told me. Father was at her house. And I ran. All across town." César smiled sadly and stared out the windshield, shaking his head, as if watching a distant drive-in screen showing a touching film. "I ran all the way to Grandmother's house. That was hard. It was up on that hill."

"I *know*."

"I had hard shoes. I got blisters, but I ran anyway. And I went in—I didn't knock. I just walked in, and there he was. He was sitting in the big chair in her living room, watching television. Smoking."

"Pall Malls."

"He looked like a giant with clouds of smoke around his head. He never looked at me. I sat down and stared at him. I don't know what I thought would happen. Nothing happened. He had gray hair. He looked a hundred years old. Watching a game show. And then he finally turned and looked at me."

"Did he say anything?"

César blew a small chuff of laughter through his nostrils. "He said, 'Which one are you?' Just like that. 'Which one are you?' So I told him. He said, 'I thought you would be bigger.' Then he walked out of the room." César opened his door and put one foot out of the car but sat there. "Why was he like that?" he asked.

"I don't know."

César shook his head. "I didn't like that," he said and got out and slammed the door.

☙

9:45 *a.m.*

Silence in the car as they returned to the house. The cakes they had pulled from the cooler would be decorated by 11:00. Pato had insisted on paying.

The gathering vatos y rucas had adjourned to the backyard. Old people still outnumbered them since old Mexicans were up before the sun and had worked a half day before these gamers and Netflix kids opened their eyes. No Mexican Little Angel had seen in his life ever slept leaning on a cactus like all the taco shop signs insisted.

La Gloriosa and Lupita were acting as Perla's sergeants,

knocking heads and moving tables. Uncle Jimbo sat over by the geraniums, smoking a cigar. He wore a straw porkpie hat and shorts out of which giant red legs emanated. Jimbo nodded and they nodded back, and he puffed away and shook a glass of Diet Coke choked with ice cubes. "Needs rum!" he noted. "And a butt-load of cherries." He had a Confederate flag pin on his guayabera to let them know he was in no mood for raza bullshit.

La Gloriosa was revealed in her full morning power, backlit, hair outlined in silver, gleaming. César flushed when he saw her. So did Little Angel. The sight of the two of them standing there like sad doggies begging for a snack irritated her, so she spun away from them and unfurled a plastic tablecloth with decisive snapping downstrokes. Each muscled arm a rebuke of their inherent weakness. She thought: *Go to the gym,* cabrones. *You flabby little men.* Little Angel hurried to his coffee box and delivered himself a dose of Colombian. César vanished into the bathroom and could be heard locking the door.

Little Angel lingered behind her, sniffing the air.

"Don't be foolish," La Gloriosa said, but Little Angel didn't know if she was addressing him or the scraggly kid who had wandered in on his way to the back room for a round of Mario Kart.

With rattles and bangs, Big Angel rolled down the hallway. He honked his bike horn. "I want to go outside," he said.

All hands on deck. They wrestled the chair out the sliding door and onto the patio.

"I smell coffee," Big Angel said.

Little Angel handed him his own cup.

"Instant?"

"No. Fancy."

Big Angel handed the cup back. "Fuchi," he said. "Get me some instant. And put Carnation in it."

The Chiweenies saw him, rushed to his chair, and danced in wagging pirouettes.

"To my dogs," he announced, "I am a legend."

10:15 a.m.

The Cookie Monster sidled up to Little Angel. "Tío, you rock."

"Thanks."

"No, I'm asking. You rock?"

"Ah! Yes. Sure."

"Hard rock or chick rock?"

"Chick rock?"

"Like freakin' short-hair dudes. Alt rock. Mormons."

I love this kid, Little Angel thought. "Oh. I see. Hard rock. Motörhead."

The youngster nodded sagely.

More brilliant convo. Little Angel was happy. What was an uncle for but this: metal Tío taking this hormonal squall seriously. "Well," he said, accessing his inner metal file: "God hates us all." He knew how to toss bait at adolescents.

"Right, Tío?"

"Reign in blood."

"Fuckin'-a, Tío!" The Monster bellowed: "SLAYER!"

They raised devil horns to the sun.

10:30 a.m., the worst time of the day

It was almost party time. Back in the bedroom, Perla and La Minnie were struggling with Big Angel. They had pulled the chair backward, against his will. Every inch made him more hysterical. He dragged his feet until the linoleum pulled off his slippers and then his socks.

None of them could remember what pills he was supposed to take at what hour. They had to trust his computer of a brain to keep track of all his mega doses. And his least favorites: the chemo lozenges. Minnie was certain he was hiding these under the bed, but she could never find them.

They muscled him into the bathroom and stripped him.

"Ay," he said. He went limp in their hands and sagged, grunting. "No."

They pulled off his diaper.

"No you don't!" he said.

Minnie carefully wrapped the diaper in a tight ball and dropped it into the trash can.

"No, I said!" Big Angel was trying to sit on the floor. "Leave me alone!"

Every damned day, the same thing. "Come on, Daddy," Minnie urged. "Stop being a baby."

Perla ran the water. She was careful—kept her hand in the stream until she was sure it was perfect. Too cold and he'd curse, too hot and he'd cry.

"No bath today!" he said.

They lifted him into the water. He kicked weakly.

"Flaco! This is the one day you need to take a bath. Your party!"

"I don't want a party."

"Be good, Flaco."

"Too hot! Ay! Too hot!"

"Dad!"

"Help!" he shouted. "Angel! Angel, come!" He thrashed. "Carnal! Help me!"

"Flaco, stop it."

Little Angel rushed into the bedroom behind them. "Angel?" he said. "You okay?"

"Don't come in here, Tío," said Minnie, kicking the bathroom door closed.

Big Angel sat in the water, hands over his face. His back looked like a Halloween costume of gray bones. He shivered in the warm water.

"You wanted a party," Minnie said. "Do you want to look good or not?"

"Good," he said softly.

Perla leaned in with a huge soft sponge foaming with soap and reached between his legs.

"Better, Flaco? Sí? Feels good, no?"

"Don't watch," he told his daughter.

"Ain't watching. I'm busy with your armpits."

He lay back in the water and kept his eyes screwed shut.

"Nice and clean," Perla said. "Como un buen muchachito."

Big Angel covered his sagging breasts with his blackened hands. "Mija?" he said.

"Daddy?"

"Do you forgive me?"

"For what?"

He waved his hand in the air. "I'm sorry."

"For what, Daddy?"

"All these things." He opened his eyes and stared at her. "I used to wash you," he said. "When you were my baby."

She busied herself with the bottle of no-tears baby shampoo.

"I used to be your father. Now I am your baby." He sobbed. Only once.

She blinked fast and put shampoo in her palm. "It's okay," she said. "Everything's okay."

He closed his eyes and let her wash his hair.

La Pachanga

sending for Perla to come to me
i didn't care if she had two sons
sending for my Perla
i didn't care if she was raising two sisters
and she came to me
finally

11:00 a.m.

Little Angel checked his watch. It was time to return to the store and get the birthday cakes. He was flummoxed when La Gloriosa tossed aside her dish towel and walked out with him, looping her arm through his.

He made a small sound like *"Ung?"*

He could feel her muscle. He tried to clench his arm so she would feel his. He smelled her hair. Felt her heat. He was back in high school.

"Ay, qué carro!" she enthused when she saw the massive Ford. She ran her hand along its long side. The Crown Vic was clearly a big winner. He opened the passenger door for her. "And a gentleman," she said.

"I try," he said lamely. Tried not to look down her blouse as she lowered herself into her seat. But she saw him looking. He made believe he was staring past her cleavage at the radio, as if remembering something interesting from his recent past.

"Did you buy this carrote?" she asked. Apparently, Mexicans really appreciated big vehicles with atrocious gas mileage.

"Just renting." He closed her door and trotted around to his own side.

"Buy one," she said as he got in. "For me."

"For you, anything."

"Eres rico, no?" she said.

"Sure...?"

"Okeh, bebeh," she said. "Buy two."

He guffawed falsely and way too loud. He was excruciatingly aware of his every movement as she gazed at him. *Don't drop the keys. Don't flood the engine. Don't crash into anything. Don't slam on the brakes. Don't fart.*

"I'm not, you know, rich," he suddenly chuckled. "Can't just buy a fleet of cars!" *Idiot, shut up*, he told himself. *Asshat.*

"I only need one, then," she said. "This one."

"Hokay." He managed to get the engine started and the shifter into *D*, and he pulled out as slowly as a cruise ship leaving port. He motored out of the little neighborhood and made the right turn that would take him to the main street. He came to a full halt at the stop sign and waited patiently until una Chevy *pee-kah* full of lawn-mowing equipment passed. He eased on out, the Crown Vic soft as a cloud as it drifted around the corner.

"Do I make you nervous, Gabriel?" she asked.

"No!"

"You driving slow."

"Okay. Yes."

"For why?"

"You're La Gloriosa."

She made a *pshh* sound with her mouth.

"You make everybody feel nervous," he said.

"No. Don't think so."

"If they don't feel that way," proclaimed the King of Romance, "they must be dead."

"Angel Gabriel. I could be your mother."

"Come on. You're only eleven years older than me."

"This family? I could be your Mamá."

"I don't have mommy issues, I assure you." Suddenly, further gallantry went off in him like a firecracker. "I have you issues." That was rather piquant, he thought with deep satisfaction.

She turned a little in her seat and put her knee up on the leather. "Y eso?" she said. "Qué quiere decir?"

A fair question: what did he mean? He wasn't sure. He rolled on down the main drag as if she hadn't said anything.

He somehow managed to drive right past the Target turnoff and on into the dry hills beyond, which were covered in tumbleweeds and manzanita and clearly awaiting one thrown cigarette to explode in a conflagration. By the time he realized he was nowhere near Target, he was lost in a housing tract apparently formed entirely of cul-de-sacs. His hands started to sweat.

"Nice," she said, pointing to various faux Southern plantation manses with pillars and porches. La Gloriosa seemed to think Little Angel had meant to give her a pleasant sightseeing drive. Real estate hunting in America's Finest City. "Mira! Me gusta!"

He grimly craned his head to search down side streets for any path out.

"I like," she said. "Ooh!"

She pointed.

"Our big carro in that drive-away. Sí?"

"Sure."

He was distracted. Thinking about Big Angel. The little notebook in his pocket representing the Big Angel universe. Lines connecting names—it was getting too complicated to read. This woman beside him. Perla. Minnie. Lalo. The Satanic Hispanic. Pazuzu. But mostly his big brother. How suddenly, on the verge of losing him, he realized he had no true idea who Big Angel was.

But Gloriosa's scent filled the car. He felt it like a caress. He spun like a lost moon.

"Go there." She pointed. Her long nail caught sun and imitated a hard candy. He followed it around the corner.

The neighborhoods over here were named, and their names were etched into signs that feigned gentile charm. Some in anachronous Olde English typeface. The neighborhoods made no sense to him whatsoever.

Marina Shores and Malibu Harbor and Pacific Landing, even though any possible glimpse of the ocean was twenty miles in the opposite direction. All that these McMansioneers could see was rocky canyons and deracinated brown hills housing vast populations of rattlesnakes and poodle-gobbling coyotes. Brown unto the white-with-heat horizon.

A phony little dock with a plaster seagull standing in some kind of dry blue-tinged concrete pool was very close to being the last absurdity Little Angel was willing to abide.

"Where in *the hell* are we?" he said.

"The beaches."

He snorted.

"Is beautiful," she said.

"You have a positive outlook," he said.

"Only selfish people are negative, Angel."

His head was throbbing. He was suddenly sure he had brain cancer. Fortunately, the mushy ride of the Crown Vic gently bore them over all bumps as if they were in a tender cradle. The car—seeming as intelligent as the Batmobile—managed to find the main street again. Little Angel was basically hanging on to the wheel and hoping the car would drag him to safety.

"I don't want to think about the funeral," she said.

"No."

La Gloriosa put her hand on his arm. Her palm was hot. He was clammy with embarrassment.

"Qué sweet," she said. "Tenk yous, Gabriel. For this nice ride."

"My pleasure," he said and glanced at her.

She smiled.

He took her hand in his and tootled down the road like somebody's grandpa.

⁂

In Target, she became a teen. They seemed to be dancing. They laughed at everything. Giant human backsides in stretch pants delighted them. Old Mexican cowboys in overalls and straw hats. She insisted on looking at flimsy bras made of shiny gauze and greatly enjoyed his misery.

"You can see through," she reported.

"God in heaven," he sighed.

They collected the two cakes. The white one had purple

and blue icing flowers on it. "What a nightmare," La Gloriosa noted. It said HAPPY BIRTHDAY BIG ANGEL. The chocolate one had yellow flowers on it. It said CARNAL.

"Buy candles," La Gloriosa said.

"And presents," he said.

They moseyed over to the toy section, and Little Angel bought Big Angel a giant action figure of Groot, from *Guardians of the Galaxy*.

"I am Groot," he said.

"Yo soy Grut," she replied. She picked out a Who T-shirt. "This is funny," she said. "Big Angel hates rocanrol."

"Los Quienes," Little Angel scored points by quipping.

They got Lalo's snacks and booze and stopped at the cooler in front to collect Minnie's sushi. Little Angel spied an in-store Starbucks and bought himself a second cardboard briefcase of coffee. Just in case. La Gloriosa had a grande skinny mocha latte, iced. No whipped cream. He thought: *Five-dollar coffee!*

"Never in my life," he said, "did I ever expect to go shopping with you."

"Are you happy?"

"Yes."

"Qué bueno." She grabbed big sunglasses off a rack and said, "Pleess?"

"Anything."

"Okeh. These and the Ford. Nice and simple."

A white woman stepped up to them and said, warmly, "You'll be out of this country on your ass very soon," then stormed toward the dog food aisle.

On the way back, Little Angel pulled over by the basketball courts. Ookie stood in the middle of the court, bouncing a ball. Nobody seemed to be hassling him. A klatch of kids just stood around or leaned on their bikes, rolling back and forth. Somebody had a boom box. The peewees apparently thought it was still the '80s.

Little Angel waved at the shorties. "Ookie's all right," he said.

A couple of kids tipped up their chins. One waved back. Ookie stood in the key and threw in basket after basket. He never missed. The kids lounged around, watching him. He bounced the ball three times—*blount-blount-blount*—then fired it in a high arc, and it rocked through the hoop, clanging the chain net. A kid grabbed it and tossed it back to him, and he bounced it some more.

"Did you know he could do that?" Little Angel said.

La Gloriosa said that she didn't.

"Excuse me," he said. He got out of the car and walked to the court. "S'up?" he said and bumped fists with a couple of the kids, did the Raza slip-'n'-slide handshake with a couple of others. "How's your mom?" he asked one of the boys.

"She's a'ight."

"You in high school now?"

"Chale—I'm at Southwestern College."

"No!"

"How's Seattle, Profe?"

"Good."

"Good coffee, right?"

"Right."

"You know Pearl Jam?"

"Not yet." Little Angel was looking over at Ookie, who was crying, snot on his lip.

The boy shot again, sank another basket. *Blount-blount-blount*. "Purple haze," he said. He bounced the ball, shot another basket. "All along the watchtower."

"What happened to Ookie?" Little Angel said.

"Eddie Figueroa caught him in his house," the kid said.

Shrugs all around from the others.

"Dude was stealing Legos again."

They shook their heads, spat.

"Smacked him up."

"Ookie—you okay?" Little Angel called.

"Little wing," Ookie said. *Blount-blount-blount*. Basket.

"Ookie!"

La Gloriosa stepped up beside Little Angel.

"Ookie," she said. "Hay fiesta."

"Party?" Ookie said, pausing in his shot barrage.

"Big Angel's birthday," she said. "Lots of cookies."

"Okay," Ookie said. He shot a basket and let it bounce away. "Voodoo child!" he said and walked to the car and got in the back seat.

La Gloriosa wiggled her eyebrows at Little Angel from behind her new cheap sunglasses.

"How did you do that?" he said.

"Women," she said. "We are very powerful."

He watched her walk.

Noon

Lalo yelled, "Minnie's eating cat food!"

She held a California roll in between her fingers and dipped it in soy sauce. "It's called sushi," she informed him. "You are not sophisticated."

"Chuchi-fuchi. Puppet chow."

Food was appearing all around them. People came through bearing aluminum tubs of grub. La Gloriosa and Lupita and Minnie and Perla had arranged for platoons of barrio ladies and their husbands to appear with party supplies. Little Angel was thwarted in his hopeless search for homemade Mexican food. In his mind, chicken mole and pots of simmering frijoles and chiles rellenos were to be displayed in pornographic lushness. But the reality of the day was folding tables groaning with pizzas, Chinese food, hot dogs, potato salad and a huge industrial party pan of spaghetti. Somebody was allegedly on the way with a hundred pieces of KFC. He noted Uncle Jimbo at his table with a paper plate heaped with noodles and buffalo wings. Somehow he had acquired bottles of mead.

Jimbo raised his bottle at him and hollered, "Skoal!"

Little Angel went over to where Perla was sitting.

She had been watching all the people coming and going. Feeling weepy about Braulio. But mostly fretting about her big warrior, her Yndio. Time was almost gone. She had been sneaking out to Yndio for years, and she didn't know if Big Angel knew it or not. She wouldn't put it past him. He knew everything, that Flaco. But he never said anything. It was killing her. Each of those proud cabrones refusing to apologize for whatever they were mad about. Each one waiting for some sign. And Mamá, in the middle, frantic. All she wanted was to see what was left of her family come together, before... Well, before.

"Perla," Little Angel said.

"Mi baby," she said.

"Are you okay?"

"I okeh." She squinted at him and said in Spanish, "You look just like your father. He was so elegant. He always brought me flowers. La Gloriosa too."

"He brought her flowers?"

"Pos, sure." *Churr.*

"Everybody loves her."

"Mi baby—you should marry her."

He coughed. "Perla!" *Course adjustment, stat.* "Where's the Mexican food?"

"What Mexican food?"

"Exactly. I was hoping you'd make something special." He gave her his best grin. "You are the best cook in the world, after all."

She stared up at him. "Yo no," she said, shaking her head. "No more cook!" She waved her hands in front of herself. In Spanish, she said, "I was a cook for everybody for fifty years. I had to. Now I won't have to cook for anybody ever again. Oh no, Gabriel. I am a refugee from the apron."

It had never occurred to Little Angel that cooking masterpieces every day had been a chore.

"Get me coffee," she said. "Sí?"

Off he went.

"I eat hamburrgurrs now!" Perla called. "Subway! Cheerios!"

He waved over his shoulder.

Jimbo swilled his mead and announced: "Hammer of the gods."

Little Angel thought it was all turning into an end-of-semester project for his multicultural studies course.

12:30 p.m.

It was as if a dump truck had spilled a ton of humanity into the yard. Bodies were jammed onto the patio, elbowing gently to get at the new macaroni salad and ignoring the mustard coleslaw.

Little Angel shoved his way out of the crowd to find more crowd milling around.

Big Angel was snoozing in the shade, hands folded over his tiny potbelly, his head bobbing slightly. Minnie sat beside him, fanning him with a bit of cardboard. She looked very sad.

A DJ had set up his rig in the backyard and fired up some P.O.D.

Big Angel opened his eyes and glared. He made the family monkey face of disapproval. He grabbed the *ah-oo-gah* horn Lalo had screwed to his armrest and squeezed the bulb for one brash honk. Then he went back to sleep.

MaryLú caused several waves of alarm when she strolled in on the arm of Leo, her former husband. "We brought mimosas!" she said.

They were dressed to kill: MaryLú had on a navy-blue dress with white dots and a pearl necklace. Leo wore a brown Tijuana suit with light yellow stripes, a cream shirt, a yellow tie with a tie tack in the shape of a dollar sign, a gray fedora, and two-tone brown-and-cream brogans. He had shaved his 'stache down to a slender worm of insinuation that seemed to nap on his upper lip.

"Muchacho," he said, giving Little Angel a wan dead-fish handshake while the moochy-lip worm squirmed to life on the crest of his smile.

Visions of half-inch-long acorns came unbidden into Little

Angel's mind. "Leo el León!" he enthused. "You are a mighty oak of a man!"

MaryLú gave him a warning glare. Leo went off to the kitchen to mix the drinks.

"Got to go inside, mija," Big Angel said. "Got to go. Now."

"Okay, Daddy."

"I'll take him," Little Angel said.

Big Angel put up his hand. "Brother," he said. "Pee-pee time. You want to see my pee-pee?"

"I do not."

"Me neither," said Minnie.

"It's your job, mija."

She muscled the chair around. "What do I get for it?" she said.

He smiled slightly but never opened his eyes. "You get all the money," he said.

"Ooh. Is there a lot?"

"Sure, mija. Fifty, sixty dollars."

Little Angel and Perla watched them roll inside.

"Ay Diosito lindo," Perla said.

Little Angel found a dapper Caucasian in khaki Dockers and a crisp denim work shirt helping himself to a cup of his cardboard box of Colombian blonde roast. *That's my coffee*, Little Angel thought. But there wasn't any time to ponder it—a wave of Mexicans swept the kitchen clean, carrying its inhabitants out into the drizzle that had begun to sift upon the DJ spinning Nortec Collective Tijuana mariachi techno. "Tijuana makes me happy," the song repeated. Kids and MaryLú danced on the damp grass with leftover funeral umbrellas and newspapers over their heads.

Paz stood before the spaghetti and KFC mounds with a look of utter disdain. She wore a platinum-blond wig cut in an Audrey Hepburn bob.

"Yeesus Krites," she said to him, scowling. "Food for peasants. Jimbo food. We have better food in Mexico City." She looked Little Angel up and down. "Food for gordos." You could tell she hated fat people by the way she poured disgust into every trilled *r* in the word. *Gor-r-r-r-dos!* She looked over at Perla. "Oye, tú. No hay cauliflower?" she demanded in Spanish: coliflor. "Carrots? Celery?" She tapped her toe in irritation.

The DJ suddenly unleashed a mash-up of "Bootylicious" and "Smells Like Teen Spirit." He said into his mike: "Smells like teen booty!"

"Qué es eso?" Paz said.

She dismissed the entire food table. "Nada bueno. Nothing. I thought so," she told Little Angel.

He sat with her at one of the tables dangerously proximate to Tío Jimbo's encampment.

"Dirty viejo," she muttered.

Jimbo had his arm around the neck of Rodney, the African American college cousin. "What kind of a name is Rodney for a black guy? You named after Rodney King?" Jimbo was asking. Rodney rolled his eyes at Little Angel and withstood this storm of whiteness. Little Angel remembered why he didn't come to family gatherings.

Paz was wearing only about six or seven pounds of gold and jewels. She caught Little Angel eyeing her tennis bracelets. She shook her wrist in his face. "You like?" Having rejected the eats, she sipped an unsweetened glass of sun tea.

Little Angel observed the coffee thief in his impeccable work shirt looming over Tío Jimbo, saying, "Are you some kind of fascist?"

He watched his family dance and wished he hadn't come.

⌖

MaryLú was breathing heavily when she sat with them. She took the seat on the other side of Little Angel, as far as she could get from Pazuzu. Her face was glistening with sweat.

"You are sitting together?" she panted, carefully ignoring Paz.

"Qué nice," Paz condescended. "You got some exercise."

"I could get lipo like you," MaryLú said. "How do you like the Botox?"

"I like it more than I like a saggy face, cabrona."

They stared at the dancers as if this vista were utterly compelling.

"You got Botox?" Little Angel said.

"Don't be an ass."

"It cost her fifty dollars in Tijuana," MaryLú told him.

"You should try it," Paz shot back. "You could almost afford it. Maybe Leo can give you some money. He still does, doesn't he?"

They breathed heavily. Little Angel sat between them like a steer trapped in a branding pen, just waiting for the burning to be over.

Finally, Paz said: "All you poor border peasants, feeling sorry for yourselves."

"We are fine, thank you," MaryLú said.

"Eating welfare food."

Little Angel was reduced to looking across to Tío Jimbo for

help, but Jimbo was busy flipping the bird at the Anglo Coffee Imperialist.

Paz took a sip of her tea. "It's embarrassing," she said.

"Come on," Little Angel finally said. "Lighten up."

Paz stared at him. "Really?" she said.

Her head hadn't started rotating yet, so he felt he had a minute or so to make his point.

"You live where," she said. "Alaska?"

"Seattle."

"Uy-uy-uy! You really are a white boy. Everything you ever wanted." *Ju eber want.* "How long since you went to Tijuana?" To his silence, she replied, "I thought so." She drained her tea. "It is too much to hope you ever went to Mexico City."

"Yeesus!" MaryLú said. "Otra vez con 'Mexico Ceety.'"

"You and your mommy. Gringos." It was almost as bad as gordos.

Little Angel saw that his brother had returned and took the coward's way out and escaped. He hurried over to Big Angel, put his hand on his shoulder, and said, "Carnal, who is that guy fighting with Tío Jimbo?"

Big Angel said, "That's Dave. He always fights with Jimbo. It's a family tradition. They like it."

"Oh," said Little Angel.

❧

The Satanic Hispanic had stolen some hair spray from Perla's bathroom and re-lifted his coif to its preferred stellar heights. He sat with Pato, who was working on his fourth platter of party grub. His face was purple and his cheeks distended, and he crammed some more Wonder Bread with butter in there.

"Gmmf," Pato said, chewing lustily. "Grnnf."

"Right on, Dad," he said. He was scanning the crowd, then did a double take. Who was that? He turned to watch her. Damn. "Check out that chick," he said.

César was always ready to (a) eat and (b) check out that chick. He craned around. "Gwabbin," he quacked through his food.

"Right?" Marco jumped up and waved Lalo over.

"You better check your hair, puppet!" Lalo said.

"Who's that chick?" Marco asked.

"What chick? A million chicks here, dog."

Marco pointed with his chin and his lips.

Lalo scoped her. She was pale and slender and had a long neck and absolutely pitch-black shades and a black Kangol turned backward to make a beret. She was smoking an electric cigarette.

"She's like French or something," Lalo said.

"How you know that?"

"Beret, homie."

They nodded knowingly.

"Dude, I'm in love. She ain't my cousin or nothin'?"

Lalo shrugged. "Ain't everybody here your cuz? But I don't recognize her. So she can't be no first cousin. She's a kissin' cousin, probly. Second cousin, like. You could marry her. Swoop on her. I will if you don't."

Marco unleashed the Cookie Monster: "SHE SHALL BE MINE."

Lalo said, "You sound like a chud," and walked away.

Lalo strode to Little Angel, across the yard, slung an arm around his shoulder, and said, "Yo, Tío, I want you to meet somebody." He reached out and grabbed a short young woman standing with a group of kids nearby. Her hair was purple in the back. "Tío," he said. "This is my girl."

"Your—?"

"My daughter, G."

"Oh!" Little Angel put out his hand. "How do you do?" he said.

"How do you do?" she said back. "My name is Mayra." She took his hand.

"That's your tío, Little Angel."

"But of course."

"Mayra's ladylike," Lalo boasted. "She's gonna be like a famous author and shit."

"Ojalá," she said.

"She's gonna be a big deal in this world, Tío. No thanks to me." She headed over to hug Big Angel in his chair.

"Hey!" Lalo called. "Don't be no teen mom!"

"I'm almost twenty," she called back.

Lalo put his hand over his eyes. "Only good thing I ever done. At least I done one thing right."

Little Angel looked away to allow him his moment. He gave his nephew a one-armed hug.

a new car—I never had one
good music—NOT rock and roll
spanish!—how could I forget??
banana slices in fideo soup (lots of lime juice)
la Minnie!!!
mi familia

The mist had burned off, though clouds still furrowed their portentous brows. Big Angel sat in the shade, receiving gifts and benedictions and hugs and hand kisses. He heard a demon roar behind him and twisted around, but all he saw was his nephew Marco. They waved at each other.

Little Angel came and sat at his brother's side. He watched people take a knee before Big Angel's wheelchair and murmur gratitude. Guys with jobs thanked him. Women getting their GEDs. Young couples.

A grizzled veterano came forward and removed his porkpie hat. "When I got out of Folsom," he said, "you took me in and fed me. Nobody else even wanted to see my face. Now I'm doing good. So thank you."

"Claro."

Big Angel turned to Little Angel and said, "Carnal, rocks remember when they were mountains."

They stared at the rocks in the garden.

"And what do mountains remember?"

"When they were ocean floors."

Big Angel, Zen master.

A woman stood before Big Angel's chair, held one of his hands in both of hers, and reminded him that he had paid bail for her son one year, and now that son was a manager at a Red Lobster.

"Carnal," Little Angel said. "This is like *The Godfather*."

Big Angel smiled and laid a hand on Little Angel's knee.

"You're like Don Corleone," Little Angel said.

"I am Don Corleone." And he gave his hand over to be fondled and kissed by strangers.

Then Jimbo stepped up. As if sent as a rebuke. He handed Big Angel a foot-long cigar. "Try that," he said.

"No!" Perla called. "Yeem! Cancer!"

"Why not?" said Tío Jimbo, his mead buzz lifting him to Asgardian realms. "What can it hurt? Celebrate freakin' gay marriage. You're all libs, right? You're gonna die anyway. Live it up."

Big Angel hated boorish behavior. "By golly," he said, turning his face away.

Suddenly, Dave the coffee burglar swept in and spun Big Angel's chair away from Jimbo, saying, "You're so rude, my friend. You have learned no social graces at all from your Latino family." He wheeled Big Angel toward the pizza boxes; all the pizzas were gone.

"You got no idea what I learned," said Jimbo. "You don't know one thing." He extended the cigar to Little Angel. "You want it?" he said.

Little Angel just stared at it.

People scattered when Pazuzu came into the yard from the kitchen. They could see the tequila buzz upon her like some electric halo of doom.

"Get out of my way," she said, and they did.

She had changed into party clothes. Her dress was a skintight orange one-piece apparently made of T-shirt material. She wore knee-high boots. She was working her backside like a rumba dancer as she marched.

"Like two potatoes stuffed in a sock," MaryLú said.

Paz stopped on the concrete apron of the porch and stared at them all. Her eyes looked bloodshot, though Little Angel was fully willing to own the fact that he was attaching occult terror to her presence. She turned those eyes on him and raised her lip in distaste. Leo could be seen absconding behind the back-yard shed. *Coward.*

She mouthed Y tú qué? at Little Angel.

"Nada," he said back. Maybe she wouldn't kick his ankles.

Paz strode to poor Pato's table and sat beside him. Little Angel watched his brother's lips say, Mi amor. She sank her nails into his left thigh. They tongued.

"Ew," MaryLú opined.

Lalo was sitting beside his dad when Little Angel went back to check on him.

"Pops," a voice behind them said.

"Yes?" said Big Angel.

"Yeah?" said Lalo.

They all turned around.

It was Lalo's son, Giovanni. Little Angel couldn't believe it. The boy had been a mere pup the last time he saw him. He had to be what? Twenty-three now? He was physically small, dark, and ferocious, with tats on his arms and neck and a flat-brim baseball cap set at a quarter angle on his head. Dodgers. Los Doyyers. Gold chains, gold gauges in his ears, a gold grill spelling PLAYA on his front teeth.

Gio had two dirty-blond white girls in tow. They looked alike, though one looked like a better-fed version of the other. They wore identical, impossibly small cutoffs. White, or denim faded almost white, and very thin; shaggy stray fibers peeked out from the shadows beneath their buttocks. One of them had a stain on what there was of her back pocket. They were already bopping and bouncing to the music. Holding their hands up and mouthing lyrics like the Supremes.

Gio high-fived Lalo. "I saw the dude about the thing," he said.

"And the thing be all, you know?" Lalo said.

"It's tight, yeah."

"I don't need this, Son. And you barely even knew your uncle."

"I got you. But, Pops, I've been on this shit forever. I wasn't gonna let it go. Now we got to deal with." Gio patted his side. He lifted his shirt and flashed the grip of Lalo's own .22 poking out of his waistband.

"You been in my stuff?" Lalo said.

"Call of duty, ol' man."

Little Angel didn't understand this conversation but knew it was nothing good. When the pistol appeared as if in a magic trick, he felt ice down his spine. Then it was gone so fast, he wasn't sure he'd seen anything.

They got all shady and surreptitious all of a sudden, heads down, hiding shadowy eyes.

"You good?" Gio said.

Lalo was shaking his head.

"Got to do what you got to do, Pops."

They walked away in a top-secret confab.

Little Angel watched them. *Not this again*, he said in silent prayer.

Minnie sidled up to him. "Crazy family, huh, Tío?"

"Not used to it," he said.

Little Angel decided to say nothing about what he had just seen.

Gio came back, leaned down to Big Angel, and gave him a cautious hug about the shoulders. "Mad props, Grandpa," he said.

"Gracias, mijo."

Gio set a small wrapped object on the stack of small wrapped objects piled up beside Big Angel.

"Brought you sompin. Happy birfday."

Behind him, Lalo was bouncing on the balls of his feet. "What you staring at, Mouse?"

"You high?"

"I ain't shit. Check yourself, puppet."

"Hungry Man," she warned.

"You don't know nothing," he said. "I don't got no problem. How many times I told you?" He was suddenly all sweaty. "You try this leg out, see how you like it."

This silenced her.

"Gio! Let's get gone," he said. "Leave the ho's." He tipped his head dismissively at the white girls.

Minnie wadded up a napkin and bounced it off Lalo's head. "So rude!" she said to his receding back. Then she turned back to Little Angel. "Say hi to these trailer-park girls."

The girls offered blankly pleasant expressions.

"Talk about rude," Little Angel said.

"Oh?" Minnie replied. "I'm rude? Girls, where y'all live at?"

"We live at the Twin Oaks trailer park over to Imperial Beach," the chubby one said. "With all the Mexicans."

"I ain't rude," Minnie said, walking away.

Before he could apologize to Minnie, the chubby white girl said, "My name's Velvette? Rhymes with 'Corvette'? My sister's named Neala? Don't rhyme with nothin'."

She made everything a question, like poets do when they decant in poet voice.

"They call me Keychain," Neala said.

"That's interesting," Little Angel replied.

"On account of my teeth's crooked and they say I could open a beer bottle with my mouth, like a can opener."

Little Angel stood there for a moment. He felt inexplicable love for these two waifs.

oye

Little Angel's notebook was getting full. He drew a Lalo page—a sad, drooping flower. On one side, a swirling bunch of dark bats. Gio. Off to the other side, on a facing page, one small hummingbird. Mayra. He felt overwhelming sorrow. His tenderness enveloped all the many pages of lines and scribbles.

oye

2:00 p.m.

Now that it was afternoon, the sun broke through the clouds in dazzling avalanches of light.

The Satanic Hispanic watched the French Girl and felt nervous. He couldn't think of an opening comment, an icebreaker, some suave shit to dazzle her. Damn it. He'd started toward her a couple of times but wussed out and rambled back to Pato and Pazuzu. He was pretty sure she was watching him back, though her dark glasses didn't turn his way or anything. But for sure her eyes did. He thought she half smiled one time.

Pato sent a message to Manila on his phone: DO YOU HAVE ANY PICTURES THAT SHOW YOUR LEGS?

Marco sat by his dad and smacked his head with his palm. Loser. Why was it always like this?

The DJ was back—he was playing some wack *oompa-oompa*

tuba Sinaloa narco music. People were dancing some Mexican thing that looked like galloping horses. He hated this Chapo bullshit. And he hated their dancing. He'd never been to a prom. Dude—he'd formed Satanic Hispanic so the chicks would talk to him, but only guys ever came to see them. Boys in black Misfits tees throwing up devil signs and banging their heads and moshing. Bloody noses, but no tasty ladies. Now this. The world's foxiest fox sitting right there, bored. Scoping him out. He rubbed his hands on his black jeans. Sweaty palms. Great.

He got himself up and maneuvered through the army of cousins in his way and stood before her and grinned.

She stared straight ahead and took a steam hit, blew vapors in his direction.

"Hi!" he said.

She paused. Smiled vaguely. "Hi?"

"I'm Marco!" he shouted, holding out his hand.

She didn't look at it. "Hello, Carlo," she said.

"Marco."

"Yes."

She was utterly unnerving. "Are you French?" he blurted.

"Why, do I look French?"

He sputtered and made slightly motorboaty sounds. "Yeah. No. Maybe. I don't know."

"And you, Carlo? Are you French?"

"Marco," he said. "Do I look French?" Scored a point there, he decided.

"I don't know."

"You don't know?"

"No," she said. "I don't know if you look French."

"What, haven't you seen French guys?"

"No, Carlo, I have not. I'm blind."

He hurried away.

✍

2:01 p.m.

Little Angel tried to go into the house and check on his brother, but Perla stopped him. "Shh, he's sleeping."

He went back outside, and as unbelievable as it seemed, the party swirled even without the presence of Big Angel.

Little Angel stopped by Uncle Jimbo's table to give back the cigar Jimbo'd foisted on him. He didn't have much time to visit, however. Paz came up behind him and pulled the back of his shirt until he staggered. "Where is Leo?" she said. "I am looking for Leo." Little Angel extracted himself from her grasp and hurried away.

Lupita watched her beloved Jimbo from the kitchen. El Tío Yeembo. Everybody loved him! Era muy popular. That great buffalo of a man. He had saved her from Tijuana, not that anyone needed to be saved from Tijuana! Viva Tijuana! She loved Tijuana. She told herself to stop thinking like a gringa. He had saved her from poverty.

Though poverty in Tijuana, well, that was its own version of suffering.

She laid into a pile of coffee cups with a scrubber. *Yes, what you hate is poverty. That's what you hate.* She remembered working in Perla's little restaurant. Big Angel, that angel, helped them secure the loan to open it. The sisters made all the food and washed the dishes, and La Gloriosa waited tables because she was so sexy; the men who came in for good food also came in for good flirting and left her big tips, which the sisters shared. Restaurant? Closet! Lupita banged the cups vigorously in a steaming pond of soapy water. Why, it had been so tiny, they could fit only four tables in there and a counter where the cooking was done. It had a room up rickety wooden stairs somebody had made with a saw and some nails. *Home*, Lupita thought. Cardboard boxes for clothes, two mattresses on the floor. They shared a foul toilet-shower with some prostitutes across the way. They had to remember to take the toilet paper out of the room when they bathed because the showerhead was above the toilet. Still, the putas were funny and shared their makeup and hair rollers. Most of the sisters' money went into the restaurant—La Flor de Uruapan. No money for lippi-sticky or fancy hairdos or nice clothes. When they needed to buy something nice, they bought something for La Glori, pues. It was an investment in their future, they thought. She was their greatest product. It was easy to take most of the leftover food for themselves and deny her— she needed to keep her figure. It was for their survival as a family, they told her, that she stay slim.

She was forever grateful to Jimbo for so many things. He had been there when Braulio and Guillermo were shot. And he had stood like a post of iron through the funerals. Poor Gloriosa. They all thought she'd die. Perla—she broke. Lupita had been at her house almost every day to try to help Big Angel keep Flaca together. Perhaps she had failed. Because her Jimbo had cracked, and she hadn't noticed till it was too late. None of them knew what it all had cost him.

Lupita watched Jimbo's head droop, snap up, droop farther, then rise slowly as he smiled at everyone. *Borracho. Is okeh, mi amor. You earned the right to be borracho.*

She ran her hands down her sides and belly. It was Jimbo

who said to her, when they were courting, "Mexican women sure do love their kitchens. You ever see a thin old Mexican lady? You get nice and gordas, all you girls." So she'd gone to La Glori for advice. Once again the baby sister saved her. By that point, La Gloriosa was an expert at dieting and maintaining the illusion that hooked men like catfish and reeled them into the pan.

Lupita's lifelong struggle. Sadly for her, her body believed it was a good thing to have round nalgas and a happy belly, and she was forced to fight against herself every day. Jimbo? Well, he had lost his handsome sailor shape right away. Frankly, it was easier for her—the fatter he got, the thinner she felt. The fatter and drunker he got, the easier it was to get him to sleep. She often snuck out after he was snoring and went over to Perla's house to help her wash dishes. But mostly to have her late-night coffee with Big Angel. Ay, qué hombre!

Everybody was in love with Big Angel. He was so broody, so dark, and had the little sideways smile that spoke volumes to any woman who saw it. What secrets did Perla know? Maybe she did not know how Big Angel heated the women. No disrespect to her elder sister, but she might not have the slightest idea what kind of man she had in her bed. While everybody knew exactly what Yeembo was. They could even imagine his sleep-apnea mask.

But poor Perla. Well, they all had their crosses to bear. Maybe Lupita was no Glori, but she was all woman. Perla fretted too much about nothing. Silly worries and doubts and suspicions and jealousies. She must have known—look at the way she wanted to kill on sight any other woman who came too close to him.

But that smile of his! Ay. Perla always thought he was amused, and every other woman felt his gaze and was certain in her gut that he was aroused. As if the very sight of her, whoever she was, pleased him deeply, carnally, and he was forced to let her know this secretly, with regrets, for he didn't want to betray his own woman, but life was life, and one could not control the stirrings of the palo that hid under the edge of the table. Oh hell, all of those brothers were alike.

Big Angel slathered his passion all over Perla. It was a delight to see, really. Delightful, so much love. Cups clanked loudly. So—much—love. Honestly, she and La Glori never quite understood what was so special about Perlita. Why her? She was old and tired even then. Their leader, their taskmaster. Big Angel was one of God's own challenges to them. A mystery they could not quite comprehend. A spiritual conundrum, a word she had learned on *Jeopardy!* She hadn't been able to get an education, but Big Angel had taught her to learn a new English word or concept every day from television.

Perla came into the kitchen. "Yeembo está borracho," she said.

"Sí."

"Pobre."

"Pobrecito el Yeembo."

Perla went back outside.

Really? Did she really need to report that Jimbo was drunk? As if Lupita didn't know that Jimbo was drunk. Jimbo was always drunk. He was drunk when they met—a young sailor asleep on the front step of their restaurant in Tijuana. He wasn't the first drunk American sailor they met. But he was the first who came back.

That night they shoveled him inside and poured menudo into him. It was part of the deal—Jimbo drank. But he was blind to Perla and, even more astounding, blind to La Glori. From the start, he was after Lupita. On his second visit, he brought her flowers. And from then on, he brought little things that got more personal and intimate, until they ended up in bed. Perfume, a bottle of rompope, lipstick, silk stockings. It didn't take all that long for the silk stockings to drop in a little tan puddle on the floor of a motel near Colonia Cacho. Lupita laughed. Ay, Yeembo! Of course she would marry him. Become an American just like that? U.S. Navy money, a gringo husband, trinkets? An apartment with a bathtub? A new fridge and a color TV and a car? They had a Vista Cruiser station wagon in those days. And her boys, Tato and Pablo, were their bartenders and servers, digging cold Mexican Pepsis and ham sandwiches out of the ice chest. It was as big as the restaurant. He taught her to drive in the Fedco parking lot and then out in the desert, tooling around the Salton Sea.

She had been so poor before Jimbo came that she had to steal napkins from the restaurant every month and fold them into pads for herself and her sisters. Oh yes. Jimbo was her savior. He didn't need to know that when he mounted her she was sometimes imagining Big Angel.

But then, that day, Jimbo watched, helpless, as his nephew's life pumped out of his body on the sidewalk in front of his own store. And he really learned to drink.

◊♭

3:14 p.m.

Marco crept back to the blind girl with two Nehis. One grape, one orange. Choice, right? That was good. *Satanic Hispanic,* he thought. *Whose panic? My panic.*

"I brought you a soda," he said.

"Thank you." She put out her hand, found the plastic cup, and held it.

"Grape okay?"

"Mmm, grape." Slight sneer.

He almost ran away again.

"You're shy, aren't you?" she said.

"What? I mean, c'mon. I'm in a metal band!" He choked down the urge to shriek *Extreme*. "Probably. I guess." He gulped his Nehi. "Yeah. How'd you know?"

Her lips twisted into a reluctant smile. She had learned the greatest trick of the interrogator. Remain silent, and they confessed everything just to fill the chasm of silence.

"Mystical blind people have psychic gifts to offset their *disability*. Didn't you know that?"

"No shit?"

"Don't be silly, boy."

"I get it. You're mocking me."

"I can smell you blush," she whispered.

He stood there with a rictus on his face he hoped looked like a grin but then realized it didn't matter. Had he brushed his teeth? He grabbed at a conversational life preserver that happened to drift across the open water of his mind: "Do you speak Spanish?" he said.

"Oh no. Do you?"

"Spanish is for PUSS—" He coughed. "For puh-people. Other people? Or something. Nah. Not a lot."

She put her hand over her mouth and smiled again.

"I sound stupid right now," he confessed.

"Only right now?"

He was dancing around in her presence as if she'd been shooting her .45 into the dust at his feet.

"All right, yes—I'm shy!"

"Know how I knew? Honestly? Because you said hi, then you ran away. I scared you."

"I think you did," he admitted.

"You don't like blind people?"

"Jeez! No! I mean, no way. I don't even know any blind people."

"If you were PC," she said, "you'd call us 'differently abled in terms of vision.'"

He looked over his shoulder. His dad was watching him. Gave him the thumbs-up. Then Pato made a fist and lifted his arm before himself and started pumping it back and forth, in and out like a piston. Paz ignored him and drained her cup.

"Dude," he said. "You're fucking with me right now."

With dreadful mock earnestness, she leaned forward and said, "I simply adore your perceptiveness, and your sweet vocabulary skills are just the thing I've been yearning for all day."

"He's a chud," Lalo said in passing.

She turned her head as if she could see him.

"Can I sit?" Marco said.

"Why, Carlo?"

"Marco. I think I want to write a song about you. So I gotta talk to you, even though you suck."

"LOL," she intoned, witheringly, and turned her face in his direction. Her lips were parted. She flushed a little. Her hand brushed her right cheek. "Really? A song?"

He nodded. *Duh*, he thought. *Blind, you dummy*. But he didn't say anything.

"Sit," she said.

3:30 p.m.

Little Angel found himself in a dance circle with Minnie and the Trailer Park Gals. Minnie was swaying dreamily like Stevie Nicks; Neala was humping and twerking away while aiming her fundament at various stunned males like a shotgun; Velvette relied on a running-man slow-motion strut that had no form whatsoever but was better than the white-boy arrythmic Phish concert "dancing" of Little Angel. Ookie danced with himself, smiling at the sky, hugging his own ribs.

Little Angel called, "The Ookster!"

This made Ookie laugh. Little Angel had never seen Ookie laugh.

Velvette spun Little Angel back around and did weird mask things with her fingers over her eyes as she ran in place, licking her lips at him while nodding encouragingly.

❦

La Gloriosa watched Little Angel dance. She didn't want to care. It was stupid. But why was he dancing with them? He never asked her to dance. She went into the abandoned living room and sat alone and told herself not to be ridiculous. He was a terrible dancer.

❦

3:45 p.m.

Everybody out here on the patio was happy, and he was dying right in front of them. *True*, Big Angel told himself. But this was what he'd wanted. Well, it was his party, he could cry if he wanted to. Ha-ha.

"Sometimes," Big Angel said, "I don't feel like I will die."

"You won't," said Dave the coffee thief, holding yet another cup of Little Angel's Colombian.

"But sometimes I know I will."

"Death is an illusion."

"It feels real to me, Dave."

"No whining."

"Damn it! Listen! Sometimes," Big Angel said, "I feel like I will die right this minute. Like today. I know I am dying today. I am going down a slide. I have only hours to live. And it feels goddamned real to me. Sorry, God."

Dave sat forward in his lawn chair, hands clutched between his knees. "God understands your anger," he said.

Big Angel rattled his footrests.

"What we need to understand," Dave said, oblivious to this outburst, "is that death is not the end. Well, it's the end of this." He waved his hand toward the Great Fiesta, where many humans frolicked beneath the sun. "But I tell you truly, it is but a transition. It is but a portal—and believe it or not, on the other side, every second is a thousand years and every thousand years is a second, and it's all a fiesta better than this one."

"Bullshit, Dave."

"Maybe. Maybe not. Only one way to find out." Good ol' Dave took a happy sip of purloined coffee.

Big Angel sighed. Rubbed his face. Thought about how much he'd miss rubbing his face. Everything was precious to him suddenly. Sighing. What a wonderful thing it was to sigh. Geraniums. Why did he have to leave geraniums behind?

Dave beamed at him. Were his teeth whitened? Big Angel

wanted to get his own teeth whitened. Except he was going to die right after the party.

"I have four children with my Flaca," he said.

"Yes."

"One is dead. Another is dead to me. El Yndio. What kind of name is that? They aren't my children, but they are. And Minnie and Lalo are here. They are mine."

"Yes."

"They all had children. Except El Yndio."

"Right."

"Their children are having children."

"Gotcha."

"Why must I leave them?"

"Believe," Dave said.

Did pinche Dave never waver? "Pinche Dave," he decided to say, "do you never waver?"

"Of course I do. Of course. Even Ignatius Loyola wavered. That dark night of the soul, man. No one's immune. It would all be meaningless if you didn't wonder and doubt. That's what makes it real. That's what makes us people. God could have sent angels to flutter around like fairies, delivering rum punch and manna all day on a cosmic cruise ship. But what would that avail us?"

Big Angel made that monkey face and shook his head. "Not fair."

"You're being dramatic." Dave leaned toward him and murmured, so only he heard it: "Bee-yatch."

Big Angel coughed out a small bark of laughter. "I hate you so much," he said.

Dave crossed his arms. "Miguel Angel," he said. "It isn't hard to die. Everybody does it. Even flies do it. Everyone here is doing it. We're all terminal." He had a tear in his eye; Big Angel could see it brimming. "Your schedule is just different from mine. Dying is like catching a train to Chicago. There are a million rails, and the trains run all night. Some go scenic and some go express. But it's a big old train yard. It's easy. What takes balls is to die well. What takes balls is to believe."

"Big steel balls," said Big Angel.

"Big clanky balls."

"Unos huevotes!" Angel cried.

"Grandotes!" Dave agreed.

Perla appeared. She sat down beside her Flaco. She tapped the table with her finger. "Balls?" she said in Spanish. "Huevos? Steel balls? No, mijo. Sorry, Dave. It takes big ovaries." She nodded at them both and waved her finger. "This life? This dying? Big clanky steel ovaries, cabrones." She clutched her belly and shook her little paunch. "Ovarios de oro!"

Big Angel raised his eyebrows at Dave.

"Amen," Dave said.

Blade Runner
more time
more time
more

&

If the spirits of Papá Antonio and Mamá América were flying over the neighborhood now, looking down on their children and their children's children, they would see:

Lalo and Giovanni in another house off a dirt alley, sprawling in a sketchy garage, with little paper envelopes unfolded before their noses and their feet splayed on a filthy carpet. Gio reaching back and slipping a small pistol out of his belt to hand to his father, who trembled and shook his head as he hit envelope after envelope, and a cholo, with teardrops tattooed on his cheeks and other face tattoos of the number 13, coming into the room with a couple of icy 40s;

Big Angel wanting to go inside for a rest, but Minnie stopping him and wheeling him against his will back toward the lawn where the dancers were filtering to the tables, saying, "Just you wait";

Tío Jimbo asleep, half lying across his table, and Lupita stroking his head;

Perla weeping silently in a corner with two Chiweenies in her lap;

A knot of vatos y rucas gathered in the driveway, passing smokes around and talking shit;

El Pato craning around to find La Gloriosa;

La Gloriosa, refreshed and re-made-up, in charge of getting Lalo's garage door open for Minnie's surprise, laughing and flirting and swirling her skirt and swaying her magnificent hair as if her heart weren't charred within her;

Pazuzu hunting for Leo;

MaryLú sitting stiffly, watching Paz and wishing she could leave;

Little Angel sitting with Ookie, and Ookie muttering, "'Third stone from the sun'";

The Biff/Buffy collegiates actually leaving;

The African American nephew learning Spanish from seven giggling young ladies;

The Cookie Monster bent in earnest conversation with his mysterious third cousin;

A chicken coming from some unknown realm, strutting among the chairs, eating potato chips and pieces of hot dog bun;

Neighbors peeking over fences;

A white Audi cruising by slowly in the street; and

A yellow school bus coming to a stop before the house, the door opening, and the vatos and rucas beginning to shout and whistle.

✑

3:56 p.m.

There is a minute in the day, a minute for everyone, though most everyone is too distracted to notice its arrival. A minute of gifts coming from the world like birthday presents. A minute given to every day that seems to create a golden bubble available to everyone. But Big Angel could have missed it because he was sore and angry that he couldn't go to bed. Jimbo did miss it because he had passed out. People on the freeway five miles from the party missed it because they were battling traffic and hating the Mexicans because talk radio told them it was all right because of ISIS and the border wall and the Chargers had betrayed San Diego and evangelicals were howling that sodomy was the new law of the land and their favorite talk show hosts were unable to control any narrative anymore and the drought was going to continue until all of California burned and vanished in dust and the rivers in the West had turned yellow or huge floods were on the way and nobody knew what to expect.

But Minnie knew all about the minute, though she could not

have explained it to anyone. It had come to her on one of those long, lonesome nights. Who knew that a night of bad sleep and discomfort and sad jams on Pandora was a gift? But it was. She found the golden bubble in her own misery.

"Wait, Daddy," she said, bracing herself against the wheelchair so her Pops wouldn't steam away like a grumpy locomotive.

"Minnie!" he said. "I am tired!"

"I know. Hold on."

"You *know*?" he snapped. "Nobody knows how I feel!"

"Yes, Daddy."

Perla fretted. "Mija?" she said. "Let him go, sí?"

"Mami! No," Minnie said. "Just watch!" It had cost her a large chunk of her savings. She started laughing when she heard the tumult from the front of the house. "Listen."

A massive bleat, a fanfare.

"What is that?" Big Angel said.

Little Angel stood up and put a hand over his eyes.

"Happy birthday, Daddy," Minnie said with perfect timing because she had come into her power and everything she would touch now would be blessed with perfection. She just knew it. So as she said it, the trumpets sounded.

"Qué?" Big Angel cried.

The mariachis marched through the garage and burst out in a line, playing impossibly loud, joyous music. All in magnificent black and silver, crimson cummerbunds, vast sombreros. White frilly shirts with red ties elaborately fluttering. Trumpets, violins, guitarrón, guitar. They formed a half circle before Big Angel and Perla, and rocked the universe.

Big Angel laughed and clapped his hands and laughed and kicked his feet and cried. He sang and sang and sang.

When they were finished, the mariachis accepted their worship like true stars and tipped their giant hats to Big Angel and trooped back out to their bus and charged into the afternoon.

Big Angel was still wiping his eyes when he kissed Minnie five times. At the end of the day, all he really knew was that he was a Mexican father. And Mexican fathers made speeches. He wanted to leave her with a blessing, with beautiful words to sum up a life, but there were no words sufficient to this day. But still, he tried. "All we do, mija," he said, "is love. Love is the answer. Nothing stops it. Not borders. Not death." He held her hand in his burning fingers, only pulling away when a shaken Perla wheeled him back to his bedroom.

♉

4:30 p.m.

Minnie turned back and watched her clan. They seemed to be moving slower and slower as she watched. MaryLú—her kids were all clean, smart, educated. Pato—his boys were sweet, even Marco the Metal Beast. Tía Gloriosa—the strongest woman she had ever met, except for Mommy. The little shorties raising hell, the old ladies and men in brown suits. God, they were beautiful.

A strange stillness fell over the fiesta. People sat quietly, talking among themselves or just thinking. The hilarity was absorbed by the music, it seemed. The density of the day came upon them all. People were murmuring their personal testimonials at every table. Suddenly remembering past moments with the Man, mourning the moment that was surely on its way, sooner than later. Everybody saw it. Everybody knew it.

Minnie was undone. She rushed inside and locked herself in the guest bathroom and sobbed.

Lupita and La Gloriosa moved languidly, policing the tables. The neighborhood ladies fussed in the kitchen and kept the empty crates and platters moving. People snuck out of the yard in odd little mincing escapes, as if their tiptoeing would make them invisible. Somehow ribs and barbecue chicken appeared, but nobody could eat any more. Pato decided, however, to give it a try.

Ookie sat far away from everybody else. He held the pilgrim chicken in his lap, petting it like a puppy. It jerked its head around, watching the people, making small clucks and groans, then put its head on Ookie's shoulder. It didn't make a fuss when Little Angel walked up to them.

"Hi, Ookie," he said.

"Hi."

"Are you okay?"

"Ookie's okay."

"Did you like the music?"

"A man hit Ookie," Ookie said.

"I know. I'm sorry."

"Ookie stold Legos."

"Why do you steal Legos, Ookie?"

Ookie petted his chicken. He smiled slyly. He looked up at Little Angel. "That's a secret."

Little Angel reached out a finger and scratched the chicken's neck.

"Ookie and Big Angel has a secret."

"Oh?"

"You are Little Angel."

"That's right."

"When Big Angel dies, will you be Big Angel?"

Little Angel blinked that one away. "I guess I'll be the only Angel," he said.

Ookie put the chicken down. He got up and took Little Angel's hand. The smaller man's grip was as dry and hard as wood. He pulled Little Angel to the shed behind the house. He fumbled under his collar and pulled out a key on a length of string and used it to unlock a padlock on the door hasp.

"It's a secret," he said again, putting his finger over his lips and pulling the door open.

He reached in and yanked a chain, and a single bulb snapped on. It swung on its cable, and shadows jerked back and forth. Little Angel could see what was inside.

"Ookie made this," Ookie said.

"What is it?"

"Look."

"You've got to be kidding," Little Angel said.

Across town, Lalo and Gio are in a panic. The candy-colored Chevy Impala burns off the blacktop and slides into another alley, this one dirt. The engine has the voice of fifty angry cats. Curlicues of saffron dust swirl in the car's wake.

"No! No! No! So bad, so bad, so bad," Lalo is shouting. He's crying. "What'd we do?" he groans.

Crows fall upon them like hordes of wasps.

"Pops," Gio says. "We didn't do nothing."

Plastered to the passenger window, Lalo is deeply into his rush: the pills and weird powder he drank in a cup of tequila have kicked in, hard, and coruscating colors run down his arms and shoot out of his pants. He thinks he rolled down the window a minute ago and vomited. But the window's closed now.

And Lalo remembers: They had pulled into the alley, and he'd said, "Where's his boys at?" And Gio saying, "It's that stupid Ruffles and his cuz. I paid them fifteen to go to Subway." And Lalo feeling guilty that his son had grown up simmering with rage and plotting wicked paybacks. While Lalo kept trying to forget.

Now he looks at his hands. Are they red? Is that blood? His hands. Is that mud from Iraq on them? Can he smell rotting flesh? The dragon writhes on his leg. He watches in horror as it climbs up into his shorts and lets its tail slip out. Blood dripping from it. Oh my God.

"Blood flew around," Lalo says.

"No, Pops. Chill."

"I busted a full clip into that dude!"

"Chill, goddamn it."

His son standing over that vato like he was just saying "Hey." The gangster smug on his Salvation Army couch in that garage. B-ball cap all cranked sideways on his fool head. Black widow spiders inked on his neck, a 13 along each side of his jaw, and those two blue teardrops in the corner of his left eye. Lalo staring at those teardrops, realizing they stood for Braulio and Guillermo. His mind blinking like a neon sign. *Youfuckyoufuckyoufuck*. The gangster laying out the drugs on his shipping-crate coffee table. "This what you came for. Best be ready to pay." And Lalo remembers arcs of blood like weird shiny pebbles that melted when they hit the walls. The slippery floor all greasy with blood.

"Blood everywhere. Gio! The radios were all static. They couldn't get to us."

"That was the war, Pops, a'ight?"

"But that dude. Just now."

"No, Pops."

Gio slams around a corner—cops could be anywhere.

"You. Killt. My. Bro." Lalo says. "I said it to his face. Right?"

Bam, bam.

"You. You. You."

He remembers noises from the gangster's lungs whistling through his ribs. No, no. That was PFC Gomez, from East L.A. They were holding a sheet of plastic over the gaping wound in his chest and pushing down till his ribs cracked. No way to get a helicopter in that alley. Dogs. Women shrieking. Hajjis on the rooftops all around.

"Gio, Gio," he cries, "what did we do?"

"Pops, knock it off." Gio is wrestling the wheel, keeping his eye on the mirror in case that culero and his homies are in pursuit.

"Gio!" Lalo gawks at Gio's eyes. They're buggin' out! His eyes are out of his head, on long pink stalks, waving like a lobster's.

He remembers the gangster's eyes. He had eyes tattooed on his eyelids. Every time he blinked, he was still staring. Lalo didn't know what he was seeing. It hypnotized him. It was the eyes. The eyes pushed him into his rush.

The car's window glass is soft and gooey against his face. Well, ain't that some shit right there. "Oh Jesus," he moaned. "We killed that dude."

"Shit no. You choked."

The car slides.

"Mijo?"

"I thought you were a badass," Gio says.

Oh my God—this boy is so cold.

A dog! They hit a dog! No, they didn't. Lalo watches it escape. Killing a dog, that would be the end. That would be the last frickin' straw.

"Payback," Gio says. "All you had to do." His voice is suddenly melting and dripping.

That whole room was melting and dripping. He watched the gangster's skull rise through his flesh like something surfacing in a swamp. And he stood, and his head kept rising and rising until it was out through the roof above the barrio, in the sky. And Lalo's in the car, looking at his own fingers. He notices how long they are. So wavy. He holds his hand before his face. It's a squid. "Where's my gun?" he asks Gio, and his long fingers claw at his empty ankle holster.

"You threw it."

Lalo flashes: They were both standing above that killer. Just another cartoon character in a Pendleton jacket. Selling poison to little boys looking to be the baddest of the bad. And Gio sliding the slender gun into Lalo's hand and nudging him with his shoulder. And the man, knowing his moment had come without seeing the gun, obviously wondering why he didn't have his own gun, dropping the Baggies of dope and pills on the table. The cups from the weird Amazon poisons Lalo had drunk starting to crawl around on the table beside the drugs. The man's dead eyes going deep with fear for an instant, and hard again. "Yeah?" he said. "This is it, huh?" Chin held high.

"You kilt my bro." Yes. Lalo remembers. "Gio," he says. "I didn't drop no gun."

"You tossed that shit before we booked out of there."

"Please," Lalo pleads with the universe.

"You gave some wack lecture, then ran, Pops."

"No."

"Yeah, you did." The words are stretching like rubber bands and snapping back at Lalo's face.

Please, please, God, if you have any mercy for me, let me wake up.

"I didn't even guess you were gonna puss out." And Gio laughs in derision.

"Oh my God!" Lalo shouts. "You my baby boy, though!" Lalo can't tell if his tweak is stretching all the sounds like it's stretching the car now. The car is suddenly rubber. It bends around corners and stretches so his lobster-faced boy moves far ahead of him, then snaps back.

"You never killed nobody," Lalo says. "You playact, little man. I killed people, for reals. It was my job. I got blood all over me. Forever. Help me!"

"Got his stash, didn't we?" Gio says. "Taught his ass to kill my tío that way, at least. What you worried about?"

Lalo kicks the mochila at his feet. It's full of weed and ice crystals and cash and chains. "Help!" he says again.

Giovanni looks at him and says, quite calmly, something Lalo cannot understand and never will. And still, Lalo tries to answer. But his words make no sense, and spit is cascading from his mouth.

"We good, Pops. All love. Proud of you anyway."

Lalo cranks his molten head and stares out the window. "Bad," he says. "So bad. Son." Or he hopes he managed to say this.

"I forgive you, Pops. You just ain't that strong."

Echoes. Weird bird noises. The meaty sound of punctures and the blood spurts and grunts when the rounds hit, burning the meat of the victims. But it's Iraq, not California. Check.

Keepin' it straight. Then Lalo sees a black-and-white. "Pigs!" he screeches.

"Stay cool," Gio says.

The cop car turns into 169 cars. Lalo closes his eyes. When he looks again, it is a VW painted like a cop car. Geek Squad. He can put that much together.

He starts to cry again. "I'm scared," he says.

Gio reaches over and clutches his knee. "Pops. Pops! Listen. Are you listening?" He lets go to downshift.

Lalo stares at him.

"Snap out of it."

Instantly, Lalo remembers: the cool pistol in his hand, seeming as ridiculous as a toy and at the same time apocalyptic. The drug writhing up his veins like some skinny black serpent. The man staring up at him with no expression but with hands shaking. His son saying, "Do it. Cap his ass." And the pistol just floating in the air, looking to him like some weird airborne tropical fish. And the tattoo. Oh God, it's the tattoo on his own arm. He's scratching at it now. Big Angel. That dumb smile. That hair. POPS 4EVER.

"What did my brother do to you?"

"Nothing. He got green-lighted, and I did what I was told. Just doing business."

All time stops for Lalo.

POPS 4EVER.

And Lalo has been a hostage all his life. Trying so hard to be Braulio. Trying so hard to be Pops. Not able to be either one. Ashamed of his father—what a silly old man. Afraid of his brother—so much more macho than he'd ever be. And all this time trying to convince people he was just like this piece of shit sitting before him.

He extends the pistol again. The man falls back and closes his eyes. And all Lalo can feel is sorrow.

Lalo feels so sorry for the world, for everything in it, all of them dying and turning to dust. He feels the drugs, feels the rush. He feels a wind and remembers how his hair would lift when he was playing baseball, how the sun felt, and how Pops cheered for him in embarrassing polyester bell-bottoms, with mustard all over his stupid mustache.

And Lalo hears his own voice again, sounding alien, as if it were his father's voice, saying: "We got to stop. We just running in circles. Payback, payback, payback. You ain't never gonna pay nothing back." The pistol drops to his side. The man on the couch opens his eyes, sees the gun has dropped away from his face, and suddenly deflates with disbelief. He is revealed: a middle-aged loser who has disfigured his own face and is not a threat to anyone in the world. Not even worth shooting.

"This ain't what we are, homes," Lalo says. "This is not us. This is the story they tell about us, but it's not true." He jerks the pistol back up. The man flinches and that flinch is the worst moment of all for him.

"This is us."

Aiming above the man's head, Lalo pulls the trigger, emptying the clip into the wall. The man falls back, clutching his chest and kicking his legs in the air, shouting in terror. Each round sounds flat and hard as Lalo fires. The smoke choking and blue. Plaster showering down on them until the gun clicks, empty. And he whips it across the room as the man ducks and weeps.

Then Gio is grabbing him and they're running. "Jesuschrist, Pops! What was that"

Lalo feels the world burning all around him. And he snaps

back into the immediate moment and finds himself staring at Gio's hands on the wheel. The wheel looks like it is made of soft licorice.

"I'm going to hell, Gio. Signed, sealed, and delivered, I'm serious."

Lalo sees his grandfather's ghost climbing in through the windshield before he passes out.

Ookie's Surprise

How could they know what Little Angel's home had been like?

He looked out the door at all of them. The incessant music thrummed in his ears. He almost couldn't hear what Ookie was muttering.

Christmas. Sure. They were jealous of Christmas. And the 'rents had knocked themselves out for him. He had to admit it: they had gone without to make sure he had his James Bond super-pistol, his *Man from U.N.C.L.E.* spy briefcase, his slot car track, his Thingmaker, his electric train. The best, of course, the baddest gift any boy could get, was a sparkling metal-flake blue Schwinn Stingray bike. They all saw that bike and thought: *Rich gringo pampered while Father left us to starve.*

What they didn't see was Don Antonio's tutorial for the soft little white boy. The fine art of learning to ride a bike. Como un hombre! Little Angel had never seen the Harley. He had no idea that his father rode such a thing. Even when they went to the Tu-Vu Drive-In and watched Adam Roarke biker movies, his father never told him. Don Antonio saw the bicycle as a way to toughen the boy. Everything was a tool toward making him a man. The belt had worked on Don Antonio's other boys, and it worked on Gabriel.

The white boy's fear of the bike, of falling—of pain, for

God's sake—shamed Don Antonio. He was damned if it would have training wheels. He balanced Gabriel on it and ran down the main street, holding him until he was going fast, then let go and watched the panicked wobbling until he crashed and lay on the curb, crying. Don Antonio walked to the kid and put out his hand. It was just like the beach. Angel Gabriel thought his father was saving him. But Don Antonio took his hand to get him back up and force him onto the bike in spite of his begging and crying. And they ran and crashed. And again. Torn pants at the knees. Blood from his left knee and his nose. And he kept crashing until he could ride.

There was no choice, so there was no problem.

After Little Angel's mother threw his father out, Don Antonio went to live with Big Angel. Little Angel was already away at college. Then his mother died unexpectedly in her sleep. She had a picture of Little Angel in bed with her. And a Junior League cookbook.

It was a simple thing, really, scattering her ashes in the ocean. Just Little Angel and his mother's friends from work—grocery checkers from Vons supermarket. There were no relatives, after all. Though Pato, loyal as ever, showed up at the boat dock and somberly climbed aboard.

Little Angel wore her name tag pinned to his shirt. The company that ferried them out into the ocean provided them with roses and a glass of champagne each. San Diego, in the distance, looked parched and crumbling to him. Dolphins appeared around the boat, and the grocery ladies took that as a sign. His mother caught a ray of sunlight as she spread out under the water, and for just an instant, she gleamed and sparkled like glitter.

5:00 p.m.

"I was so bored before you came over to say hello," she said. "Our family is afraid of anybody who's different."

The Cookie Monster's hair had fallen. He rested his chin on his fist at the table and stared at her pale face. Her name was Liliana.

"I'm different too," he said.

She patted him like a good doggie. "Of course you are."

"Dude."

"You can call me Lily," she said.

"For sure." *Lily—how freakin' awesome was that?*

She was his third cousin on his dad's side, daughter of a dentist in Mazatlán. Safe enough for kissin' cousins, like Lalo said. Studying at UCSD. Blind since birth. His exact age. She had been to Paris. She had confused him by saying it was beautiful. How did she know? Did it smell beautiful? Probably not. His dad had been to Paris and said it smelled like pee.

"I can't wait to hear your band," she said.

"Well," he boasted, "it's pretty dark."

"I love dark music!" she said. "I have a new stage name for you. Nice and dark."

He had thought about stage names before; she got closer to perfect every second. "Hit me," he said.

"Nihil Jung."

"Neil Young?"

"No, silly! Nihil. Right? Jung? Carl Jung? Oh, never mind. It's college humor."

Ow.

"Are you fat?" she said.

"Yeah. Totally fat," he said.

She laughed. "Say it in your devil voice."

"Aw, man."

"For me, Carlo. Shred it. Shred the fatness."

"Marco. People are listening."

"Exactly. Isn't that the point?" She patted the table with her palm. "Sacrifice yourself for me."

"I AM FAT!!!" the extreme demon roared.

They fell across the table, giggling like four-year-old twins sharing a bubble bath. Several people craned about to stare at them. Marco waved. He was very happy.

"Are people looking?" she said.

"Everybody's looking."

"Kiss me quick." She scrabbled her fingers across the table and found his hand. "While they're watching."

He gave her a peck.

"Ravishing," she said and squeezed his fingers. "So I had this dream last night," she said. "Listen, listen—this is crazy. I hate it when people tell me their dreams, but this one is really weird. I was in this field. It was a summer day, okay? Like, all sunny. Birds singing—just a perfect day. And the fields were all golden, and the sky was blue. And there were big green trees. Little pretty puffy white clouds.

"I know what you're thinking. Like, how do I see it, right? I don't know how! I just see it in my dreams! Anyway, but then this thing happened. There were people in the sky. People hanging above the field on cables. Like ornaments. Surreal."

"The Rapture," he suggested.

"Hardly, you asswipe," she replied.

"Screw you."

"You wish."

He stared at her face. It was animated, full of joy. Yeah, she made expressions that seemed otherworldly, but he understood she had never seen another face to know what tics were "normal." Her lips were pink and shiny, and he was dying to see her eyes, even if they couldn't see him.

"How did I see those things, Carlo?" she asked.

"Marco. I don't know." He bent down and smelled her hand.

"Stop sniffing me, you freak!" she said. But she didn't take her hand away.

He kissed her knuckles.

"Oh my," she said.

"I can't," he said. "Explain it."

"Me neither. But I would give anything to be inside your head for a minute," she said. "I would give anything to see if what I saw was real or not."

"Like if what you think is blue is really red."

"Or some color you never saw."

"Or not a color at all."

"Blue, boy! Blue—it's the color of wind blowing through flowers. Right?"

He kissed her hand again. "Absolutely."

"You're crazy about me, yes?" she said.

"For real."

He stood. As they left the party, they were holding hands and still laughing.

They swiped Pato's car and didn't come back.

At first, Little Angel was unsure about what he beheld, but the magnitude of it slowly came to him. Perhaps it was the colors that threw him, for Ookie had built this with no regard for matching hues. It was all a rainbow.

"Ookie made it," Ookie said.

Little Angel stood there, holding his hand, breathing. "How long did it take, Ookie?"

"Couple years. Yeah. Couple."

Forms made of plastic rainbows.

There was a worktable in the shed. Beyond it, an open space that would have held rakes and wheelbarrows, even a car, but Big Angel and Ookie had cleared all that out when Big Angel could still walk. Big Angel had cut out pictures from newspapers and magazines, and he had tacked up a street map on one wall.

"Are you experienced?'" Ookie said.

There were sheaves of notes and drawings stacked up on the table. Loose sheets all penciled in and colored with crayons.

"Ookie's blueprint," Ookie said.

It was huge. The expanse of the Coronado Bridge swooped away to the right. Around its nearer base, Ookie had meticulously built a model of San Diego. He had made Lego skyscrapers, hotels, even the embarcadero with a model of the *Star of India* docked at the pier. Little streets and avenues. Some of it sketchy—blocks barely begun. Some of it insanely detailed. Broadway was alive before him. The old Woolworth's building was exactly as he remembered it. And down the blank riverbed that was the I-5 highway there stood a small wire model of the Eiffel Tower. Little Angel was befuddled for a moment, until he saw Ookie had affixed paper letters to it: KSON. He laughed. Yes—it was the country music station's broadcast tower. South of the big bridge. And it all came rushing back to him—he too had thought, when he was a child, that it was the Eiffel Tower.

"Ookie!" he said.

"Yeah." Ookie laughed and clapped his hands.

"Ookie!" he said.

"Purple haze!"

Against the left wall was a model of this neighborhood. Lomas Doradas. Ookie scuttled over there. He pointed. "Big Angel's house." Little Angel nodded. "Ookie's house," pointing to the next block.

They sat on the floor and stared at the plastic city. Ookie pointed out his best towers.

"That's El Cortez hotel," he said. "That's the Gaslamp Quarter, Ookie's favorite."

The new Horton Plaza shopping mall was not part of Ookie's city. It was the old Horton Plaza. With a fountain and little benches and plastic palm trees. It had been gone for decades. But Little Angel saw that it was better than the fancy stores there now. With its string of tumbledown movie theaters and its sailors and bums. Buses on the sides. Little cars lined up on Broadway.

"Ookie steals Hot Wheels," Ookie confessed.

They laughed.

"Ookie needs buses."

"Matchbox," Little Angel said.

"Buses?"

"I think so. Trucks, cabs, everything. I'll look it up."

They shopped for Matchbox buses for a few minutes on his iPhone.

"Look, Ookie! Delivery trucks. Fire trucks. A mail truck."

"Buy."

"Hey—a VW hippie van."

"Buy all for Ookie."

They high-fived when they found little groupings of pigeons made to scale for model train setups. Cops. Businessmen in

1950s hats. Little Angel ordered and ordered and entered Big Angel's address. He had no idea how long he sat in that room with Ookie. It was one of the best days he'd ever had, though. He hugged Ookie, but Ookie shoved him away.

"Airplanes!" he cried, holding up a little metal 747.

They rigged it up on a wire and hung it from a crossbeam to look like it was coming in for a landing.

"Look," Ookie said and held up a little Dodge Charger. "Crosstown traffic," he said. He handed it to Little Angel and nodded at his city. "Go on."

"Really?"

"Yeah, yeah. Put."

Angel got up on his knees and placed the car on Seventh. Ookie squinted and shook his head. Angel moved it to Broadway, close to the water and the almost completed Union Station. Ookie nodded.

"My brother helped you do this," he said.

"Big Angel. Yeah. He told me the secret."

"What secret?"

"It's a secret."

"What secret, Ookie?"

Ookie tapped his noggin. "Ookie," he said, "is a genius."

"You should always listen to Big Angel. He's always right."

"Scuse me while I kiss the sky!"

They held hands and studied paradise in reverent silence.

today

The Confessions

Ookie left the padlock unlatched so Little Angel could go back in and look at it again later. Little Angel was in a hurry to tell his big brother he had seen the secret city. What he'd seen was more astounding than that. He'd seen his brother for the first time. His brother, knowing his life was running out, had locked himself in a garage with a crazy boy to help him realize a dream no one would ever see. If there had ever been any doubt, Little Angel was now firmly in line with the Big Angel worshippers. Fully aboard. Big Angel: bodhisattva.

It was dark.

Little Angel paused at his sister's table. MaryLú was sadly drinking a glass of red wine. She was lit semi-romantically by a burning anti-mosquito torch. She was sighing. She couldn't understand why these party people didn't stop to think for a minute. She didn't know why they had all forgotten about her mother and forgotten why they were there now. Everybody was dying and nobody cared.

"Where's the patriarch?" he asked.

She put her hands together beside her cheek and closed her eyes, doing a variation of the family monkey face; this apparently also represented napping.

"Where else?" she said. "My poor brother."

He moved on; he'd sit in the room till Big Angel woke up. It was about time to say good night. He imagined his nice quiet hotel room. He felt like a weakling, but enough was enough. He could not imagine how his family could carry on in all this activity. They exhausted him.

For a moment, he imagined La Gloriosa asleep beside him, her head on his chest, her hair across his face.

The thought that this circus went on day after day stunned him. When he was a kid, alone with Dad and Mom, he had wished there was this kind of family tumult in his house. But, no. In Seattle, he had a quiet white-and-blue condo looking out to Vashon Island. He watched the Bainbridge ferries cut across Puget Sound. He put out bread on his porch railing for the gulls and the crows. He once saw a fox pop out of the woods beside his complex and mince onto the beach. Barring Seahawks games, his life was quiet. He didn't even really like his girlfriend staying over.

He noticed Paz glaring around at the partiers.

Perla was slumped a bit, crushed by sorrow she knew she could not bear. She was going to die right after her man, she was sure of it. Though she would end up living on for many lonely years, guiding the family. But seldom cooking. A glass of bubbly tipped in her hand. Beside her, two old ladies played cards. He hugged her and kissed the top of her head.

La Minnie stood with her arms crossed, looking at nothing. He went and put his arm around her.

"You did good," he said.

"Think so, Tío?"

Poor El Tigre had had to go to work. No boyfriend for her. She was flying solo.

"You liked the mariachis?"

"Genius."

She smiled at the ground.

"Where's Lalo at?" she said.

"Left with his son. Said something about a dude and a thing."

"That can't be good."

They watched Pazuzu stick her finger in MaryLú's face and lecture her.

"Gotta go," Sheriff Minnie said, hurrying to them.

Little Angel wondered where Pato was until he discovered him in the living room, asleep on the couch.

Down the hall and into Big Angel's room.

There he was, the Mexican Buddha, in his blue pajama bottoms and gym socks. He was wearing a white undershirt. Not asleep after all. Dave the American coffee bandit sat on the end of the bed.

He rose.

"Gabe," he said. "Hi." He held out his hand.

"Dave, right?"

They shook.

"They call me Little Angel."

"So I hear. I just found out about you."

They looked reproachfully at Big Angel.

"I'm their best-kept secret, Dave."

"Not fair," said Big Angel. "We have a life, you know."

"Me too," said Little Angel, a little alarmed that this moment had already gone a tad sour.

Dave watched the brothers. He said, "Maybe you're their precious jewel."

Big Angel's voice cracked. "Good one, Dave."

He studied the two of them, standing there, his focus intense, sucking every second of life out of the air.

I'm not even tired, he told his dead mother.

"Look," said Big Angel. He had a small stack of books by his foot. "Dave thinks I can read these."

Dave ignored him. "We're just hearing confession here," he said to Little Angel.

"Confession?" said Little Angel.

"Got to speed read," Big Angel said.

Little Angel picked up the books. Thomas Merton, *The Seven Storey Mountain*. Brennan Manning, *The Ragamuffin Gospel* and *Ruthless Trust*. Frederick Buechner, *The Sacred Journey*.

"Light reading," he said.

"If we had more time," Dave said, tipping his head at Big Angel, "I'd have given him some Buddhist texts too."

"Dave wants me to learn to trust," Big Angel said.

"It's late, I admit," said Dave. "But a worthy pursuit, even at the last minute."

"Trust what?" said Little Angel.

Dave sat back down and smiled at Big Angel.

"God," said Big Angel.

"Partly," said Dave.

"Cancer?" said Little Angel, just a tad sharply.

Dave said, "You should bequeath these books to your little brother."

Clock ticked.

"Right?" Big Angel said. He looked at Little Angel. "I told this cabrón. I don't have time to read these. All my life is just three words over and over: today I die."

"You're being morbid, Carnal."

"That's what I've been telling him," said Dave.

Big Angel's left hand was starting to shudder. He hid it under his butt.

La Gloriosa came into the room with a glass of murky orange-brown fluid. "I brought agua de tamarindo for you," she said as she put the glass on Big Angel's bedside table.

"My favorite," he said.

She patted his head.

"Not cold?" he said.

"No."

"Cold feels like I swallowed a knife," he said.

"I know."

"Since chemo."

"Sí. Take your pills."

"Hurts my teeth. Hurts everything."

"Sí, amorcito," she said.

"Hello, Father," she said to Dave as she went back out.

Dave raised his hand and blessed the air behind her.

"Father?" said Little Angel.

"He's my priest," Big Angel explained.

"Indeed," said Dave. "Father David Martin, SJ."

"Es un Jesuita," Big Angel said. "Going to do my funeral."

"Oh shit!" said Little Angel. "Sorry, Padre."

"No worries. Jesuits say it too. Every Jesuit in the world said 'Oh shit' when Francis was made pope." He nodded at the prone patriarch. "We are deciding when to do last rites."

"Are you dying tonight?" Little Angel said.

"I am," his brother replied.

Dave shook his head. "I think he has more time."

"He's pretty sick."

"I am right here, pendejos. Don't talk about me like I'm not here."

258 • LUIS ALBERTO URREA

Little Angel dropped the books and sat on the end of the bed too. "God," he said. "This is all too much for me."

"Carnal—I'll have cake first. Don't worry. We got time."

"Shut up."

"Maybe dance too."

"Not funny."

"You don't need to tell me what's funny."

"Brothers, you have some business to attend to," Dave said. He raised his hand over them and made the sign of the cross in the air. "I do this a lot," he noted.

"Does it work?" said Little Angel.

"It got you here."

"Boom," said Big Angel. "Owned."

"Lalo teach you that?"

"I'm an OG," Big Angel said smugly.

Dave clapped his hands once and said, "Okay! Call me, Miguel—or have Perla call me. You know. And I'll call you, Gabe," he said. "Your brother gave me your number. You will help me at the funeral."

"Wait," Little Angel said. He was going to say *I'm leaving*. But he stopped.

"Thanks, guys," Dave said. He waved at them and strode from the room, maintaining a splendid pace through the house and front yard until he was far down the street and climbing into his SUV and whistling.

ᡠᖯ

Random-selecting thoughts, Big Angel announced, "I never took drugs."

"No?" Little Angel replied. "Me neither."

"Not even marijuana."

"Same."

"I thought you were a hippie. I am going to start smoking marijuana," Big Angel said. "Eat it in cookies. What do you think about that?"

"Why not? They say it helps."

"They say it makes you laugh. I want to laugh."

"I hear magic mushrooms make you very happy."

Then Little Angel said, "I saw what you did."

Coming so soon after confession, it hit Big Angel with a cold rip of panic all down his back. "What did I do?" he blurted.

"In the shed."

"What?"

"Ookie."

"Oh!" Big Angel lay back. "I did lots of things," he confessed and let a slow leak of relief breath whistle out. "Yes. Ookie's city. That was good."

Little Angel moved up and lay next to his brother. Together they stared at the ceiling.

"I can't believe you did that," Little Angel said.

"My little secret."

"People will find out."

"I know. When I'm gone. That's a good thing. They'll see what Pops did." Now his right hand was trembling. He tucked it under too. *Mother,* he thought, *maybe I am tired after all.*

Big Angel was aware of the sad steps of the dance. It cost him great effort to speak now. When you died, you died in small doses. You had trouble speaking. You forgot who was beside you. You were suddenly furious and in a panic of outrage. You wished you could be saintly. You wished you weren't so weak. You suddenly felt better and fooled yourself into believing that

260 • Luis Alberto Urrea

a miracle was about to happen. Well, wasn't that all a dirty rotten thing to pull on somebody.

He produced a smartphone and struggled to control his hands and tap on it.

"What are you doing?" Little Angel said.

"Texting Minnie." The phone pinged. "She's coming."

In a minute, Minnie hurried into the room. "You rang?"

"In the closet," Big Angel said.

Minnie squeezed past the bed and said, "The chud is back. He's outside. He's wasted. I'm so pissed."

"Qué?" Big Angel said.

"Nothing, Daddy. Just talking to my tío." She turned back to Little Angel. "Lalo. I told him to stay clean. He doesn't listen."

"Lalo?" said Big Angel. "Is he using again?"

"It's okay," she said. "I got this."

Big Angel kicked his feet.

"Really, Daddy. Lalo's just having a tough day. Everybody is."

"I'm sorry."

"No! No, no."

"It's my fault."

"Stop it, Daddy. No such thing."

"Carnal," said Little Angel. But he didn't have anything else to say, so he left it hanging.

Minnie rattled around in the closet and came out with a small flat plastic storage box with a snap-on lid. She laid it beside Big Angel's feet. She went back into the shadow and came out with a heavy brown wool overcoat. It had brass buttons and looked floor length. She nodded at Big Angel and smiled, and she squeezed Little Angel's shoulder as she slipped past him.

"Have fun, you two," she said and went back to managing the fiesta.

"This is our father's police overcoat," Big Angel said. "I give it to you."

Little Angel just stared at it.

"You can touch it," Big Angel said.

Little Angel reached over and took up the coat; it was heavy. It smelled faintly of mothballs. He studied the buttons—they were tarnished, but the eagle battling a snake on a cactus was clearly visible. He stood up, held the coat to his chest, and looked down at himself. His shoulders were wider than his father's had been. And the long coat reached only two inches above his knees.

"I thought he was a giant."

Big Angel wheezed slightly. "So did I."

"He was tiny!" Little Angel said.

"My size," Big Angel said.

"Sorry."

"I used to think I was so big. I thought I was a big man."

"So did I."

The line fell flat and hard.

"What is that supposed to mean?" Big Angel said.

Little Angel shook his head. "Nothing." It wasn't what he had meant to say.

Their entire life as a family had relied on playacting, he suddenly realized. He dropped the coat back onto the bed.

"It sounded harsher than I meant for it to sound. No harm, no foul, right?"

"I have disappointed you."

Little Angel turned away. "Come on, man," he said. "Let's not."

"I must have failed you. Is that right?"

"Jesus, man."

"Tell me now."

"Knock it off."

"Go on! You have a complaint? Last chance, pinche Gabriel."

"You fucker. Stop waving your death in everybody's face."

Death? Big Angel thought. *Really? What do you know about death?* "Nice," he said.

"Look—"

"Don't say *look* to me, mister!"

Little Angel walked out of the room. *Who do you think you are, my mother?* He walked to the kitchen and hugged La Gloriosa, who was startled.

༄

Little Angel returned to the room and sat on the end of the bed. "Look—" he said.

Big Angel raised his hand. "I know," he said. "I was not a perfect brother to you." He put up his other hand. "Don't say it. I don't want to hear it. 'You did the best you could.' That's talk for losers."

"Hey, now. Tone down the harshness there, Angel."

They didn't look at each other.

"Maybe I wasn't a perfect brother either," Little Angel gallantly announced.

Big Angel laughed. "Maybe?"

"Shut up." Little Angel was furious, and he didn't know why.

Big Angel laughed again—cruelly, Little Angel thought.

"Who cares, all right?" the younger brother said. He hated it when his voice sounded like some sitcom teenager in his head. He wanted his big brother to take him seriously. "Nobody cares about all this ancient family bullshit. Just enjoy your day!" He leapt from the bed and towered over his brother. Grabbed the coat. It was astonishingly heavy. "You wanted this goddamned dramatic event, so get out there and live it up."

"Really, Baby Brother?"

Little Angel meanly noted his brother's accent made the word into *rilly*. "You're having a great time. Just be honest. Enjoy it. You set this all in motion for yourself, yeah? Who cares how I feel about things?" Little Angel wanted to embrace the coat and toss it to the floor in equal measure. He laid it back at his brother's feet yet again.

Big Angel was so furious he was almost healed. "You don't like my party?"

"Sure. It's *great*."

"Prick."

"Back at ya."

"You were always a crybaby," Big Angel snapped.

"I know. Like when you taught me to swim at the beach."

Big Angel reddened. "You had everything," he said.

"Are we really doing this?" It was Little Angel's turn to laugh. "Everything," he said. "You think it was all happiness on my side of the street."

"Now we get to it!" Big Angel said. "You dare—!" He just pointed at his little brother. "I didn't have food, cabrón!"

Minnie rushed in. "Tía MaryLú!"

"What," both brothers said.

"It's a disaster," she cried.

"Porqué?" said Big Angel.

"Tía Paz tore her wig off! This whole party's turned to shit!"

"MaryLú wears a wig?" Little Angel said.

In spite of everything, both brothers laughed.

"Ain't funny! I had to pull them apart! Paz kicked over a table. MaryLú ran off with a napkin over her head." She hurried back out.

The brothers wiped their eyes.

"I know you were happy not to be here," Big Angel said. "You didn't have to deal with all the struggles we had. All this excitement, it never ended."

"You don't speak for me."

"I speak for all of you. I am the patriarch." He had meant for it to be funnier than it was.

Little Angel cleared his throat and looked away.

"I always had one question for you, Carnal." Big Angel pounced: "What did you ever have to cry about?"

"Well, Miguel. He left us too."

Big Angel took a noisy gulp of the tamarind La Gloriosa had brought. "He left us first. For you," he said.

"For me? I wasn't even born yet, for God's sake. I thought you were a computer guy. Figure it out."

"Father said your mother was an alcoholic. That she picked lice out of her hair and snapped them with her nails."

Little Angel guffawed. "That's what he told us about your mother."

Big Angel was trembling. "Take it back," he said.

"I didn't start this."

"Father was forced to marry your mother. Because he was a gentleman," he snapped. "She was knocked up."

Stunned silence. They couldn't even hear the party. They couldn't hear the kids in the room next door or their video games.

"My— What?" Little Angel said.

Big Angel looked away. "Now look what you made me do," he said.

"What did you say? Just now."

"Forget it."

Little Angel stood. He sat back down closer to Big Angel. "Holy God," he said.

"Your mother was pregnant with you. That's why they got married."

"Liar."

"Oh, it's true. And you call me a liar again, I'll get up."

"And what?"

"I can still fight."

"Ooh, I'm shaking."

Big Angel rocked forward and grabbed a fistful of Little Angel's shirt. "Hey!" Big Angel bared his teeth. "I can still show you!"

"I don't want to hurt you." Little Angel put his palm against his brother's chicken-bone chest. "Come on, now."

"Teach you!"

"Don't—wanna—hurt—you."

They wrestled on the bed. Big Angel landed several loud, smacking blows on his baby brother's face.

"Stop it, you dick!" Little Angel said.

Perla rushed in and spanked Little Angel with her slipper. "Están locos?" she shouted.

"Flaca," said Big Angel, occupied with ripping Little Angel's pocket off the front of his shirt. "Please leave us alone right now."

"I am so sick of all of you!" she said and stomped back down the hall.

They collapsed on the bed, panting.

"I kicked your ass," Big Angel said. He sat upright and gulped from his glass of juice, then passed it across the bed to his brother.

Little Angel didn't want Big Angel's tepid tamarind juice, but he recognized a gesture of reconciliation when he saw one. He took the glass and drank some down. "I went away," Little Angel said, "to make something of myself. I thought I was going to change the world."

"And what happened, Carnal?"

"Nothing."

"Oh, come on."

Little Angel took a deep breath. "I know you hated me for leaving. I know you thought I looked down on all of you. Well, maybe I did. All my life I thought I had to escape to survive. Maybe even to escape you. And now you are leaving me, and I can't imagine the world without you. I always thought I didn't really have the father I wanted. And all this time it was you.

"To be here now, to see what you have made, humbles me. The good parts and the bad. It doesn't matter. I thought I was going to save the world, and here you were all along, changing the world day by day, minute by minute."

Big Angel was going to say something but decided against it.

changing the world
poco a poco
a little better
right here, right now

7:30 p.m.

The Satanic Hispanic lay in his unkempt bed, hoping Moms wouldn't come home. Lily lay against him, her head on his chest. They were naked. She totally snored. He ran his hand up and down her narrow back. Her bottom was like two soft fruits or something. Like, handfuls. Her shades were on the table with his *Deadpool* action figures.

His hands smelled like her. He had never smelled that before. He held his hand over his face. He couldn't tell anybody in his family about it. It smelled really good. He didn't think he was ever going to wash his hands. Because he could smell her later. He could be right here again. "Oh," he said. Maybe he'd tell Little Angel about it. Little Angel wouldn't think he was a perv. He probably knew some poem about it. But Pato? His own dad—nah. Pops would try to sniff his fingers.

After they had made love—she had, incredibly, mounted him and allowed him to see her slender body as she moved—she had nestled against his chest and scratched at his body hair. "I'm glad you aren't a waxer," she said.

He actually snorted but felt like that was too unsophisticated.

"I'm a dreamer," she said.

"Yeah, no kidding." He made a small laughing chuff. "People in the sky."

"No. Not that. A dreamer. Like, the DREAM Act."

"What's that?"

"DACA? You never heard of it? For undocumented students?"

He hove up on his elbow. "Dude—you're illegal?"

Her eyes were closed. "Marco," she said, finally using the right name. "You almost were not a moron for a moment." She found his chin and kissed it and rolled over to sleep.

ap

Lupita muscled Tío Jimbo onto the couch and tucked a nice blanket around him. She paused in the bathroom and touched up her makeup, rinsed out her mouth, stole a cigarette pack from Jimbo's stash. She stared down at him. He almost looked at peace. She hurried out to the car. She wasn't about to miss the birthday cake.

❧

Ookie was feeling good. He wandered down the street. He hadn't seen his mom for a couple of days. But his pockets were full of cookies. His ghost show was on TV pretty soon—Ghost Bros creeping around freaky places going, "Is that you?"

He was tired, though. He was going to eat whatever was in the fridge. If he could stay awake, he was gonna go into Myrna Bustamante's backyard later and steal the Legos in the sandbox. But he also had to watch out for his toy cars. They were gonna be delivered. Good old Little Angel. Goody, good. Cars and buses and pigeons.

"Wild thing," he said, "you make my heart sing."

❧

Giovanni had all that dude's drug money wadded up in his pocket. He tried to fist-bump Lalo, but his father was limp in a lawn chair, staring at his splayed feet.

"Later, Pops," he said. "You might wanna get out of town for a minute."

Lalo raised one finger.

"Whatever," Gio said.

❧

Minnie and La Gloriosa cleaned the tables. They had never seen so many paper plates. Where had they come from? Red plastic cups.

"Just keep working," La Glori said. "Don't let your mamá do anything."

Perla had joined the card game.

"Daddy and Tío are fighting," Minnie said.

"Men are idiots."

None of the comadres argued with her.

❧

Back in the bedroom:

"I'm done," Little Angel said. He got up to go.

"Sit."

"No."

"Carnal! Sit down for a minute. Please."

Rage and sorrow, rage and sorrow.

"I am trying to walk out of your house."

Walk through the house, away from this barrio, away from this family. For good this time. No big brother, no beautiful niece, no relatives, no Gloriosa, no damned father. No history. Just that big ridiculous cop car outside. Just that. Just drive. He would drive to Seattle. He would drive north until he could turn right and vanish into the western American mountains. He would bury himself in snow. He would keep going north. He would drive to the end of the highway, to settle in Homer, Alaska. To watch eagles work the shore. To write poems. He could meet a poet there—a woman with great hair and good coffee. He would get so far it would take a week for a postcard to get out. But he couldn't even step away from the foot of Big Angel's bed.

"If I go," he finally said, "I will never come back."

"Sit. Down. Carnal," Big Angel said.

Slowly, he sat.

"You already left us forever," his brother said. "I had to die to bring you home." Big Angel started taking his pills. Noisy little gulps of tamarind juice. "I destroyed my own family," the patriarch said.

Little Angel tried to tune it out. He didn't want to listen. But he did. What more was there? What more could anyone take with them at the end of the day?

Big Angel started into it all. Braulio. Chentebent—that part of the narrative carefully redacted. Struggles with his mother. At last, from parts unknown, El Yndio entered the family ring.

"I never understood Yndio, Carnal. I was...bad to him. I was trying to be a father for the first time, but who did I have to copy? Our father. I was trying to be him. And goddamn it, I am not him. Sorry, God.

"All that trouble between us. Why did I never learn to say I was sorry? What is wrong with me?

"Do not answer that, cabrón.

"We were strong males, Yndio and me. We fought for Perla's love—I see that. He must have thought I was an invader. Taking over his perfect world. I thought he was a spoiled little bastard. Mama's boy.

"And, you know, he was strange.

"I know you gave him those records. That crazy music. You, cabrón, it was you! No, it's okay, Carnal. I understand everything. Yndio wanted to be famous. He wanted to be a star.

I told him he was crazy. Acting? Singing? What? Long hair? What kind of man did that? Men earned money and made a home with a good woman and had babies. Men were serious. That's what I thought. I told him to be an accountant. Don't laugh. An accountant, or maybe manage a 7-Eleven.

"He said, 'What about Grandpa? Playing piano all night!' 'Yes,' I said. 'But that's like a hobby. After his real work is done.' Yndio was furious. 'My life is not a hobby!' he said, and he knocked over his chair when he left the room. So dramatic.

"And then he moved away for good. I don't even know where he lived. He had those tattoos, and he dressed all in white. That hair. My father didn't like that. Our father. They didn't get along.

"Well, a year later, Yndio got a job, singing at a nightclub! In Hillcrest! Not far from Dad's place—that Rip Room, where he played piano. A place called Lips.

"He gave us an invitation. What did we know? I made Perla go. It was Perla and Dad and me. We got all dressed up. It was our boy's first big performance. No, listen! Yes, sure—strange people there. But I thought, you know—they're like you. Crazy hippie people. Gringos. Lipstick on boys, I don't know—leather. Stop laughing. We had drinks. Perla was scared of all the crazy people. I think this was why our father had a stroke. It's not funny.

"Yes—Yndio came out on stage. His new name was Blackie Angel. Another pinche Angel! He came out from behind this silver curtain. As Cher. He was in some kind of bikini bottom, and he had chi-chis! This is not funny. He had makeup and feathers in his hair, and he was singing Cher songs! He came up to our father and humped him! Jajaja! Ah, cabrón! Papá just sat there, sipping his drink. Like nothing happened. Yndio rubbing his crotch on Father's shoulder. Then Yndio turned around and shook his nalgas at us. It was worse than Mamá and the parrot! And then he grabbed his chi-chis. I knew what he was doing. He squeezed them and pointed them at us. He was shooting milk all over us in his mind. Carnal! He was washing us out the door.

"Poor Perla kept staring at his panties. She grabbed her heart and shouted, 'Where is his pee-pee! He lost his pee-pee!' Yndio leaned over and whispered in his mother's ear, 'I tucked it in, Ma.'

"Stop it! You're making me laugh."

✑

The next day, Big Angel had found his father dead on the bathroom floor.

"Heart attack. You knew that. But now you know why."

Big Angel was so somber, Little Angel couldn't help himself. "Didn't Dad like Cher?" he said.

They bent over laughing, though Big Angel cursed him and said, "Not funny!"

"Kinda funny."

Big Angel hit him with a pillow. Winded, he took another sip of his tamarind, then put his glass down. He was smiling insanely, leering, his feverish eyes like dartboard targets. Filled with fury.

"Carnal," said Little Angel, wiping his eyes, "that is the best story I ever heard."

"I tried to be good to my boy."

All Little Angel could do was nod; he didn't want to start laughing again.

"Tell me," Big Angel said. "Did I do anything good in your life?"

"You gave me the books." It was instantaneous.

"Yes. All the books—that was pretty good. I gave you good ones."

"And bad ones."

"True. But all books are good, man. Imagine no books."

"I still have them."

"Ah. Bueno. But what was the best thing I ever did? Aside from giving you books?"

Little Angel rubbed his eyes with his palms and ran his hands over his forehead to smooth his hair back. "Well," he said. "You called me one morning and told me to get ready because you were coming for me. And to tell my mom I'd be gone all day. It was mysterious. It's not like you came for me all the time. You wouldn't tell me why, but you told me to bring a coat. So you showed up in a while. You had La Minnie with you. She was just a little kid. And we drove off. You had ham-and-cheese sandwiches."

"On bolillos!" Big Angel said.

"Right. Ham and cheese on bolillos with chiles and mayo. And Mexican Pepsis."

"Mexican's better."

"And we drove east, to the mountains. It had snowed up there. Living in San Diego, we never saw snow. So you said, 'We are going to make a snowball.'"

"And we did!"

"That's what we did. Yep. There was about an inch of snow. We got out of the car and scraped up some and threw it at Minnie. She started crying. Then we got back in the car and drove home."

They laughed some more.

"Yes," Big Angel said. "Good. Now tell me the worst thing I ever did."

"Come on."

"Tell me, Brother. Was it the beach?"

"No."

"What?"

"It was the year Dad died. We had nothing. I know, I know—it didn't match your suffering, blah, blah, blah. And we had nothing. No car, no money. No food. Kind of a theme, isn't it? And it was Christmas, and Mom didn't know how we'd afford presents or a Christmas dinner. And you called. That was your thing, I guess. Surprise phone calls."

Big Angel sighed. "I know."

"You said, 'Don't worry about a thing. I am your big brother.'"

"Yes, I know."

"'I am the patriarch.'"

"Yes."

"You said, 'We will come for you Christmas morning.' You fucking said you'd treat us to a huge Mexican Christmas fiesta. Family."

"Yes."

"'Don't buy a ham,' you said. 'Don't worry. Perla is making the best feast you ever ate.' And Mom cried. She was so relieved."

"I am sorry."

"No, wait. You wanted it, so here it comes. You never showed up. We got up and played Christmas music all morning and drank coffee and promised each other we'd give presents next year. Yeah? And you never came."

"I am so sorry."

"We had some bread in the house, so we ate some toast. Marmalade—Mom always had marmalade. She thought she was French. I hate marmalade. It wasn't much, but we were saving room, we told each other, for Perla's great meal. And when five o'clock came around, I finally called. I was like, 'When are you coming?' Do you know what you said?"

"Yes. I said I was too busy to come get you."

"You said that it was *too much trouble* to come get us."

Big Angel sat staring at the wall. "What did you do?"

"I dug in the couch. I shook out my bank. I raided Mom's purse. Then I walked a mile to 7-Eleven and bought a little canned ham and a can of corn. Jesus! How Dickensian."

"Thank you," Big Angel said. "For telling me."

"Ancient history."

"I don't think so."

"It's all right. You're a good man."

"I am a bad man."

Little Angel turned to him. "I forgive you."

Big Angel sobbed once.

"Hey! Look at how many people love you. Look at everybody you have helped."

"Men who do good deeds only wish to atone for their sins."

Minnie came in, followed by Perla. "Why are you crying, Daddy?"

He picked at his blanket and avoided her eyes.

"Mi amor," Perla said. "Are you done fighting?"

"Who won?" Minnie asked.

Both men raised their hands.

"Ya es hora!" Perla said. "Let's get cake."

"Time for the cake, Daddy."

He put up a trembling hand. "Just a minute." *Yust.*

"Flaco," Perla said.

"Flaca—un minuto, sí?"

The women reluctantly exited the room.

Big Angel struggled upright from his pillows. "I did worse," he said. "I have so much filth in my past."

"Stop."

"I snuck into your house with MaryLú. You were in kindergarten. Papá and your mother were working. We broke all her jewelry with a hammer."

"What?"

"And then we cut up your mother's nice clothes with scissors."

Little Angel's mouth hung open.

"We left it all for her to find."

"You—"

"Yes. And Papá had silver dimes and quarters in cigar tubes. I took them."

"I—"

"Tell me how good a man I am now."

Parrot

The brothers lay side by side, shuffling through so many memories. So many imperfect scenes. It felt as though they had opened a box of old photographs, each of the pictures torn and tattered. But for all their lives, they had hoarded one perfect memory. One joyous, inappropriate memory that they kept as their own secret like a holy relic. Now seemed the moment they needed it most.

"Remember the parrot?"

It was decades ago. Big Angel had been in possession of his green card for only six months, and he was already exhausted. Being American was like getting a good shellacking—whatever that meant. He'd heard it, and it sounded right for how he was feeling. These people did things all day long. They were frantic. They ate lunch in their cars and never had a siesta. They even went to church in their cars. Or on their TVs. And they were making him embarrassed about being Mexican. It was creeping into his mind. He didn't know what to do with himself. He was self-conscious about everything. His pants were cheap and outmoded. His posture was somehow slack and not heroic like the mad posture of the marching gringos. He hung his head too much. He wore white socks.

He was turning gray inside. Like boiled meat, he thought. He could not find energy in himself and had taken to drinking black coffee all day. Until his stomach felt sour and his abdomen sloshed nauseatingly as he walked. But he never walked. He sped among herds of cars up and down the endless ribbons of California highways, cursing and chain-smoking. For that was his other vice: Pall Malls. Like his father. But consumed at an industrial pace. Smoked quickly, and the next butt lit from the glowing cherry at the end of his previous butt. He even tried to hold his smokes like Americans did. He held them between his thumb and middle finger. He'd seen Esteep McQueen do it in a movie. And he used that infamous F-U finger to flick the spent cigarette away like a shot rocket.

And he was ashamed of his father. What a beaner. Making believe he was some piano master on Ed Sullivan. Moved away to white suburbs up north of the border. Living with neighbors named Wally and Ralph and Ginny and Floyd. White faces turning red every time he drove up there. He was pretty sure of that. His father had married a woman from Indiana named Betty, for God's sake. And that little brother. Riding his Stingray bike around in dirt lots and jumping it off cardboard ramps like some pudgy daredevil. Stole his name.

And now this ghastly development. Once a month, Mother deigned to cross the border for her regular inspection of her children's lives. Angel had to drive down there in his Rambler and collect her. He was the eldest—it was his job. But he and his mother…It was complicated. He hated these visits. And he had lost his taste for Tijuana. It was all embarrassing. Mamá América. Who would name somebody América but Mexicans?

And his damned father had gotten it into his head that "Little" Angel was too much of an Americano. He was so gringofied that he needed regular doses of Mexico to save his soul. So somehow Big Angel had to first drive all the way north to Clairemont to pick up the kid. Double hell. An hour on I-5, going nowhere. The kid somehow thought his big brother would love stopping at Winchell's Donuts every time to buy him chocolate donuts. *Not really*, he wanted to say. But he remembered those many Saturdays watching the kid's lonesome fantasy life with his stupid television shows and his comic books.

Father would drive down in a day or two to collect Little Angel. He didn't fool Big Angel one bit. Big Angel knew his father too well. He was coming down every month to sniff around at Mother. He could not believe that he was denied. He could not abide the thought that he could not creep into her bloomers once again, at will, and enjoy what he had once enjoyed whenever he wanted. And to her credit, Mother stayed in her back bedroom or went to César's house instead of dealing with him.

Big Angel lit his fresh cigarette with the end of the previous one and shot that butt out into the air as if trying to light a brush fire along the road. He steered with his knees as he engaged in this complex operation.

⚭

Tijuana then was not anything like the modern technological mecca it has become. No fancy discos or IMAX cinemas. No river channel. No art scene or microbreweries or cafés serving French roasts. There were donkeys spray-painted with zebra stripes that made Little Angel ridiculously happy, though. They still lurked on certain corners, wearing sombreros and withstanding tourists taking selfies. Years later, it seemed the only constants in Tijuana were the Border Patrol and the burros.

They entered and immediately descended into the murky funk of the Tijuana River—a broad muck-choked alley beneath rattling wooden bridges. On either side of the road, the notorious slum called Cartolandia. Now, eradicated. Then, an expanse of hovels made of scrap and tarps and cartons.

Big Angel paid no attention to any of it. He was trying to formulate his plan of attack. How would he take charge in the USA? He had a family to run.

They pulled up before Mother's yellow house perched on the edge of a dirt hill, overlooking some dusty park and, in the distance, Cine Reforma, where sometimes Little Angel conned his brother into suffering through Mexican vampire and Mil Máscaras vs. various monsters movies. The top of Mother's wall was glittering with embedded shards of shattered Pepsi bottles to shred the arms of imagined gangsters hoping to creep in and steal her underwear.

She was in her room, packing and repacking her overnight bag. Vicks VapoRub was the main commodity she smuggled across the border. And in the living room, the green parrot raised psychotic maelstroms of noise in its domed cage. Everybody in La Paz owned a green parrot. They all had names. They had named this bird after themselves: Periquito de La Cruz. Big Angel thought: *He's hardly a "little parrot."* That bird was fat. It would announce its presence all day with the monomania of unbridled ego. "Periquito, periquito, periquito *Cruz!*" This last delivered in a screech that rang in Big Angel's ears.

"Shut up," Big Angel said. He would have lit up another smoke right then, but his mother forbade cigarettes in the house. And then Little Angel. Fifth graders being almost as smart as parrots. He joined in, shouting at the parrot.

"Cruz!"

"*Cruz!*"

"Cruz!"

"*Cruz!*"

Fortunately, Mamá América came forth and observed the scene. "Ah, the bird," she said.

"Mother," said Big Angel. "Let's go." He was eager to escape before the two idiots started their duet again.

"Son," she said. "Have you noticed there are no parrots on the other side?" El otro lado—the other side.

He said he hadn't noticed.

"All those Mexicans, and no green parrots."

"Gringos like canaries."

"I have a parakeet," Little Angel offered, to be helpful. "He's called Peppy."

"I've been thinking," she said. "I think I will start a business."

Oh no, Big Angel thought. These old women with their negocios. These women would find things to sell, or they would sew something, or they would cook tamales. Big Angel's favorite definition of *Mexican* was "Out of nothing, food."

"I will import parrots to the Mexicans in exile. Pay a few pesos here, sell them for a hundred times what I paid."

Big Angel grabbed her bag. "Sorry, Madre. But, no. This is illegal. You are not allowed to carry parrots into the United States."

Both brothers should have taken note.

"We shall see" is all she said.

☙

Long before they got to the border crossing, Mother spoke again. "Take me to the fruit market."

"You can't take fruit either, Mother."

"Who said anything about fruit?"

Big Angel cast a fretful glance back at Little Angel, then took the detour east.

The fruit market was in a warren of old buildings surrounding a parking lot. The ground floors of these edifices housed soup counters and tortilla shops, candy sellers and taco stands. And, of course, fruit. Fruit of all kinds. Watermelons and lemons. Papayas and mangos. Bananas, stalks of sugar cane. And vegetables: eggplants like dinosaur eggs, jicama, chiles. The parking area was clogged with trucks at all hours and hustling men with rags tied on their heads, moving produce. The blacktop was sticky with a centimeter-thick coat of ancient fruit mashed and sunbaked and remashed over the years. And in the far corner, to Big Angel's horror: a bird vendor.

"Madre, no," he said.

She marched away.

"Are we in trouble, Angel?" the kid asked.

"I think maybe so," Big Angel replied in English.

"A green parrot, young man," she said to the bird seller as she fished a few colorful pesos out of her pocketbook. "If you would be so kind. Un periquito bien mancito."

"What did she say?" Little Angel said to his brother.

"Tame," Big Angel said. "Mother wants a tame parrot." He lit a Pall Mall and started to slouch as if the sun were melting him.

The helpful fellow produced a blinking little green parrot that sat astride his finger mildly and turned its head in every direction, observing the activity all around them. He climbed upon América's extended finger and fluffed his feathers. Big Angel puffed his cigarette and observed. Mother handed the man his money and began to compliment the bird in the faux-sweet baby talk all Mexican women used to delight babies and small dogs.

"Ay qué guapo el periquito! Ay, mira nomás qué bonito!"

The little bird grew proud and stuck out its chest and preened vainly.

As she spoke, Mother reached into her purse and produced a small bottle with an eyedropper on top.

The brothers nudged each other.

She unscrewed the cap with one hand, fingers working like a spider. She squeezed the bulb atop the dropper and lifted it. They saw it was full of clear liquid.

She tapped the parrot's bill. "Andale, pajarito," she cooed. "Abre el pico, mi rey." The parrot opened its beak, and she delivered four drops into it. "Tequila," she noted, screwing the cap back on the bottle.

The three gathered males watched as if hypnotized.

The bird swayed. He wobbled his head. He lay his head over. The bird was wasted.

She laid it in her free hand, where it might have snored on its back. She reached again into her infernal pocketbook and produced a sheet of newspaper. Little Angel would for some reason remember that it featured jai alai scores. And she laid the sheet on the seller's bench and the drunk parrot upon it. With both hands, she then wrapped the bird tightly, forming a paper cone. Tail in the pointy end, green head sticking out of the open wider end, like a parrot sno-cone.

Mother América retrieved the cone and, with a self-satisfied flourish, astounded them all by pulling open the neckline of her sensible blue dress. She took the somnolent bird and inserted it into her cleavage. Big Angel had never noticed his mother's endowment before. Suddenly, she seemed to be blessed with an expanse of pillowy flesh. And she tucked the parrot into that cleavage, adjusting herself as it sank from view, finishing the operation by using her thumb on its head to get it well positioned in the shadows.

She adjusted her bust and said, "Let's go to San Diego, boys!"

☙

The border in those days was different. No huge wall. No drones, no infrared towers. What awaited the de La Cruz family was a raggedy line of wooden booths manned by Immigration and Customs agents sitting on stools in the heat, bored to despair as they breathed limitless clouds of car exhaust, and more cynical every day as every single driver said, "No, I don't have liquor in my trunk!"

Big Angel pulled up in his Rambler.

"Be calm," he said. Mother beside him with her pocketbook in her lap. Little Angel in back, toying with his Baby Bobby matchbook to distract himself from his absolute terror that they were about to go to federal prison for life. Gangster Grandma seemed as serene as a Tibetan monk.

All Big Angel could see of the agent was his belly. It was a good belly. It floated outside Big Angel's window. It turned away once, as the agent eyed the following vehicle. Then swung back.

"Papeles, amigo?" the voice said.

"Yes, sir," Big Angel replied. "Green card." He held up his magic ticket to the USA.

The agent bent down, and a red face appeared. He glared at América. "Papeles?"

She held up her passport. "Pasaporte."

The red face swung back to Little Angel. "How 'bout you, bud?"

"U.S. citizen," he cried.

The agent patted the top of the car and rose, his belly back in the window. Little Angel was afraid the big man would yank out his pistola and blast them all.

"Okay," the belly said. It started to turn away. "Have a nice day."

Which is when the parrot awoke. The belly was three-quarters of the way turned when the parrot announced its displeasure. "*Qwock!*" it screamed.

The belly froze.

"*Kwee-yock!*"

The belly turned back to them and stopped. Big Angel stared straight ahead, his jaw muscles furiously rippling in his cheek.

"*Yeeeeek!*"

The agent's big red face lowered itself to the window and gawked.

Mother América turned to him with the blandest expression on her face. "Isn't that strange?" she said. "I wonder what it could be?"

And then her bustline began to move. The agent's eyes bugged out. Suddenly, with further mutterings and screeches, the parrot wriggled out of her cleavage, its head rotating as it appeared.

"How interesting," Mother América said.

The angry and hungover parrot burst forth and cursed them, then leapt out the open window and flew away. All of them — government agent, Mexican nationals, and the U.S. citizen in the back seat — watched it flutter north, across the border.

Las Mañanitas

The women came back in and began to wrestle Big Angel into his chair.

"Forgive me," he said as they wheeled him away.

Little Angel caught up to him. "It doesn't matter, hermano," he said.

"It matters."

Minnie rolled Big Angel away and parked him in the kitchen. She rushed out to the yard to collect partiers.

Big Angel grinned through the pain of crossing his arms behind his head so he could strike a nonchalant pose. "It's funny, Carnal. I used to starve, you know? I used to want to eat all the time. And when we got here to this country, I ate. All the time. I got fat! That's why Perla started to call me Flaco. Funny."

Little Angel could see Minnie's shadow on the patio.

"Pero sabes qué?" Big Angel said. "Now I am starving again. I hate to eat. I eat to feed the cancer. The pills make me sick. My stomach hurts all the time. But I dream of food. Like I'm ten again. Really. I never dream about making love, but I dream about carnitas and tortillas."

Minnie's shadow moved away.

"Well...okay. I dream about sex all the time," he admitted. "These are the great thoughts of Miguel Angel. Pig meat in a tortilla. And nalgas. For when you write a book about me."

"I should."

"You should, yes."

"Pinche Angel," Little Angel said.

"Take me outside," Big Angel said. "I don't want to do it in here."

Little Angel maneuvered him to the big door.

"I was always tremendous," Big Angel announced.

"Let's go."

"Tell me," Big Angel continued, ignoring him. "Pato said my father cooked for you. Yes? What was his best dish?"

"Chili."

"Chili? Like gringo chili?" Big Angel was appalled.

"I called it heart-attack chili."

"Más. Detalles, por favor." He wanted the details.

"He started with a pan and lots of oil," Little Angel said. "He diced and fried red onions. Fried them till they turned clear. Then he poured in a bag of rice."

"Rice!"

"He fried the rice and put in tomatoes and garlic. Fried that till it was clear too, then poured in water and tomato sauce."

"Spanish rice."

"Right. That would simmer, and he'd get another pan."

"Ah." Big Angel was flushed. It was as if he were hearing a pornographic yarn.

"He chopped more onions, then diced and fried five pork chops."

Minnie came back in. "Daddy!"

Big Angel held up a finger. Pointed at a chair. She sighed and sat down. He nodded for his brother to continue.

"Once the chops were cooked, and the Spanish rice was done—you had to pour water in over and over and let it boil away—he put beans and all those other ingredients in a pot. Refried beans. But wait. That wasn't all. After that, he chopped up a pound of Monterey Jack cheese."

"No," said Angel.

"No," said Minnie.

"Oh yes. And peppers. Then he stirred the whole thing for an hour. Until the cheese had vanished into the cement. You couldn't eat more than a couple of forkfuls, honestly. Except him. He could eat a huge plate. And the next day, he ate it cold. He put it on toast, in tortillas, ate it right from the pot."

Big Angel clapped his hands. "Mija," he said to Minnie. "That was your grandfather. Un hombre tremendo!"

The brothers basked in love for their dad.

"Recess is over, boys," she said. She gestured, and they rolled.

"Forgive me," Big Angel said.

"You do the same," Little Angel replied.

Into the yard.

"Hey," Little Angel called. "What's in the box you gave me?" He gestured back toward the bedroom.

"It's what I was going to give you that day," said Big Angel. "That Christmas."

Minnie rolled him away.

"Go look."

Little Angel wasn't going to open the box. To hell with Miguel Angel. To hell with all of this. He opened the box. Inside, a signed first edition of Raymond Chandler, *The Big Sleep*.

The people in the backyard started to cheer.

8:30 p.m.

Little Angel stood at the back of the crowd, clinging to the shadows by the kitchen door. The revelers had diminished in number. Pato was snoring on the couch inside. Some of the ladies had laid their coats over him. His cell phone, unheeded, pinged over and over with texts from Manila.

Gauzy scarves of cloud slipped across the moon. Dog barks echoed in the canyons. Little Angel listened to the crickets like a haiku poet, reaching out to them as if they were lovers whispering hope.

Big Angel was tinier than ever, sitting in his chair, gazing at these looming people. Lalo was sprawled in the lawn chair beside his Pops. His head lolled, and he sometimes lifted his chin and sneered and then let it drop again. Big Angel stared at his son with the inscrutable grin burning on his face.

Lalo opened his eyes and stared at his father. He let out a cry. "Daddy!" He started to weep.

"What, mijo?"

"Daddy, I'm so sorry for what I done."

Big Angel reached as far as he could. "Whatsa matter, mijo? Come here."

Lalo leaned over and put his face against his father's bird chest. "I'm so sorry."

"You're okay, you're okay," Big Angel murmured.

"I been so bad."

"You are a good boy, Lalo. You are my good boy." Big Angel kissed the top of his son's head, and Lalo fell back into his squealing aluminum seat. "Hey," Big Angel said. "I like your tattoo."

Really? Little Angel thought. *It's over? This is it? Everything ends like this?* He didn't want it to be over. Not like this. Wasn't there supposed to be some climax? What novel, what opera, ended in birthday wishes and an early sleep? He knew if the party ended, his brother would be gone. He leaned on the wall and crossed his arms. His eyes stung.

The women came out of the kitchen, bearing the cakes. Minnie, Perla, Gloriosa, and Lupita. Four candles blazing: a wax seven and zero on each cake. Great uproar, applause. Children and little dogs jumped around Big Angel's wheelchair as the cakes approached. He folded his hands over his belly. Was his head bobbing?

The women put the big cakes on one of the folding tables, and Minnie wheeled her father to the table. He looked around at the partiers with a wry little eyebrow lift, leaned forward in his wheelchair, drew in a great rattling breath, and blew out one of the candles. It took four tries before he got them all out. Then Big Angel fell back breathlessly as they applauded him. Perla fussed over him as if he'd just won a 5K foot race.

And the spirit moved. Of course it did—any birthday party had a "Happy Birthday" song. Any Mexican birthday party had the Mexican birthday song, "Las Mañanitas." There was no obvious signal, but the whole bunch started singing as one.

> *Estas son las mañanitas*
> *que cantaba el Rey David*
> *las muchachas bonitas*
> *se las cantamos así.*

They moved toward him, tidal, as if the moon drew them. Closer and tighter. A whirl, a protection of bodies. Big Angel vanished from sight in the center of the flood.

And they threw their heads back and sang.

Despierta, Angel, despierta,
mira que ya amaneció,
ya los pajaritos cantan
la luna ya se metió.

But it was apparently not loud enough for them. They started over, unleashing gusts like Little Angel had never heard. They roared, they shouted, they launched operatic and mariachi voices, and they lost notes in sobs halfway through the lines.

Little Angel hung back, standing in the music, watching his brother. He had never really heard the rest of the song, yet everybody there seemed to know it.

Qué linda está la mañana
en que vengo a saludarte
venimos todos con gusto
y placer a felicitarte.

They went on and on, and when they finished singing, they applauded hard and long and kept clapping as they parted, and Little Angel could see him again. They clapped and whistled until Big Angel lifted his hands like a spent boxer and clutched them over his head and shook them and mouthed, Gracias. He actually had tears in his eyes. The sparkle of them pierced everyone like needles.

Little Angel put his hand over his own eyes.

Big Angel was staring at his brother. He didn't want Little Angel to know he was feeling sorry for him. He ate some cake.

So that's it, Big Angel thought. He had got what he wanted. And now it was over. Everything. Over. He had thought it would be more, hadn't he? Pinche Angel. He chuckled at himself. He had thought he would be healed.

He couldn't find his father's or his mother's ghosts in the crowd, so he watched his little brother. He couldn't take his eyes off him. Poor Little Angel, he thought. He had no idea what life was going to do to him. He wouldn't find it in books.

La Minnie over there. Lalo slumping around—he wished Lalo would stand up like a soldier like he used to. La Gloriosa was somewhere. He could feel her even when he couldn't see her. She was sacred and didn't know it. When her wings unfurled, they would be wide and dark, almost black, and she would fly above all the flames when the world ended. And there was his poor Flaca. Cleaning the kitchen. He had failed his wife as well. If there were a chance to renegotiate with God, he would lobby for more delight for Perla. Maybe Dave could swing one last novena. Or tell him what prayer might move God.

But.

No.

He shook his head. *Too late, baby. Estamos jodidos.* He and God already had that talk. By golly. Tonight was the deal he'd made at the end of it all. *Goddamn it—sorry, God.* They never warned you to never make a deal with God.

Every man dies with secrets. Big Angel was certain a happy man was a man who died with the worst things safely hidden. A life was a long struggle to come to terms with things and to keep some things from others. This was his deepest secret, and it wasn't even a sin. He just didn't want anybody to know he couldn't get off the floor.

"Oh yeah," he said out loud. "You put me on my knees."

He was in a time bubble—the party rumbled around him, but he was not there. He was back in his room a few months ago. There had been much carrying on in his house that day. It was, ironically, he thought, a Sunday. Just like today.

Dave had just left after eating all the food in the kitchen and wheeling him back to bed and tucking him in. Kids and dogs and Lalo and everyone outside, yelling. *Why*, he remembered thinking, *is everybody yelling all the time?* Laughing and shouting. He wanted some water, but nobody could hear him. He felt around and couldn't find his cell phone on the bed.

"Hey!" he called, his voice muffled and reedy. "Minnie!"

He smacked the mattress. It was time for his pills. He scrabbled around on his bedside table, popped open one bottle, and gulped his pill with a mouthful of flat, warm Coke. It made him want to throw up. But where was the other bottle? It was definitely time for two pills.

He looked around. *Oh great.* The bottle was up on top of the dresser a few feet from his bed. *What asshole put it there?* He'd scold somebody for that.

"Hey!" He reached for it, but he knew damn well he couldn't reach that far. "Help me, pues!"

Nothing.

He cursed and fussed and knew—he knew perfectly well—that somebody would wander down the hall when they remembered him. Somebody would bring him water. Somebody would fetch his pills for him. But he wanted what he wanted when he wanted it.

He gritted his teeth, put one skinny, blotched leg down, and winced when the cold floor sent a long needle of pain up his calf. Right from the ball of his foot to his knee. "Ching!" he muttered. He braced himself with his left arm and reached with his right, and his free foot hovered in the air above the floor; he knew that was a tactical error. The geometry was way off, and as soon as his braced arm started to jackhammer from the strain of holding him up, and just as he reached across that immense gap between mattress and plywood dresser with his other hand, and just as the pain of the cold went ahead and shot up into his balls, he fell.

He landed on his knees. Hard. His head banged into the edge of the dresser. The parchment skin at his temple tore, and cool blood made its instant presence felt all over his face. It was greasy.

He wasn't worried about the wound. He was worried that he'd shattered his knees, and he whimpered and cried. He thought cancer had hurt, but this was more vivid, and he could not get up, so the pain screamed louder and louder in his crushed joints as he ground them into the hard floor. Then the blood dribbled to the floor between his hands. He cried and yelled.

"Help! Oye! Me caí de la cama! Help me!"

Now, Angel, he told himself. *We're stuck. Think.*

He reached up, grabbed a fistful of the sheet, and tried to pull himself up. He dropped back to the floor, where he knelt with his ass in the air and his hands on either side of his bowed head. Who was he kidding? He had no muscles left in his arms. He was truly trapped—jammed between the bed and the dresser. Unable even to move his knees under him to try to lever himself up. He pulled the collar of his T-shirt up to his temple and tried to stop the bleeding. His blood looked almost blue to him.

"God," he said, "this hurts."

God said nothing.

"I need some help," he offered.

God might have been taking another call.

He looked around for ghosts. But he had been abandoned to his fate. For a moment, he was afraid Chentebent might come through the wall, grinning. The pain made him tremble all over.

"All right," he said.

He laid his head on the floor. He'd wait. Someone would come. He was Big Angel. He was not going to die like this.

But what if he did?

What if nobody came until bedtime? He would be gone for sure. His body couldn't take this. His heart already felt like it had been hit by a hammer.

"God? Are you there?"

And it hit him then: *You are on your knees, pendejo. Confess.* God had put him there, and there would be no getting up until he had done what he needed to do.

"I am dirty," he began. "I am so dirty."

It took him three hours.

Lalo was on his way to the back room to play Grand Theft Auto when he found Big Angel. Lalo had a little buzz on, nothing too rad—couple beers, couple shots. He stared at his old man down there like he was praying to Mecca or something.

"Yo, Pops," he said. "Why you sleepin' on the floor, G?"

He picked up his father, laid him on the bed, and covered him up. He didn't notice the crust of blood on Big Angel's face.

He wandered back out of the room, grabbed the video-game controller, and started capping fools and crashing cars.

Big Angel slept, exhausted beyond the agony in his knees. And God gave him a gift of revelation: he dreamed the farewell party. He saw it all. He awoke in the morning to Perla's cries of terror. She had seen the blood on his face and on the pillow, and they burst from the house, dragging him against his will to the emergency room, and the whole time he was refusing to die because of this very event. These cakes. This singing.

He exited the time bubble that had held him. Everyone was laughing and talking and still eating and throwing cake at each other. And Big Angel stared at Little Angel, feeling immense pity. *You have never been put on your knees,* he thought. *And if you don't do it for yourself, God will slam you to the floor and make you square your account. Just wait, Baby Brother.*

I am so sorry.

Apparently, all this noise hadn't awakened Lalo, who slid farther down in his seat near Pops, hung out his feet, and snored. He rubbed his face with the back of his hand.

"Chuds."

❧

Outside, the sleek white Audi idled at the mouth of the driveway. El Yndio sat behind the wheel. His new tattoo read: PRODIGAL. All down the inside of his right forearm.

He checked his phone. There was a voice message from Moms. "Mijo—ven. Por Dios. Come inside." He didn't delete it.

His window was open. He listened to them sing to his father. How many times had he driven up and down this street, monitoring the family? How many parties? How many arguments had he heard? How many door slams?

Every year he had stayed away made the wall between them feel higher, unscalable. It was almost impossible to admit that he was embarrassed by his own behavior. How could he ever admit that he had exiled himself?

He wanted to get out, he really did. He wanted to get out of the car and walk through the crowd and see Minnie and his mother fall to their knees when they saw him. Wanted to flaunt his long hair and muscles and expensive white jeans. He wanted to stride up to his father and forgive him.

And be forgiven.

That was the secret Yndio didn't dare speak to anyone, and hardly acknowledged even to himself. He had walked as far away from Big Angel as he could, living a life Big Angel could not understand and would never condone. It felt like defiance. But like every true prodigal, Yndio's deepest fear was that his father would close the door in his face.

He hung his head on the rim of the window and listened to the roar of the last lines of the song. And the barking of the neighborhood dogs. He wanted to say good-bye. But he could not. The window went up silently. The white car sat quiet in the night.

ص

It was over, they were telling themselves. Well, except for the cakes. Los kekis, pues. Everybody wanted cake. None of them more than Big Angel.

He had two plates before him and a plastic fork in each hand, and he laid into the white and the dark with a furious joy. He had frosting on his chin and even on one cheek, and he didn't care. Perla tried to wipe his face, but he shrugged her napkin away with his shoulder and gestured at La Gloriosa to put another slice on each plate.

"They won't call you Flaco anymore," she said. "They will call you Gordo."

"Good," he said and gestured at his plates. "Más."

Minnie supervised the various girls and morras and rucas to help her distribute droopy plates to everybody. "No more food fights, you brats," she warned.

Perla's great cutting knife was so covered in clots of frosting that she took it to the kitchen for Lupita to wash.

Big Angel looked up at La Gloriosa and said, in Spanish, "I always loved you."

She flushed. Turned away. She gave thanks that none of these kids really understood Spanish. "Love you too," she said lightly. She excused herself and backed away and walked out of the yard. All she wanted to do was breathe.

∂ρ

When Little Angel came for his second piece of cake, he sat beside his brother. They looked at Lalo, who was laughing in his sleep. They shook their heads.

"You know I always loved you," Big Angel said.

"Back at you."

"Don't go back to Seattle."

"I have to. I have work. I have a life."

"Who will take my place?"

"Not me."

"You're the only one. Lalo's not a patriarch. Yndio's gone. Poor Pato—he can't do it. I choose you."

Little Angel glanced at him and shook his head. "Maybe it's time for a matriarch," he said and pointed at La Minnie. "She's the boss now," he said.

Big Angel tipped his head and stared up at his daughter.

❧

La Gloriosa leaned on the garage door and stared up at the night sky.

The street was silent. She didn't recognize the glistening pearl car nosed onto the driveway. Nice. Not big enough, though.

She was talking to her son. She didn't want to be disturbed. He was up there. Guillermito. None of that "Joker" nonsense. She wished him a good night every night.

"Mamá loves you," she whispered.

❧

Yndio had decided to drive away again. He checked his rearview mirror. Copper pools of light seemed to float on the sidewalks and blacktop every twelve feet, receding toward the distant glittering border. Lily pads on a black river.

He noticed a lone man moving quickly toward the house. He watched the man cross the street, turn up the driveway, and head to the backyard. Before Yndio hit the ignition button to drive away again, he saw the man reach back and pull a pistol from the waistband of his pants.

"Oh hell no," Yndio said.

For the first time in ten years, he opened the door.

✐

The gunman stopped at the edge of the party. He had flipped up his collar to hide the tattoos on his face. Lalo, that puto, lived here. He stared hard at the crowd. He hadn't expected some birthday. But this was even better. He was going to do Lalo with his own gun in front of his whole family. Teach them all a little lesson in respect.

He even knew what he was going to say: *Here's how you spell payback.* He had to count it out on his fingers, wanted to make sure he had enough bullets for each letter of "payback."

The gunman was looking at Lalo. Bringing it hard. He had the dude's own .22 pressed against his thigh. He scoped all the raggedy-assed peeps in the yard, eating cake.

He was still burning with shame about the scene in the garage. There was no way to hold his head up with pride if he didn't do something about it. And it had to be personal.

Really? That's what he was going to say to Lalo as he pulled his gat. *Really, bitch?*

And a double tap right in the head. The rest in the chest. The partiers would freak, and he'd just walk fast right back out the gate. Be gone before they got it together enough to look for him or call the cops. Then Gio would come looking, but there'd be some surprises waiting for him.

He had no idea, and nobody in the crowd noticed, that Yndio was moving in the shadows, calculating the possibilities. Yndio knew that he could rush the dude and overpower him, but who would be hurt if the guy started to shoot? Yndio stared at Pops in his wheelchair and was shocked at how frail he looked. *What would you do?* he thought. How would Pops play this out?

The gunman stepped forward. Checked the old dude in the

wheelchair putting a hurt on the cake. And the other old dude beside him, just sitting there. Looking all yuppie, chocolate on his face. Sheeit. Both of those old-timers had little notebooks in their laps.

He brought the pistol around and cranked the body back and jacked a fresh round into the chamber. That cold sound stopped the party in an instant. Silence. All faces swung to him.

People started to see the gun. Repelled by its force, they instantly surged away from it. Chairs tipped over. Chickenshits ran. The whole yard clearing out.

Minnie looked up. She smiled a little and blew a strand of hair out of her face. "Wha—?" she said, then saw the gun. She should have been heroic. She wanted to be heroic. But she found herself scrambling backward. Anything to get distance between her and the pistol. In her rush, she slammed into Yndio, who silently grabbed her shoulders, moved her aside, and kept going forward.

Big Angel was leaning toward his brother, saying, "I wanted to see Seattle."

"Maybe you will."

The gunman held the pistol in both hands and kicked Lalo's foot. "Hey," he said.

The brothers looked up. No response from Lalo.

The dude turned the pistol on the Angels.

"Stay," he said. "Don't say shit." He kicked Lalo, hard, in the leg.

"Hey..." Lalo complained. His head lolled back, and he regarded the gunman through slit eyes. "Check yourself...puppet."

Big Angel started to smile. Oh my God. It was a miracle. This little asshole. A revelation. God had spoken. He had to remember to call Dave if he survived this. He knew in his crumbling bones that he would survive.

He saw his father. He saw Chentebent. He saw the sailor who had come to their yard seeking blood. He heard his father's voice as if the ghost of the old man were right behind him, the words he spat so many years ago. He saw his own end—not small, not wretched, but heroic. Vast. A legend that would never fade from his family's minds or lips. And he rose.

He held out his hand to Little Angel, not for help, but to keep him in place. He forced his way slowly out of his chair.

"What do you think you're doing?" he asked the man.

Instead of pulling the trigger like he knew he should, the gunman looked over and said, "Sit down, old man."

"Chinga tu madre."

How much disrespect was he supposed to take this day? These assholes were so mouthy, he was losing track. This had been the most ridiculous, messed up day of his life. This family. They were all crazy. And they all talked too much. The gunman's plan to regain his lost self-respect had all seemed so clear: kill Lalo with his own gun in front of his family. But then the old man had opened his mouth, and the gunman was confused. He hadn't come there to kill them all or he'd have brought more bullets. Thug life. Too much work.

"What did you say?" The pistol swung back to Big Angel.

Little Angel was caught in his seat as if pinned to it—staring in disbelief and confusion.

Big Angel was shaking all over, but shaking from pain and rage, not fear. "You heard me," he said. "You little shit."

Many of those left in the yard had never heard Big Angel swear.

He didn't grab for his wheelchair. Just rocked in place. Anchored to the pendejo with the gun by his wrathful gaze.

The gunman stared back at him. "Back off, grandpa," he said. "For reals." He shook his head and took fresh aim at Lalo's face. Made a disparaging sound.

But Big Angel was already moving. Slow. It was only two feet. Sliding glacier-like to the side, nearly tripping over his son's splayed feet, until he straddled Lalo and held his own body between his boy and this gangster trash.

All was silence.

"The fuck you doing, viejo?"

Big Angel still had a plastic fork in his hand.

Little Angel was seeing everything in the clearest detail. The fork was covered in black cake and dark frosting. And he saw Perla trying to break through the crowd. She was shouting, but there was no sound. And he saw Minnie staring in disbelief at this scene and at the white-clad beast approaching them.

Yndio?

Big Angel raised his fork at the pistolero and pointed it at him. They aimed at each other.

"Get out of my yard," Big Angel said.

The dude's gun wavered. "Get out my way, fool," he said. He glanced at Little Angel and back at the patriarch. "Dude," he said sideways. "You don't want gramps capped, you best sit his ass down now."

Big Angel snapped his fingers in the man's face. "Hey, look at me. If you want to shoot my boy, then shoot him. Go ahead."

"Say what?"

Big Angel smiled, showing all his teeth. It was the smile of a wolverine. The gunman had never encountered this before.

"But I'll rip your eye out with this little fork." Big Angel put his fingers on his sparrow-bone chest. "Maybe you better shoot me first. Shoot him through me, you little prick."

"What?"

"Shoot here. I'm dying anyway." He shrugged one shoulder, lips tugged down. Shrugging in Spanish. "Put the bullet through my heart. Right here. See? It'll come right out and hit Lalo." He patted his chest. "Kill us together. I'd like that."

"I'll do it."

"Do it!"

"I'll do it, old man."

"Good! Do me a favor. Right there. I won't feel a thing."

"Daddy!" Minnie cried.

The dude looked over his shoulder. The crowd was starting to move again. Toward him. Some screaming old lady was knocking people out of her way, running from the kitchen. Oh shit—she had a huge knife in her hand.

"But if you don't kill me, I vow that I'll cut off your mother's head. And your father's head. I can't wait to do that. And I'll go bowling with them."

Perla's voice came from behind: "Son! Save your father!"

They were starting to shout at him. He swung the pistol at the crowd. Damn. He looked back at Gramps.

A man's voice: "Sorry I'm late to the party."

Big Angel turned his head and then looked again. Out of the shadows, Yndio appeared and put his arm around his father's shoulders.

The old man looked up at him. "Hi, mijo!" he said.

They fell into family theater as though they had been in rehearsals for a month.

Yndio felt vast relief. He should have known this was how it was always meant to play out. He performed his role with no hesitation.

"Hi, Pops. What's this here?"

Big Angel's small grin filled Yndio with pride.

"Oh," Big Angel said, as if they were talking about the weather. "Some pendejo is going to kill us all."

El Yndio was flying now. They were going to do this Big Angel style all the way.

"Kill me first, asswipe," said El Yndio. "That's my advice."

These people were all crazy. The dude lowered the pistol and spun around to make his escape.

Minnie moved to block him and said, "Hey, bitch." He looked over his shoulder for just a moment, a brief pause that was all it took for Yndio to strike. His right fist streaked into the side of the man's face and cracked his jaw and cheekbone. The dude lifted off his feet and hit the concrete so hard the pistol flew out of his hand. Minnie stepped on it, holding it to the ground.

Big Angel turned to Little Angel and said, "Look at my kids."

The crowd closed on the gunman and started kicking. He scrambled on his hands and knees and withstood a gauntlet of pain until he was able to pump his arms and legs and speed toward the gate on all fours, then on his knees and then stumbling into a run.

Out in front, La Gloriosa watched him run and fall, run and fall, caroming off cars as he went. "What's your problem?" she called.

⌘

Perla got to her man just as he collapsed. She and Yndio. She was about to crack like a porcelain plate. She cried, "Angel!" and "Yndio!" and "Flaco!" and "Mijo!" Yndio took Big Angel up in his arms. He weighed nothing. He was all balsawood and paper. They put him back in his chair.

Perla was crying.

Little Angel picked up his brother's notebook and stood there, helpless.

Yndio looked at his hand. His knuckles were bleeding. His hand crunched as he opened and closed it. That hurt, but felt good at the same time.

"Hero," Minnie said.

He put his forehead against hers.

Perla slapped him.

"Ma!"

"Ten years!" she shouted, then fell upon her husband again.

Minnie bent to the pistol and picked it up. Turned it back and forth, recognized it as Lalo's. Walked over to Lalo, watched him snore, and said, "Jerk." She went to the rain barrel, pried open the lid, and dropped the gun in the black water. "Try to find it now, Hungry Man."

And that was it for Big Angel. The string was cut. He felt and saw sparks rise around him. Now he knew why he was not dead yet. The sparks whirled. He thought he had stayed alive to enjoy his own wake. He thought he was still alive to make his amends. He thought he was alive to try one last hour to unite his family. But now he knew. What a pretty little tornado of light.

He was alive to save his boy's life. His youngest son. He had just done the most heroic thing in the world. He grinned now with joy, not rage. He had outdone the heroics of all those detectives in all those books. He had outdone his own father. He had shown Little Angel what he was made of. In front of everybody.

And God had even forgiven him by bringing Yndio home. To his family.

He started to laugh. His shoulders shook. He wiped his eyes. "I said, 'Shoot me here!'"

"Loco!" Perla scolded.

Little Angel let out a long breath and started laughing too. "Damn, Brother!"

"I know!" Big Angel said. He reached to Yndio. "You punched him like The Destroyer!"

"Who?"

Big Angel waved his hand, then touched Yndio's arm. "Like a mule kick, mijo."

Yndio flushed. Well, yeah. He had to admit. He had busted that homie up with one blow. Damn. He felt proud. He felt good every time Big Angel called him "mijo." Why was he all shaky? Everybody kept staring at him—he'd thought he would like that, but it was making him nervous.

"Yndio, I am so tired," Big Angel said. "Can you help me get to bed?"

Yndio reached down and gathered up Big Angel in his arms. The family followed him down the hall, just to watch him carry his father.

"You need to go on a diet, Old Man."

Big Angel actually laughed. "Good one," he said.

"Just kidding around," Yndio said. "You know."

They entered the room.

"I missed you," his father said.

Yndio remained silent.

"Did you miss me?"

Yndio laid the patriarch down.

"I was afraid I'd never see you again, Son."

"You knew where I was," Yndio said, not unkindly.

"So did you, mijo. So did you. Thank you for carrying me."

They all watched this conversation, holding their breaths.

Big Angel called to his brother, "Carnal, visit with me before I go to sleep."

Yndio was astounded when his uncle crawled into bed next to Pops.

"We've been doing this," Little Angel told him.

"Cool," Yndio said, but honestly he was a little appalled.

"Mija," Big Angel said, and Minnie climbed into the bed.

Yndio stood with his fists clenched, watching this scene unfold. This wasn't the family he remembered. His mind flashed on Braulio—he imagined his bro having a cruel laugh over this display. He stared again at his father.

Perla stood behind him, running her hand up and down his back. "You," she said. "Go."

"Nah," he said. "That's all right."

"Go, mijo."

"I'm okay."

"Where is Lalo?" Big Angel said.

"Right here, Pops."

Lalo didn't wait to be invited and crawled up onto the foot of the bed and curled around his father's feet.

Perla wasn't about to climb into bed with everybody. She moved away from Yndio but beseeched him with her eyes. His face was burning. Perla moved to the head of the bed and stood close to Big Angel's side and reached her hand out to him. Big Angel took it, pressed his lips to her knuckles. She patted his mad hair down with her palm.

"Son?" she said.

Yndio turned away but couldn't step out the door.

"Son," Big Angel finally said. "Why aren't you in here with me?"

Yndio finally turned.

And they all made room for him in the family bed.

Coda

And that was the end of the story.

In a week, Little Angel stood holding Minnie's hand, staring in disbelief at his brother, turned away from them in a hospital bed. The smell of antiseptics. His temples black, his hands dark. Tubes and hoses running into and out of his body, his mouth. A monitor making a terrible, constant cry. Flat.

Big Angel, curled in on himself, one hand up, one down. Already seeming dense, denser than he'd been in life. Absorbing the light out of the room.

Perla, collapsing slowly to the floor, seeming to float as if she were made of down as her boys tried to hold her up.

⌁

There were other things, though. There were always more details trailing any good story. Like tin cans on the back bumper of a newlywed's car. Rattles and pings and wonderful small moments spinning in the wake of a great life. Things they would talk about forever.

How Big Angel's funeral was more beautiful than his mother's had been.

How the cousins brought white doves in cardboard carriers and let them fly over the grave. And Lalo said, "What—they bought pigeons in a box?"

How Father Dave's sermon was so beautiful, so brilliant—full of things nobody could remember later but that had made them cry all the same.

How the mass was lovely, and the little rat-faced priest stood aside for Father Dave.

How the pallbearers were all in white. Yndio and Lalo at the head of the coffin. Pato and Marco in the middle. Little Angel holding up his back corner, looking across at Minnie. Her hair was pulled back. She stood tall. Pants and a satin vest. Nobody was going to tell her women didn't carry coffins.

How Perla never wavered, never needed her sisters to hold her. And how she made good on her promise to abandon the kitchen.

How El Yndio shoveled the first dirt into the grave.

How they laughed and cried as they passed his notebooks among themselves.

How that night, after reading his lists, Minnie smelled his aftershave in her living room. Just one gust, there and gone. "Daddy?" she said.

And later, how Perla cut apart all of Big Angel's pajamas and used them to create small teddy bears for each of the kids. Her children, and her children's children. Even Giovanni, that little cabrón. And her two sisters. Little Angel hoped to get one but was too shy to ask. It was Minnie who sent it to him.

What they really talked about, though, was the later mystery of Flaco and Flaca's wedding anniversary. Months after Big Angel was gone. How the biggest, most beautiful flowers arrived on that day. How the note was signed by him. And how a handwritten letter from him was delivered that same day by UPS. A letter that Perla never showed anyone but that put her in bed for two days.

Nobody ever knew who had helped Big Angel arrange that miracle. They half believed he had found a way to reach back to them from heaven. Big Angel—they remained in awe.

ঔ

After they had all crept from Big Angel's bed on that last night after the party, Little Angel went looking for La Gloriosa but couldn't find her. Instead, he found Minnie standing alone on the patio, crying.

"Tío," she cried and fell against him. She sobbed into his shoulder.

He patted her back, her hair. "It's okay," he said.

"No, it's not!"

He held her tight as she snuffled and cried. When she calmed down, he let her go.

"I got snot all over your jacket," she said.

"It's all right." He took her hand. "I want to show you something," he said.

It was time for a little magic. Ookie's paradise. Just to gild Big Angel's legend a little more for his dear niece.

"Come on." He led her across the yard. They stopped outside the shed. "You're not going to believe this," he said, and he swung open the door.

Inside, Leo the Lion stood with his back to them. His trousers and flowered boxers were pooled at his feet. His pale buttocks wobbled as he thrust.

Pazuzu was sprawled facedown on the worktable. She was snarling, "Faster! Harder! Ride it, cabrón!"

Leo rutted away like a donkey gone mad. He leaned back and spanked her generous behind with one hand.

Little Angel and Minnie backed away and shut the door.

"Thank you, Tío," she said. "That was very special."

Later that same night, lying in his hotel bed, Little Angel was nervous. He had no idea what was going to happen. He didn't really know what it was he wanted to happen.

Leaving the party, laden and somber, he had found La Gloriosa leaning on the wall. She was shivering.

"Is it over?" she said.

He nodded.

"You don't even know me," she told him.

They simply stared at each other.

"What don't I know?" he said.

"Anything."

He was weepy and small. He took her hand.

"My name no es La Gloriosa," she said. "My real name is Maclovia. Did you know that?"

He admitted he didn't.

"You like?"

"Maclovia. Beautiful. Yes."

She squeezed his hand back. "Take me away," she said.

He gave her a quizzical look.

"I can't go home. Not now." She rested her head against his chest. "Take me with you."

And now, as he lay in bed, she was coming out of the bathroom, wearing one of his T-shirts. It hung just above the bright rainbow of her underwear.

He swallowed. "Wow," he said, fully returned to his thirteen-year-old self.

"Nothing crazy," she said. She stood beside the bed and looked down at him. "Get up," she said.

He rose. He wore running shorts and a black T-shirt.

"Take off your shirt," she said. "I want to see you."

He paused, searched her face for a moment. He should have done more planks, he realized. But he pulled the shirt over his head. He tried to suck in his gut, but it was too late for games. So he just stood.

"Shorts," she said.

He laughed a little, embarrassed.

"Show me," she said.

His face turned a vibrant pink.

"Do it," she said.

He dropped the shorts, kicked them away. He wore black briefs.

She raised an eyebrow. "Muy sexy," she said. Her gaze was frank and open.

He pulled down his underpants and tried to keep his hand from covering himself.

"Qué grande!" she said, because that is what you said to the men. Though it really looked like a bedraggled bird sitting atop two eggs in a nest. "Are you crooked?" she said.

He blushed ferociously.

She pulled her shirt over her head, threw it aside, and stood topless before him. "Is okay, Angel. Look." She pointed at her left breast, which was lower than the other. She dragged off her underwear.

There they were.

"We are not children," she said.

"No."

She put her finger upon the scar at the edge of her pubic hair. "My baby, Guillermo," she said.

He pointed to a scar on the edge of his abdomen. "Appendix."

She took his hand and pulled him onto the bed, then crawled in beside him. She showed him her leg. "Veins," she said.

He pointed to his chest. "Man boobs."

She pulled the sheet over herself. He hugged her close; she put her head on his shoulder. Her hair was rich with her perfumes, and her own scent, and cilantro and rain and wind.

He breathed her in.

She pressed up against him, and they were ageless. They were a hundred years old. Her mouth against his collarbone.

❧

She spoke.

How Big Angel's son Braulio and her son Guillermo had been more than cousins. Best friends. Almost twins.

How that night they had been running around having fun. It was a Saturday. They'd borrowed Big Angel's car. She knew they'd eaten pancakes. The whole family was pancake crazy. How they'd joined some girls at the Bay Theatre down in National City. There was a Tom Cruise movie. Lots of crazy boys from Tijuana came up to see movies. Who knew who all was there. But somebody was. Somebody bad.

Uncle Jimbo had a little liquor store by Plaza Bonita mall. Just a silly little shop where he sold Wild Turkey and cheap cigars and magazines and lotto tickets. She and her sisters scolded him for it, but he loved for the boys to come in. When they were underage, he thought it was fine for the boys to have a beer once in a while. So he'd let them into the cooler, and they lurked in there behind the cold cans, stealing Buds and feeling like wild men. As they grew older, it became their week-end ritual.

After the movie, they went to Jimbo's. She didn't know why. Who could ever know? Beer? Jimbo kept the really naughty magazines in the storage room beside the counter. Stuff he couldn't show the public—it was a good family-type shop. So maybe they wanted to look at girls after cuddling with their ru-cas in the balcony. But somebody caught them outside and shot them both.

It was Jimbo who called the police, who sat with her poor Guillermito as he died. He covered both boys with cleaning cloths and sat on the curb until the cops came. And he drank himself blind.

"I never told my baby good-bye," she said. "I never said 'I love you.'"

And when she was done speaking, what they had thought would happen became something more tender, even beautiful.

♒

On that last night, after the partiers had finally left, after the women had picked up the mess and Minnie had tossed Lalo into his bed in the garage and driven to her house at one in the morning, Big Angel and Perla lay together.

"Flaca," he said. "Be naked with me."

She was out of this habit and embarrassed. But they un-dressed and lay close to each other, close enough so they could feel each other's heat.

"Flaca," he said. "No hay más."

"Sí, mi amor," she said.

"This is it," he said.

They held hands there in the dark.

"I like being naked," he told her.

"Ay, Flaco. Me da pena."

"What could you be shy about, Flaca? How many times did we make love?"

"Ay!"

"Guess."

"Ten thousand times."

"That was the first month!"

She smacked him lightly.

"And then, after you had the baby—"

"Don't say it, Flaco."

"You had milk."

"Flaco!"

"Milk everywhere!"

"Cochino!" she scolded.

He was so happy. "So delicious. Coming out of your body. So hot on my face."

She thought: *I am as old as the hills, and he still makes me tingle.*

He turned his head to her. "I loved that," he said, his voice almost as low as it used to be.

She put her head against his arm.

He put his hand on her face. "I'm sorry I can't anymore," he said.

She shushed him.

"I can't be a man for you."

"You are always a man for me. My man. Be quiet now."

He sighed. "May I touch your fountain?"

She nodded against his arm and opened her legs for him. His hand went to her like a shadow—she could barely feel it.

"You on top," he said. "How I loved that."

"You're bad, Flaco."

"So I could look at you."

"Ay."

They remembered. Even though his body was aflame, though agony had wrenched his veins into knots, he thought he might be able to perform his husbandly duties after all. One last time. He just might. It moved a little.

But, no.

"A good life," he finally said. He lay back and withdrew his hand and clutched the warmth of her in his empty palm.

She lay beside him, making that happy sound lovers know so well. "What was your favorite part?" she said.

"Of the party?"

"No, Flaco. Of our life."

He responded immediately: "Everything."

She thought about it. "Even the bad?"

"There were no bad times," he said. "As long as you were there."

She kissed him. "Poeta," she said.

"I did bad things," he confessed.

"Yes, you did."

"I remember the first time I saw you," he said.

"Was I pretty?"

"The prettiest girl I ever saw. And you still are."

"Ay, viejo." She was going to say more, but his phone chirped.

"Qué es eso?" he said. It chirped again. "Who the hell?" he said, irritated now. He scrabbled among his bottles on the table.

"Leave it, Flaco."

Still it chirped.

"Could be an emergency, Flaca." He opened it. Squinted at the screen.

"Ay, cómo eres," she scolded.

"It's my brother," he said.

"Pato?"

He shook his head, then answered it. "It is midnight!" he said. "I'm dying!"

"Listen," Little Angel said. "You are not going to die tonight."

"Yes, I am."

"No, you're not. That's a drama-queen move. The Big Exit. Come on, Carnal. What would Raymond Chandler do?"

Big Angel looked at Perla and whispered, "This cabrón is bothering me. He doesn't want me to die."

"Don't think you're so special, boy," she called into the phone. No te creas. "Nobody wants my Flaco to die."

Big Angel grinned.

"Hang up," she said.

"Carnal," he said into the phone. "We are naked. Okay? Leave me in peace."

"Go away," Perla said.

"Go out in style," Little Angel said.

"By golly," his big brother replied. "That's why I'm naked."

Perla was doing her naughty laugh.

"Get up early tomorrow," Little Angel said. "I'm not kidding. I'll be there at eight. And get dressed. All right? Don't be naked. I just threw up a little thinking about it."

"Pinche idiota," Big Angel said.

"Got shorts? Dress in shorts and sandals."

"Shorts? I don't wear shorts."

"Stay naked, then. Make a spectacle of yourself."

"Qué chingados?"

"I am taking you to the beach."

"*What?*" It sounded like *gwatt*. Big Angel thought of a hundred protests. Then he smiled. And he laughed almost silently. He turned to Perla and nodded. *Little Angel*, he mouthed and shook his head, as if she didn't know.

"Sí," she sighed, tired of Little Angel. "Es tremendo."

"I want to go to La Jolla," Big Angel said. "Where the rich people go. I never went to La Jolla."

"There's an IHOP there," Little Angel said. "We can get pancakes."

"Qué?" Perla kept whispering.

"Okay," Little Angel said.

"Okay," Big Angel replied.

"Eight."

"I'll be ready."

"No dying."

"Not yet," Big Angel said. "But when I'm gone and you see a hummingbird, say hello. That will be me. Don't forget."

"I will never forget," Little Angel promised.

They clicked off without saying good-bye.

Big Angel hugged his woman tight. "Bueno, pues," he said. "I will die tomorrow. But we're going to the beach first."

She couldn't help but think: *These men are driving me insane.*

Big Angel drifted to sleep thinking of the trip in the morning. Little Angel would drive them out of the neighborhood, out past the basketball courts and the McDonald's, down the ramp onto the 805. He would turn on the radio and smile at his big brother. Far Tijuana would recede behind them and grow invisible. They would head north and west, and when they arrived at the shore, they would watch great waves traveling forever across the open copper sea.

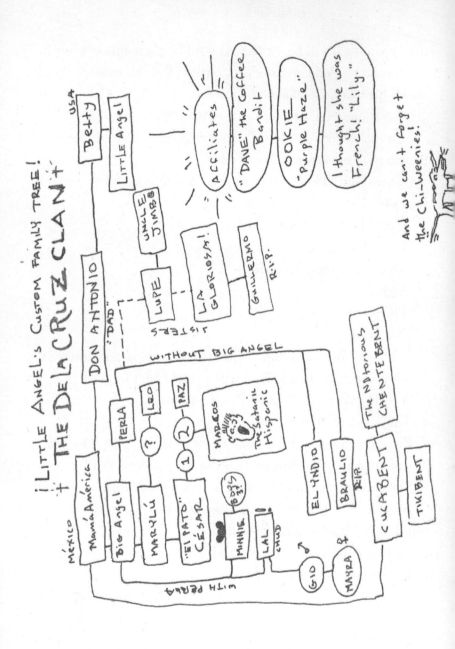

¡Little Angel's Custom Family Tree!
† THE DELACRUZ CLAN †

And we can't forget
the Chi-weenies!

Author's Note and Acknowledgments

Dear Literary Companion,

There are no Angels in my family today, Big or Little.

When my eldest brother was in the last month of a terminal disease, he had to bury his own mother. Her funeral happened to be on the day before his birthday. He knew it was to be his last, though I believe he kept that certainty to himself. Crystal, one of his army of granddaughters, had urged the family to give "Pops" a blowout party, the kind of ruckus he would have delighted in during better days. And we did. And he did. Everyone was aware that this was a farewell, but, hey—we're Mexican: Some curandera or angel or UFO pilot could descend during the cutting of the cake and heal him.

His name was Juan. He was whittled down in size but not in ferocity or presence. Small as he was thanks to the cancer, he burned with light and good humor. The party / living wake was astonishing. A Mexican *Finnegans Wake*. Around every corner, there seemed to be a remarkable scene of comedy or tragedy. Avalanches of food. Storms of music. Generations of ordinary people come to take a knee and thank this man for his seventy-four years of life. Juan sat in his wheelchair in the middle of this swirl of bodies and stories and behaviors—some of them glorious in their inappropriateness—like some king. Which, of course, he was.

Because of his illness, he got weak at various moments and took to his bed. He asked me to get in bed with him, which I did. We reviewed many of our stories there—he took great credit for my becoming a writer due to his foisting of old E. E. "Doc" Smith space opera paperbacks on me when I was a kid. Soon, la familia found out there was a bed party going on, and suddenly Juan had a shifting dog-pile of bodies in bed with him. He smiled a lot that day.

Within a month, he was gone, and we were back to bury him.

That being said, I must remind readers that this is a novel, not the story of the Urrea family.

Of course, Big Angel could not exist without the example of my brother, or of his beloved wife, Blanca. I often felt as if he were dictating ideas and scenes from beyond the grave. In fact, when I shared passages with my niece, we were a little spooked that what I had invented was a reflection of actual scenes from real life that I had no way of knowing about. But, no—there is no Bent family, no Ookie or Paz or Braulio. Nor are we from La Paz. There was no deadly fire that I know of. And, sadly, no Pato or MaryLú.

I stole the Lego image from my son-in-law, Kevin.

Readers in San Diego will know there is no such neighborhood as Lomas Doradas.

We have no Gloriosa, though I wish we did. We have no Hungry Man, though I could only write that character thanks to the sense of humor and general goodwill of my nephew Juan. No blind "French" girl or trailer park girls. (I met those in New

Hampshire.) No Leo. Dave the Jesuit knows who he is. I wish we had an Yndio—though someone did run away with the Cycle Sluts from Hell back in the day. But that's another book entirely.

On a historical note: The scene with the pistolero and Big Angel was remembered from my own father facing off against a gangster at a quinceañera party. And the parrot scene—ah, the parrot scene. That was inspired by my grandmother's very short tenure as a parrot smuggler. I didn't know at the time that I was lucky to see such an event.

We do, however, love pancakes.

Not long after Juan's funeral, I was invited to have supper with another of my heroes, Jim Harrison. He was near his own death at the time. When he sat beside me, I asked, "Are you all right?" His reply became a line in the book: "I will never be all right again."

As we ate, and Jim enjoyed a lineup of liquors that covered the color spectrum from clear to amber to deep red, he suddenly said, "Tell me about your brother's death." So I did. At length. Jim just stared at the ceiling and listened. When I was finished, he turned to me and said, "Sometimes, God hands you a novel. You'd better write it."

My wife, Cinderella, lived these things and read a thousand drafts of this book. There were moments too close to home that she typed for me as I blurted them. She lay in the bed with us.

Thanks to the team; editor, Ben George: We engaged in hand-to-hand combat over this book, and his vision of it was grander than mine—thank you; Reagan Arthur, forever. Maggie Southard and her publicity team at Little, Brown steer me with a cool and cheery hand. My best agent and taskmaster (wrestled through several drafts with me before poor George had to), Julie Barer of The Book Group. Love and praise. Mike Cendejas at the Pleshette Agency navigates the turbid waters of Hollywood with me. Michael Taeckens believes in me. That is appreciated more than you know. And Trinity Ray and Kevin Mills keep me on the road, talking year round. Keep putting my kids through college, brothers!

If you write, steal well: I owe the Urrea family, the Hubbard family, the Glenzer family, the Somers family, and the long-ago García family; thanks for quips, anecdotes, and laughter that blended into my narrative.

Finally, thank you to the many friends who read chunks of the many versions of this book to offer advice and critiques. You know who you are. I must thank tireless Jamie Ford for good superpowers. Thank you, Erin Coughlin Hollowell. Thank you, Jonna and Steve. Thank you, Dave Eggers—we each auctioned off characters in our new books for an 826 benefit, then Dave offered good take-no-crap advice later. And Richard Russo, who read it and, in conversation, noted that I had told him something I had not put in the book. His response will always stick with me: "Are you nuts?" I added it.

Finally, Cinderella knew it was a book before Jim Harrison did.

From Byron, Austen and Darwin

to some of the most acclaimed and original contemporary writing, John Murray takes pride in bringing you powerful, prizewinning, absorbing and provocative books that will entertain you today and become the classics of tomorrow.

We put a lot of time and passion into what we publish and how we publish it, and we'd like to hear what you think.

Be part of John Murray – share your views with us at:

www.johnmurray.co.uk

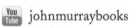 johnmurraybooks

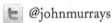 @johnmurrays

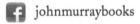 johnmurraybooks